PALADIN'S ODYSSEY

BY BRUCE FOTTLER

MW01519069

Copyright ©2014 by Bruce Fottler

All rights reserved. No part of this publication may be reproduced, distributed, or transmitted in any form or by any means, including photocopying, recording, or other electronic or mechanical methods, without the prior written permission of the author, except in the case of brief quotations embodied in critical reviews and certain other noncommercial uses permitted by copyright law.

Paladin's Odyssey is a work of fiction. Names, characters, businesses, places, events and incidents are either the products of the author's imagination or used in a fictitious manner. Any resemblance to actual persons, living or dead, or actual events is purely coincidental.

ISBN: 978-1502829030

Printed in the United States of America
First Edition

Cover art by Norman Soul (under Shutterstock license).

A special thank you to my Beta-readers: Ric Derdeyn, Lauren Espe, and Melody Fottler.

An extra special thank you to my editor: Joyce Conkling.

Other novels by Bruce Fottler:
Chasing Redemption
Dover Park
The Juncture

Table of Contents

CHAPTER 1

August, 2059
Auburn, Maine

Winston Churchill once said: *"In wartime, truth is so precious that she should always be attended by a bodyguard of lies."* I've always believed this to be so, but I've also struggled to determine when the bodyguards should be retired.

My name is Joseph E. Paladin, former major in the United States Army, retired colonel in the Maine Republic Militia, and one of the founders of the NAC (New American Confederation). As I write this memoir, thousands are gathering in Bangor, Maine for the unveiling of a statue to commemorate my life and achievements. I haven't seen it yet, but I'm told it's over five meters tall and will reside as the centerpiece in the lobby of the new capitol building.

The historic commission approached me over a year ago seeking pictures, particularly those I had from the early days. They took a special interest in a photo that showed me riding at the front of an old diesel locomotive as it slowly pulled the first supply train into the Auburn freight yard. It was early morning back in 2019, and we had returned from our first trip to the Loring vault. To my recollection, not many people were there to greet us, as the mission was supposed to be kept secret. I've never shown this picture to anyone before and I don't remember any being taken. Someone I've never met before sent it to me about twenty-five years ago. If the commission decided to use that image, I'm curious to see how it could translate into a statue.

I should be feeling a tremendous sense of gratitude over the recognition, but I'm honestly unnerved over all the fuss. I've never been comfortable with all the attention that my past exploits seem to draw. I've been told on countless occasions that the people of this great new nation hold me in the same esteem as the old country held Thomas Jefferson or George Washington. This has always been difficult for me to fathom and it's taken me many years to come to a reluctant acceptance of how I'm perceived. It's not that I think people are praising me for things that didn't happen. Despite some exaggerations that have blended into the truth over the years, most reports of my known accomplishments are accurate.

In all honesty, I'm feeling an overriding sense of shame over it all. Every time I labor over my Bangor speech, I can't help obsessing over a secret that I've kept hidden away for decades. I was once told by the person who directed me to keep this secret that there are times when truth needs to be protected by a falsehood. There was little question that protection was germane at the time, but I feel too many years have passed since it's been relevant. Now that history is congealing, I feel the truth needs to come out before legend overshadows fact.

I've sustained a false identity for decades. I'm not really Joseph Paladin.

My actual name is Walter Johnson, but no one has called me that in over forty years. It's a name that died when I assumed the identity of Major Joseph Paladin, United States Army, during the turbulent aftermath of the great flu pandemic. The real story is complicated, and I'll attempt to recount it with as much brutal honesty as my aging mind can recall.

* * *

My strange odyssey began back in 2015. Ironically, apocalyptic tales were popular at the time. I often scoffed over the absurdity of these tired doomsday cliches which played out in books, movies, and television shows that many of us eagerly consumed. The end of the world made for an entertaining distraction, and maybe a frightening nightmare or two. However, once we put down the book, walked out of the theater, or shut off the television, fantasy would relinquish its toehold. But there was always the lingering thought in the back of our minds that wondered: Are these doomsday scenarios plausible? Could something as infinitesimal as a virus bring a powerful civilization to ruin? How could our vast knowledge and wondrous technologies completely fail to stop something so miniscule?

After all, terrorism was our primary concern back then. After airliners flew into skyscrapers, our daily lives were never the same. From that point forward, we fretted over numerous dire scenarios including chemical, radiological, and cyber attacks. Our attention was fixed on human threats, and wars flared as a result.

Then came the great flu pandemic in the winter of 2015, eclipsing all other cataclysms in human history.

I lived in a large suburb of Boston called Waltham and worked as a purchasing agent at a bio-tech company. It wasn't a challenging or terribly exciting job, but it paid the bills. I had recently moved into my own apartment after sharing a place for five years with my old girlfriend, Veronica. She was an out-of-my-league-goddess who left my buddies wondering how an average-looking guy like me scored someone like her. When we first met, she was pleasant and irresistibly attractive. I enjoyed showing her off and she drank in every ounce of attention. Our shallow relationship began to sour after the first year, and died a slow, agonizing death during the years that followed. In fact, I'm pretty sure she cheated on me a couple of times. The plug needed to be pulled on our high-maintenance sham, and it took me far too long to do anything about it. It was always difficult for me to break from the familiar. That's probably why I slaved away at the same tedious job for nearly as long. I clung to consistency as though it was a security blanket, no matter how miserable the situation became.

After five years, what little remained of our relationship was nothing more than a cheap accessory to Veronica and a bothersome burden to me and my bank account. I finally broke it off with her in late fall of 2014. She was shocked and livid. My friends were mystified that I had pushed a smoking-hot girlfriend away from me. I didn't care. I was relieved that Veronica had finally been excised from my life.

The new year of 2015 started with great hope and promise. At the age of thirty-two, I felt I was still young enough to get back into the singles market. I wanted to explore all the possibilities I had missed while wasting my time with Veronica. However, five years of complacency had taken a toll on me. I was five-ten and a pudgy two-hundred pounds. My once full head of light blonde hair had darkened and begun to recede. Of course, I figured it was nothing a gym membership and a good hair stylist couldn't fix. It wouldn't be long before I sculpted myself into something that camouflaged the monotonously average person I actually was.

At the end of January, hospitals were reporting a tougher than normal flu season. Too many people had taken a pass on the annual flu vaccination and had paid a harsh price. This caused a run on the small vaccine supply that remained, so new batches were rushed into production. A tough flu season wasn't uncommon, so most people took the news in stride and continued with their routines. I remember being satisfied that I had been vaccinated at my company flu-shot clinic back in November. Working at a bio-tech company that helped develop the vaccine had advantages. Problem solved, at least for me.

At the end of February, things changed. The media networks ran alarmist reports of a new mutation of the H1N1 flu strain. I remember jogging on a treadmill at the gym while watching the news-crawl use terms like *Super-Flu Pandemic,* and *Spanish Flu Redux.* Everyone watching shared a chuckle while someone requested the channel to be changed. The news media's quest for ratings through brazen fear mongering had already strained their credibility. Because of this, too few took the current reports seriously when they first broke, causing a tragic delay. The new and lethal flu strain had a few extra days to spread through an apathetic population. After all, we were being vigilant against terrorism, not a flu epidemic. The Boston Marathon was coming up and it was the second year after the bombings. We were all still *Boston Strong.*

By the time we all woke up and paid attention, it was the beginning of March. The death toll rapidly rose. Worldwide estimates at the time were over 100,000 dead. Hospitals were quickly filling, followed by the morgues. Terms like *cytokine storm* and *morbidity* became commonly used. This terrible new flu strain mimicked the Spanish Flu of 1918 with a frightening fidelity. Once infected, the sick would be dead within a couple of days; sometimes sooner. The young and healthy seemed especially susceptible because the flu caused immune systems to overreact, which became deadlier to those with stronger immune systems.

Adding to the woes was a discovery that the newest batches of flu vaccines were ineffective against the new strain. They were different from those dispensed back in the fall of 2014. The fall vaccinations actually contained effective antigens, which was due to a bizarre production mistake by the company I worked for. It would take several more weeks to produce new batches of effective vaccines.

These new vaccines would never see the outside of their factories.

FEMA mobilized with the National Guard and state health crisis units. Breathing masks of any sort became an instant must-have item. Grocery stores and gas stations were overwhelmed, despite a warning from government officials to stay isolated and not to hoard. The entire world slowly lost its sanity as panic overtook social order.

By mid-March, martial law was declared. The estimated worldwide death toll soared to over one million. One press report was bold enough to disclose that for every one flu death, another died because of civil unrest. I suspect the death toll due to violence must have been much higher than that. Our President tried to calm us, but too many news pundits were eager to call him out on the dire realities. It was too obvious that our government was in full spin control; trying to project a confidence that they were on top of the situation. Nothing was further from the truth, and no matter how many helicopters and drones they put in the air, we all sensed that the situation was actually spinning out of control. It was too easy to mistrust our government in the aftermath of so many political scandals and appalling approval ratings.

I was hunkered down in my small Waltham apartment. It was located in a complex of aging, brick-faced, three-story buildings tucked away in a tightly packed neighborhood. We were surrounded by older, modest ranch-style houses with as many telephone poles as old oak trees in their front yards. I liked it because it was located close to the main roads, which offered me several alternative routes to work. My building was quiet and my neighbors generally kept to themselves. Despite the rising chaos in the world around us, a sliver of calm managed to prevail on our small street.

It didn't bother me to occasionally venture out for supplies because I was one of the lucky few who had received the right vaccination. However, reports of escalating violence started to worry me. The predominantly empty grocery shelves also gave me an ominous feeling that our normal way of life would never return. As I watched the endless media coverage, a depression started to envelop me. Their brigades of medical experts weren't shy in sharing all the grisly details about how the flu performed its deadly rendition. It seemed absurd that these reports were typically accompanied by sanitized illustrations because using actual pictures was deemed too graphic. I once saw someone being wheeled out of our apartment complex, suffering from advanced flu symptoms. The EMT's tried to hold a once-white towel over a nose that bled profusely. There was even a small trickle of blood coming from his ear. Uncontrolled hemorrhaging was a typical symptom associated with this new and terrifying killing machine.

The EMT's stopped responding to emergency calls a short time later. A shelter-in-place order was issued for those who were infected, people were urged to stay away from hospitals, and medical practices closed their doors. From that point on, once you contracted the flu, you were on your own. Many died gruesome deaths in their own beds. Too many children watched their parents shut themselves away and then listened to their ghastly moans, sputtering coughing fits, and heaving, eventually followed by a terrible silence.

I was consumed by the thought that I couldn't survive in a world without convenience. I knew nothing of being a survivalist and never watched those outdoor reality shows on television. The closest relevant experience I had was a couple of years I spent as a Cub Scout. I was nothing more than a spoiled, middle-class kid raised in the suburbs. I needed my car, my electricity, well stocked grocery stores, drive through service, and my data-phone. There was little doubt it was all slipping away. I sat and wondered when the electricity would finally go out.

I worried what would become of my parents who resided in a Florida retirement community. I last talked to them at the end of February and they were healthy. They too had received the right vaccine, even though they were part of an age group that had a better survivability rate. I also had a younger sister in Texas but was never able to contact her. Long-distance calls became nearly impossible. Soon, all phone service was restricted to emergency use only. I lost contact with all of my friends, many of whom lived only a town or two away. Internet services were intermittent and most websites fell offline due to lack of administration.

I remember a silly but vivid nightmare of being stalked by zombies, which probably came from a popular television show I used to watch. After waking up, I knew that my reality had become worse than my nightmares. I actually yearned to deal with slow-shuffling zombies rather than a world full of people acquiescing to panic. My sobering reality was that I was holed up and unarmed. Anyone could have broken through my flimsy door and taken anything they wanted. Funny, I had always been a proponent of gun control until that point.

By April, the National Guard formed numerous disposal teams. They came around in trucks marked with large, red bio-hazard insignias. Some were military vehicles, but most were commandeered commercial trucks. I suppose the military were reluctant to use their own vehicles; whatever they used had to be disposable. The teams would sweep through a neighborhood knocking at all the doors to check for bodies. I even heard stories about mercy executions. Several people claimed to have seen soldiers ending the lives of anyone they found close to death. Some thought it was out of compassion, while others were convinced that the soldiers just didn't want to make another trip back to pick up the bodies.

The disposal teams left large spray-painted markings on all the exterior doors after checking. I noticed the color of the markings varied, so I asked one of the soldiers what they meant. He warned me through his mask to stay away from anything in neon orange. It indicated infected people in the residence. A team would return later to recover the bodies.

One time, I stood in the parking lot and watched five bodies being removed from the apartment building next to mine, all wrapped in heavy black plastic. A chill shot through me after looking into the back of one of the trucks, those black bags were stacked to the ceiling. The horrible smell of death couldn't be sealed in with them. I ran back to my apartment and spent the next half-hour puking into the toilet while hoping my next door neighbor didn't think I contracted the flu.

I was soon on a first-name basis with neighbors I had hardly acknowledged a few weeks before. We banded together to keep watch while maintaining a polite distance from each other. It was clear the police presence was becoming ever more sparse. One resident owned a handgun and it gave us a feeling of safety. His name was Bill, and we kept a very close eye on him to make sure he stayed healthy. He was six-two, musclebound, and not socially graceful. He was often gruff, but we happily endured his social shortcomings. Bill and his gun needed to stick around.

At the end of April, the disposal teams stopped coming around. Most cell phone service was gone and the few remaining television stations were tuned to the emergency broadcast system. They didn't say much about what was really going on; no surprise there. Fewer helicopters were in the air, but Air Force jets occasionally roared overhead to let us know that our government was still alive and kicking. The National Guard set up food distribution centers because the grocery stores had shut down. We walked or rode bikes in order to get to these places, weaving in and out of the piles of garbage that hadn't been collected in weeks. Gasoline was scarce and no one was allowed to travel out of town. A water-boil order was soon issued, but the water service failed entirely a week later.

Unknown to us, the worldwide pandemic death toll had jumped from the last reported one million to a staggering one hundred million. Social order in most countries was quickly breaking down. In the United States, law enforcement and National Guard ranks were being depleted. The flu was no longer the primary culprit. Desertion was rampant. Self-preservation was fast becoming the order of the day.

Meanwhile, in many underdeveloped countries, far more people were being killed by war, hunger, and unsanitary living conditions than by the flu. The United States would soon be ravaged in the same ways.

The world as we knew it was passing away.

CHAPTER 2

By the summer of 2015, the National Guard disappeared. The police were nowhere to be seen. The birds had the sky to themselves as it was void of any sort of aircraft. The power failed and the only portable radio in our apartment building had depleted the last of the batteries. My world shrank into an area that encompassed only our apartment complex, and we knew little of what was going on elsewhere.

The United States government rapidly evaporated. The teams of doctors and scientists that we all thought were feverishly working on solutions in secret facilities were never heard from. Nothing came from the underground bunkers that our leaders supposedly took shelter in. Exactly what happened to the local and national leadership remains an unprecedented enigma of our time, because no trace of them has ever been found. Many historians have since hypothesized and debated several theories. I'm still being asked questions about this subject, but I really don't know much more than what's already been reported. While I've heard all the theories over the years and have had access to several high-level confederation investigations, I don't have any unique knowledge that would help solve this great mystery. It's as perplexing to me today as it was back then. My only guess is that the flu got too far ahead of any efforts to contain it, mainly because our infrastructure quickly crumbled in the panic. Whatever the reasons, I hope someday, someone will be able to finally find the answers.

I vividly remember an eerie quiet on the day Bill rode back from where the food distribution center had been located. He announced that it was gone, went up to his apartment, packed, and left without another word. We never saw him or his gun again.

A dozen of us were left in a three-level apartment building. No water. No electricity. No news. Food was scarce, so we risked foraging through the various homes with neon orange markings on the doors. While I knew that I had received the effective vaccination, I was still careful about what I came in contact with. Most of our group didn't take any chances and wore masks. We did well, as most other survivors avoided these places. They were too busy trying to pick over stores whose shelves had already been emptied. We found plenty of supplies in forbidden spaces, and I worried more about eating spoiled food than about coming into contact with anything contaminated by flu virus.

After a month of sweltering summer heat, our apartment building was down to six people. Of the six no longer with us, one died of what looked like flu, but I'm fairly certain it was something else. Chloe had been a middle-aged woman who complained about every irrelevant thing. I guess it was her way of coping, but to be honest, none of us would admit that she'd be missed. We buried her in a side yard of an abandoned home. The other five decided to leave in order to get closer to Boston, hoping to find some sort of relief center. Rumors were the only thing we had plenty of, and most of them seemed too good to be true. Many said that Boston was a fortress where all the soldiers and police had gone. I decided to stay with what I was sure of, probably because I was yielding to my tendency to cling to consistency.

The nights became increasingly frightening. There were the howls of dogs and the awful screams of fighting animals. I've heard feral cats fight, foxes scream, and the cries of fisher cats, but what I heard on those nights took it to a whole new level. From time to time, gunfire rang out. In a way, it reminded me of hearing distant fireworks people set off around the Fourth of July. At least that's what I tried to envision.

The gunfire actually came from gang warfare. Several gangs were fighting to control territory and supplies. Rumors of their cruelty abounded. One story told of how members of the local One-Two-Six gang would sever body parts just to get at a book of matches. I desperately hoped they never found out that I had a whole case tucked away in my place.

* * *

Fortune finally tilted my way one day in August. Our motley band of apartment dwellers was rummaging through homes a few blocks away. We had stayed away from that neighborhood due to persistent rumors of gun-toting neanderthals occupying the homes. When we finally dared to venture in, we found the whole area abandoned. There wasn't much to be found in the first two houses, but a horrid rotting smell greeted me in front of the third home. I was about to skip it over when I caught sight of a body lying on the floor in the entryway. Normally, I'd have given it a quick glance and been on my way, but something caught my eye. An object clutched in the victim's hand glimmered in the rays of the morning sunlight coming through a side window. It was a revolver. After looking over the body through the broken window, it was clear that this unfortunate soul had been shot at least twice and left for dead. He probably had been just trying to protect his home. I entered, carefully moved his finger from the trigger, and pried the gun from his hand – all while trying not to puke over the smell. I rushed out, cradling my new treasure but quickly tucked it away so no one else would see it.

Although I'd been with these people for a few weeks, I just couldn't be sure how they'd react to my new gun. Desperation was already wearing on us, and I sensed it would be best to keep this find to myself.

I made a closer inspection of the gun after I got home, but I didn't know much about firearms back then. The gun looked small. It was actually a twenty-two caliber revolver. I opened the cylinder and found bullets in all the chambers. It was a good thing I decided to take them all out to check them over, because I found that only three bullets were unspent. Despite the shortage of ammunition, the small revolver gave me a profound sense of security.

* * *

The day finally came, near the end of August, when my apartment comrades decided to move on. Everything we needed to survive was becoming much harder to find. It forced us to scavenge in dangerous areas marked by numerous spray-painted gang tags. Despite the troubling signs of gangs, the consistent thing we noticed was the absence of people. It was painfully obvious that most survivors had already left town.

I resisted leaving. The others begged me to come with them because I'd be left alone if I didn't. I repeatedly refused and wished them well. My last sight of them was as they turned the corner of our street and disappeared behind the overgrown weeds. I've spent far more time with many other people since, but I still think surprisingly often of that odd band of characters I hardly knew - two middle-aged men, a teenaged boy, and two thirty-something sisters who would never leave each other's sight. They all disappeared, and I never saw them again.

Left alone with my small gun, I was tempted several times to leave and try to catch up with them. My stubbornness won out. I spent a few days loathing myself over how I couldn't depart. I thought I had a convincing reason to stay, but I soon came to a sad acceptance that I was afraid to leave. Despite the dangers surrounding me, it was the only place I felt safe. Looking back, I'm convinced something kept me there. My frustrating timidity had a larger purpose.

* * *

A week after the others left, lack of water became a serious issue. I always had a good reserve built up, but a recent stretch of hot weather had forced me to consume more than I had anticipated. I had also given my departing comrades some of my supply. There had been no rain, so I had to make a trip to the Charles River. We had developed a reliable system to process drinking water out of the murky river. It involved retrieving a couple of gallons, boiling it, and running it through a series of water filters we had scavenged from a local hardware store. No one ever got sick after drinking it.

It was late afternoon when I was walking through town to get to the river. I was near Main Street when I heard a scream. It sounded like a young girl in distress, and seemed to originate just around the corner from where I was standing. I froze until another yelp echoed out. I then firmed my grip on the baseball bat that I typically carried with me, felt to make sure my gun was still tucked away, and sprinted off to investigate. I heard more screams, and running footsteps. Carefully peeking around a corner, I saw a teenaged girl who had been chased down by two pursuing gang-bangers. The girl looked out of place. She appeared too well dressed and groomed to be a pandemic survivor, assuming anyone not part of a gang was left around town. She was a pale Caucasian with long red hair around her freckly face. I watched while the older of the two men nodded to the younger one while holding the girl's arms behind her. With a smile he kicked opened a door to an abandoned coffee shop and dragged her in. The younger one smiled and stood guard. The girl's screams soon grew louder and more intense.

I stood there wondering what to do. The sensible thing was to walk away, but my heart raced faster with each shriek. I determined I would take an alternate route to the river when a flash of anger overcame me. I suppose it was pent-up frustration that boiled over from staying behind, but I just couldn't leave that girl to them. My hands suddenly stopped shaking and I tightened my grip on my bat. Before I knew it, I had charged around the corner at the gang-banger standing guard. He was turned away from me and the girl's screams covered my approach. He turned in time to greet my baseball bat with his face. He was propelled backward, hit his head against a brick wall, and went down hard. He didn't get up, either knocked out cold or dead.

I drew my gun and slowly entered the shop. The older gang-banger had the girl pinned on a table, naked. She was putting up a fight, writhing and trying to kick at him. His pants were down and he was about to start in on her when he caught sight of me. My gun was pointed at him and I shook my head. We stood and looked at each other for a while before he glanced to his gun lying on a nearby table. A terrifying thought went through my mind: I might actually have to shoot this guy. He scowled and reached for his gun, but a single crack rang out before he could pick it up. He looked at his chest with the most bewildered expression I've ever seen. I had fired, but to this day I can't remember pulling the trigger. All I remember is him slumping down and falling lifeless to the floor. It was my first kill, ever. I stood there stunned as the girl got up and gathered her clothes.

"Are you all right?" I asked, trying not to look at her as she quickly got dressed.

"What in the hell took you so long?" she fired back in annoyance.

Her reply perplexed me. I stood there in total confusion, not knowing how to respond. She sneered as she buttoned her shirt.

"Well? Are you waiting for a thank-you kiss or something? I should have your ass kicked for waiting so long." She paused and pointed to the dead man's crotch. "One more second and he would've had that filthy thing in me."

I said nothing as she marched past me to the door.

"My car's parked down the street where they ran me off the road. I can drive myself back."

The click of her shoes was all I heard after she exited. I turned to take one last look at the man I had killed, but his handgun suddenly caught my attention. Although I didn't know it at the time, it was a forty-five caliber semi-automatic pistol. All I saw was something that looked far better than the gun I already had. I picked it up and looked down to his body. While I should have been satisfied with the new pistol, the thought of having only two bullets left in my revolver came into my mind. I searched his clothing and found two extra magazines full of bullets. I had hit the jackpot. Suddenly, the shooting and the girl's odd rebuff didn't matter as much.

I walked out past the kid I had dropped earlier with my baseball bat. He was starting to twitch and grunt. A sense of relief came over me that I had killed only one person that day. I left him behind and went straight back to my apartment, elated by my fortune. I kept thinking about how I could finally mount an effective defense if I needed to.

* * *

It was difficult to sleep that night. The adrenaline rush was long gone, but thoughts of what I had done consumed me. Killing a real person wasn't anything like those first-person video games I used to play with the cool graphics and loud music.

Something also stirred in the distance. I heard sporadic gunfire early in the evening. It was distant, but close enough to get my attention. It stopped, and an unnerving quiet enveloped the area. Not even the animals were out fighting. Then came the fireworks. Starting around midnight, the sound of shooting came and went in waves through early morning. It sounded like a war had erupted north of Main Street, on the other side of the Charles River. An occasional booming explosion mixed in with the crackle of gunfire. Even though I was on the third floor, I couldn't see anything. Whatever was happening was too far away.

A memory came to me as I lay in the dark, trying to sleep during a lull in the distant clash. On the day after I graduated from high school, I had been sitting in my old backyard. It was a sunny afternoon in early June and I lounged in the shade of an oak tree. There wasn't a cloud in the sky. I felt neither too cold nor too hot. I wasn't thirsty, hungry, or longing for anything at the time. There were no pressing obligations on my mind. The pressures of school were behind me, my summer job didn't start until the following week, and the start of college was still a couple of months away. I relaxed, closed my eyes, and enjoyed a brief experience of perfect contentment.

I'd never felt anything like it since, and on that lonely night in Waltham I hungered for just a sliver of that glorious June afternoon. A terrible despair washed over me when I realized something like that would probably never come around again.

* * *

By dawn everything had gone quiet and seemed to stay that way. I had barely slept and was still in need of water. Considering how recently the distant uproar had settled down, I waited until the afternoon before daring to venture out. Everything was still quiet. Whatever had happened was clearly over.

I heard voices as I carefully approached Main Street and immediately ducked down a side street to skirt the area. Normally, I would've retreated back to my apartment, but I desperately needed the water. I was fairly certain I could find a detour around whoever it was without being seen. I had done it many times before. I was good at staying out of sight.

I was wrong.

I nearly walked into someone holding an assault rifle. He wasn't wearing any uniform, but the way he handled his gun gave me the impression that he was well trained. Suddenly, my nifty new pistol didn't seem all that comforting. He told me to raise my hands and lie face down on the ground. I put down my empty containers and did exactly what he demanded. He patted me down and quickly found my gun. After stepping back, he instructed me to stand and walk ahead of him.

The fact that he didn't shoot me on sight gave me a ray of hope. There was a good chance I'd make it out alive, but I also wondered if it would've been better for him to execute me on the spot. He wasn't a gang-banger, but I'd heard horror stories of abductions by survivalist nut-jobs.

I was led around a corner into a small group of armed men congregated around three vehicles. One of the vehicles was a Humvee. The other two looked like they used to be unmarked police cruisers. One of the men stepped forward. He was older, perhaps in his fifties, sporting a high, tight buzz-cut. He was tall, a bit overweight, and his serious demeanor didn't settle well with me. My captor handed him my pistol. After giving it a quick look-over, Mister Buzz-cut turned back and waved at someone who was still inside one of the cars.

"Is this him?" he growled.

The red-haired girl I had saved the day before peeked out from the back seat. "Yeah, that's him."

He nodded as the girl closed the car window. With a satisfied sigh he handed my gun back to me.

"What's your name?" he asked.

"Walt," I replied as I hesitantly took my gun. I couldn't understand why he was giving it back to me. I guess it was painfully obvious that I wouldn't have a chance to do much with it, considering all the heavy artillery that surrounded me. I certainly wasn't stupid enough to even think of trying anything rash.

"I'm Pat Donahue," he said as he reached out for a handshake. He allowed a smile to surface over his grim expression. "Hey, lighten up. Calm ya liwa, you're among friends."

Calm ya liwa was one of those odd Boston expressions that I rarely heard. I never learned it's origins, but it simply meant to relax.

"Thanks for saving my niece yesterday," Pat continued.

"You're welcome."

It was a rather pathetic reply, but it's all I could think to say at that point.

Pat turned to his men. "That's long enough. Let's pack it in and roll."

Everyone walked back to their cars and got in.

Pat waved for me to follow him. "You, too, Walt."

"Me?"

"Trust me, you don't want to hang around here after we leave."

"My place is only a few blocks over."

"Son," Pat replied with a patronizing chuckle, "Waltham is not a place you want to call home anymore. It's best you come with us."

I nodded and reluctantly joined Pat in the back seat of the Humvee. He handed me a sealed bottle of spring water. I sat and stared at it; it'd been months since I had last seen one.

"How long have you been stuck here?" Pat asked as I took my first gulp of the cleanest tasting water that had passed through my lips in a long time.

"Since the flu started."

"And you hung around?" Pat asked in a surprised tone as he looked me over. I couldn't blame him for what he must have been thinking. I was a sorry sight. My hair was a tangled mess, my scraggy beard hadn't seen much attention, and I hadn't bathed in days.

"This is where I live."

"That's unfortunate."

"So what's going on? It's hard to imagine it getting any worse around here."

Pat smiled. "You have no idea who you shot yesterday, do you?"

I only shook my head in reply.

"His street name was *Reaper*. His real name was Manuel Ortiz. He was the leader of the One-Two-Six gang. Please tell me that you at least noticed the fracas that erupted around here last night."

"I heard something coming from the other side of the Charles."

"Something?" Pat replied with a laugh. "It was a goddamn war. You started something that's going to come burning through your neighborhood real soon. Reaper's death set off a nice little chain of events. There were three gangs shooting it out with each other last night. It started when the One-Two-Six started fighting with each other for control of the gang. Two rival gangs tried to jump into the party. I expect more gangs to join in the big game tonight. It should be one hell of a mess. Waltham is now a highly contested territory."

"What gang are you from?" It was a bold question that came out of my mouth before I even had a chance to think about it.

"We're no gang, chucklehead," Pat snapped back in an authentic Boston accent, the type that I've heard poorly faked in numerous movies. "I lead an organization comprised mostly of former law enforcement, firefighters, and assorted city workers. They call me The Godfather."

I gave him an odd look.

"Yeah, I know it's a cheesy nickname, but it's useful. It gives the gangs around here something to think about, and we have a shitload of them to contend with."

"Do you think I could go back to my place, you know, to get some things?"

Pat smirked as he glanced me over. "Just so you know, I was a detective with Boston P.D. before this shit-storm came down on us. I can tell you don't have much to go back for, or you would've been carrying something a bit more formidable than that handgun you probably lifted from Reaper yesterday. Then there's the desperation of getting your water from the Charles. God, of all places to draw water from. I'm surprised you're not already dead from drinking that sewage."

"I just have some sentimental items I want to take with me."

"Look, Walt, I expect most of Waltham to be burned to the ground soon. Best to put as much distance between you and senti-ment as possible."

"So you came back for me before it all burns?"

Pat chuckled. "Not really. No offense, but finding you was a bonus. Consider yourself a lucky sonofabitch. I came here to make an appearance."

"Appearance?"

"Did you think that we were the only ones in the area? We were watched, and I wanted to make sure they all knew who I was."

"Why?"

"I'm laying bait to draw in several other gangs so tonight's party will be an extra big event. Seeing me here should give them the idea that I'm interested in claiming this town, which I'm not. At least not yet. But they'll think so, and I hope word will spread so they'll all come chargin' in to claim it first. I'll wait for them to kill each other off. They're pretty damn good at doing that - nothin' but a bunch of dumb-ass punks."

As we slowly negotiated the debris-strewn roads back to Boston, Pat elaborated on the current state of affairs. He described how the entire region was fragmented into territories controlled by numerous gangs. No one had heard anything from the emergency state bunker in Framingham, or any other government agency. Aside from some crackpots transmitting on rogue stations, the radio and television stations were dead. There had been no contact with the world outside of the Boston area for weeks.

Pat ran what he called the Bay State Alliance, or BSA, as most came to call it. It controlled most of Boston and Cambridge but lacked the resources to assert control elsewhere. Gangs sprang up like weeds, and they had little difficulty attracting members. They weren't motivated by drugs anymore. Everything was about survival. Most were ethnically driven, and Pat freely described them with all the racial slurs I'd ever heard, and a couple of new ones. Racism was one of the few things that prospered during that time. Only sadism prospered more.

Pat was proud of his Irish roots and he openly despised non-white races, particularly Blacks. It was rather disappointing to see how so much hatred had been lingering under what once had been a thin veneer of police professionalism. His career was done, so there was no point in hiding anything. The only reason he had taken me with him was because I happened to be Caucasian. If I had been any-thing else, he would've made his appearance, thanked me, and let me return to my apartment with that nice bottle of spring water for my trouble.

Pat told me how he lost his daughter to the flu and took in his niece, Kathryn, after his brother succumbed. She was a drama queen who tested his patience. She had sneaked out for a joyride, eventually got lost, and ended up driving past Reaper. He obviously saw a nice, working car, and a sexual conquest would be icing on the cake. Kathryn assumed that Pat had sent me after her because I sort of looked like the many guys who worked for him. Despite her childish, uppity demeanor, I'm certain young Kathryn had taken a harsh lesson to heart.

The flu pandemic had burned out, Pat said, at least in our area. Most people were dying of violence, starvation, and a broad spec-trum of illnesses related to poor living conditions. Pat claimed that he was trying to bring unity back to a lawless region. While his BSA was fairly well equipped, they were outnumbered. He figured his intelligence would offset this imbalance. In his mind, while the gangs were good at playing checkers, he played a patient game of chess.

It turned out that Reaper's death was the first domino to fall, allowing Pat to make some subtle but bold moves. It only took a little push to set off a battle for Waltham, and his publicity stunt the day we met would draw several other rival gangs into the fight. The resulting carnage would weaken them and lead to even more conflict. The BSA would wait and eventually mop up in the aftermath.

CHAPTER 3

"So, Walt, what did you do before everything went to hell?" I remember Pat asking as we crossed the Longfellow Bridge into Boston. The lack of traffic was stark. Bridge renovations had halted. Through the many gaps in the construction fence, it looked like the workers just shut off their construction equipment and walked away.

"Purchasing."

"Ah, so you worked with inventory?"

"I guess you could say that."

"Good, I have the perfect job for you because I'd like you to stick around. You're part of the BSA now."

"Job?"

Pat sighed and looked out over the river. "Walt, it took a hell of a lot of work to bring order back to this place. When everything first broke down, it was a goddamn free-for-all. People looted everything and capped anyone who got in their way. A bunch of us ex-police banded together and fought hard to put a stop to it. We killed and drove out a lot of wicked bad people. Our justice was quick and harsh. We found the hoarders and reclaimed everything they took. It turned out to be a shitload of badly needed supplies, so we put a warehouse system together back across the river in Cambridge. It's where we store and dispense all our supplies. My people nicknamed it *The Supermarket.* I'm always looking for trustworthy people to help manage the inventory. Shit like that has a way of growing its own legs, if you know what I mean."

"I do." And I really did. I could hardly believe the office supplies that regularly disappeared from my old company.

"Great to hear, because I really don't think you're cut out for enforcement. I'm going to put you up in a nice place over here in Beacon Hill. I'll get you hooked up with Tony Walsh, my procurement boss in charge of The Supermarket. Once you get settled in there, I'm sure you can have your pick of houses over in Cambridge if you want. Vacant housing is something we have plenty of around here. You just have to be willing to clean it out first. All I ask is for your loyalty. We're all trying to survive here and we can do it best by sticking together."

* * *

I met Tony Walsh a few days later at The Supermarket, which was located in what had been the Massachusetts Institute of Technology. Most of the buildings on campus had been hastily converted into warehouses. I once heard that they wanted to do the same for Harvard, but at the time it was located too close to Arlington and the burbs. Securing anything located that far from the city proved too troublesome.

Tony was the epitome of a sly, corrupt boss. He embraced nepotism, as everyone else did in the BSA organization. He had been a plumber and union representative in his former life. His personality was easygoing, but his shifty eyes gave me pause the very first time I met him. He was the type who would never say no to his superiors and always had a good excuse for the numerous times he wasn't able to keep his word. I think he could have talked his way out of cancer, or at least would've tried. He also looked like he'd suffer a heart attack if he climbed a staircase too quickly. In a world without electricity, there were a lot of staircases to contend with. So he had a healthy staff of young lackeys to run his errands.

The Supermarket operation mainly warehoused food, fuel, medicine, and weapons. There were several collection teams that went through areas to salvage anything of value. It was all sent back to The Supermarket to be sorted. Overall, it was a much larger operation than I first imagined.

I was put in charge of the day shift in the main building that received, recorded, and sorted the daily deliveries from the collection teams. Once sorted, the supplies would be transferred to any number of other buildings on campus for storage and eventual disbursement. The BSA had thousands of people under its rule, and more migrated there on a daily basis. The Supermarket concept was something that set the BSA apart from everyone else. Pat seemed serious about taking care of his people.

There was only one building I was not allowed to access: the armory. I had no issue with that. Weaponry, and the responsibility for tracking them was something I didn't want to mess with.

* * *

Pat was genuinely grateful that I had saved Kathryn from a heinous experience, but I always had the feeling he was most pleased with the opportunity I had handed him by killing Reaper. He hated owing people, so taking me in and getting me set up with a job at his Supermarket was an easy way to repay a debt. He also made sure I was put up in a nice brownstone on Beacon Hill. I liked it so much that I never did move to Cambridge.

Like Waltham, there was no electricity or running water. It was, however, a much nicer and safer place to live where clean water was delivered every morning. The sewage system hadn't backed up like it had in my old apartment, so I could manually flush the toilet with a bucket of water. That might seem like a minor consolation, but at the time it was a pretty big deal. Having toilet paper again was also a huge perk.

The BSA had firm control of downtown Boston, most of Brookline, Cambridge, and some of Watertown. Just south of Boston was a mishmash of ethnic gangs controlling pieces of Dorchester, Jamaica Plain, Roxbury, and Mattapan. The Italian gangs had control of almost everything north of Boston, Charlestown, and Revere. The suburbs were a complete mess. Control out there shifted on a daily basis. No one could keep up with what was going on a mere ten miles from Boston, nor did anyone really care.

Hundreds of refugees came into the city every day and Pat set up special selection boards to deal with them. These boards would decide who could stay and where everyone else would be sent. Typically, Caucasians were allowed to stay. Everyone else, unless they had a skill that was in demand, did not. It was no surprise that most non-Caucasians who were deemed skilled were attractive young women. The rest of them were expelled south to contend with the gangs. It was far from a perfect existence, but it was still much better than what I'd had back in Waltham.

* * *

My Supermarket sorting teams were a collection of people with BSA connections. Unfortunately, that's about all the good that could be said about them. It became immediately apparent that they were stuck in those jobs because they were too dimwitted to contribute anywhere else. It seemed that anyone high up in the BSA organization stuck their dumb-ass cousin in The Supermarket to keep them out of everyone's hair.

My first order of business was to develop idiot-proof procedures. The work wasn't that hard, but it did require some thought. However, in time I came to appreciate the basic nature of my workers: they were just too stupid or afraid to steal. They'd also snitch on anyone who did. It made my job a lot easier, despite the constant bungling I had to endure.

I soon discovered that some collected items stayed off the books. Tony had a little side-business going. At first I noticed an occasional truck making a transfer to another truck but soon stopped paying attention to it. Making waves was the last thing I wanted to do as the new guy. I did my job and minded my own business. I made sure that everything ran as smoothly as could be expected. Each item was received, well documented, and got to where it was supposed to go. I didn't give anyone a reason to think that I wasn't doing my job.

I really had nothing to complain about. I had a nice home, regular meals, and a purpose. I was once again content with my life as it was.

Meanwhile, Pat's strategy for dealing with gangs was succeeding. Several of them had committed to the conquest of Waltham and ended up paying a hefty price in attrition. This set off several additional conflicts as other gangs tried to seize on any perceived weaknesses with each other. At first, all I saw was an influx of used weapons as BSA enforcers slowly cleaned up in the aftermath. Then came recovered supplies as each gang fell and new neighborhoods were captured. Pat was particularly harsh in the areas south of Boston. He drove the residents out of the area like they were rodents and routinely executed the gang-bangers. It was driven by racism in its most ugly form.

* * *

As I settled into my new job, I was forced to embrace a difficult reality that my operation was too honest. Tony expected his people to act dishonestly by skimming items for themselves. To him, this was acceptable so long as you didn't take too much. On the other hand, showing honesty was a clear indication to him that you had something to hide that could cause big problems. Tony had little patience for those kinds of problems, and I quickly learned not to attract his attention in that way. He had a simple philosophy: if you weren't skimming, you were unhappy - and he was deeply suspicious of unhappy people.

So I had to learn how to skim. Not only that, I had to learn what to skim and how much.

What had once been commonly available items could easily fetch a handsome price. One of my workers once held up a case of feminine hygiene products and jokingly declared that he could use it to get laid every night for a year. He was actually underestimating its value. I could have easily bought a woman with it. In fact, for a bottle of ibuprofen, I could have probably bought my own harem of sex-slaves.

I didn't really need much, so I was at a loss as to what to skim. Then there was the guilt I felt over taking things I really didn't need. Despite the stability the BSA brought to the area, there were still far too many people who were in need. The thought of skimming needed items away from them caused me profound remorse. At first, it was surprising how deeply this affected me. Before the pandemic, I wouldn't even think about people in need. I'd occasionally see a homeless person, but the only thought that came to my mind, before ignoring the person, was how I was glad it wasn't me. Now poverty was all around me and I couldn't ignore it. I felt strangely compelled to do something to help. I suppose all that Sunday School my parents forced me to endure as a kid really had made a difference.

The solution to my skimming dilemma came a short distance from where I lived. There was a neighborhood nicknamed *The Pit*, located in what used to be known as the Back Bay. The rows of old Victorian brownstones were crammed with non-Caucasian BSA citizens who were deemed worthy to stay. They were all good people bunched together by the order of our racist godfather. Many of them were actually American-born and highly educated. They were as American as I was, but their living conditions were deplorable. They would often get the leftovers from our BSA order, if there were any. They had only two working fire hydrants to draw their water from, which forced them to ration it at dangerously low levels. Sickness was too common. In that neighborhood, it seemed that just as many bodies were carried out as new citizens were moved in.

It upset me how poorly the residents of The Pit were treated, but I was in a position to do something about it. However, I also had to be extremely careful how I'd channel supplies into that neighborhood. Getting it into the right hands was only part of the problem. If Tony ever discovered that I was directing my skimmed goods to non-whites, he'd mount my head on his wall for Pat to enjoy every time he visited. To further complicate things, if too many people found out what I was doing, I'd have a mob of candidates at my front door every morning. Discretion was critical. Fortunately, I was helping some highly intelligent people who understood exactly what needed to be done as well as the consequences of not keeping it on the down-low. I only wish I could have done more for them at the time, but I did end up making some important friends.

* * *

In September 2015, I met Glenn Bradshaw. He was a refugee who had walked in from Newton during the prior month. A former vice president of marketing, he was deemed skilled by a selection board and assigned to supervise the medical supply storage building in The Supermarket complex. His job was particularly challenging because most of the recovered medical supplies needed to be carefully vetted. Even the smallest imperfection in some items could be deadly. Medication was particularly difficult to categorize and expiration dates were hard to judge without original packaging. I helped him to develop strict but simplified criteria for the medical sorters. Glenn appreciated the assist because he was far more accustomed to working with educated supervisors. It took him a while to learn how to dumb things down.

Glenn was affable and easy to work with. Like me, he was just happy to be there. He had experienced a particularly rough time during the height of the flu pandemic, which claimed his wife and young daughter. He was thirty-eight, stood at an even six foot, and was in excellent physical condition. His positive attitude and congenial personality won him many friends, but it didn't play well with Tony. Tony was jealous of Glenn's magnetic personality and felt threatened. Tony didn't like it when someone else was more popular around The Supermarket than he was.

* * *

I recall a lunchtime talk with Glenn in late October. He was frustrated over dealing with all the BSA cronies, just as I was. Tony wasn't making it easy on him, either.

"Aren't you getting tired of all this shit?" I remember Glenn asking me as we sat on a bench during a warm autumn day. We had just finished our lunches and were trying to enjoy the colorful foliage.

"Yeah, since it all started," I cynically replied.

"I mean here, now, at this place," Glenn persisted.

"Hey, don't let Ass-Clown get to you," I implored, using our new private nickname for Tony. Tony was annoying, and had a talent of wearing people down. It looked like Glenn was beginning to buckle. He looked disheveled and had allowed his full head of black hair to grow too long. Dark circles were also prominent under his eyes.

"He forced me to ship an expired lot of pain meds over to the hospital yesterday."

"That's not good."

"That's why I called over to warn the pharmacy. Do you know what the lead pharmacist told me? She said to mind my own fucking business and let the people who know what they're doing make that decision - total bullshit."

"You think she's working an angle with Tony?" I wondered. "Because I wouldn't put anything past him."

"She's a hack, so anything's possible. There's just too many of them to deal with."

"Agreed."

"It's not like we're finding and keeping the good people, anyway. I heard the selection board turned away one of the best ophthalmologists in the country last week. It's all because she was Indian. If she'd been young and hot, they would've kept her around."

"Yeah, I've heard a few of those stories." I was down-playing it.

I'd actually been hearing way too many similar stories through my contacts at The Pit. It really all depended which selection board she went through. There were several, and only one of them seemed to care about which people to keep around. They could be bribed, but their price was often too high.

"You know that old guy with the silver hair I've got working for me?" Glenn continued. His dander was up and he was on a roll. "Do you know he's an M.D. with over thirty years in a successful family practice? He should be over at Boston General instead of inspecting pills with the village idiots. But I suppose we'd rather have a bunch of well-connected hacks practicing half-assed medicine."

"Maybe I can have a talk with Pat about him," I suggested. I would've, too. Despite my deteriorating opinion of him, I was still on good terms with The Godfather.

"It would be a waste of time. There's already a shitload of people around here who are in the wrong place and doing the wrong things. It's such a goddamn waste of talent. In fact, this whole BSA thing is turning out to be a monumental fuck-up. And what part of this mess is considered an alliance? It's not like we're actually allied with anyone." Glenn paused as he leaned back and let out an exasperated sigh. "I'd feel better if someone at least acted like we had a plan, because I don't see any real progress being made. There's no long-term vision. All we seem to be doing is surviving by picking over the remains of our past civilization. We just conquer and consume. What happens when we run out of neighborhoods to loot?"

Glenn was right. He was also making me uncomfortable. Talk like that could get both of us into serious trouble. I remember looking around to check if anyone else might have overheard him. Plenty of people would snitch on us in a heartbeat in order to get a reward.

"Can I show you something?" Glenn asked me in a low voice.

"Show me what?"

Glenn rose and gestured for me to follow him. We walked across the campus to a section that I thought wasn't in use. We approached an old building that had vines growing up over it. He led me to a side door and pried it open. We squeezed in before he closed it behind us. It took a minute for our eyes to adjust to the dim lighting that leaked in through the vine-covered windows.

"This way," Glenn beckoned as he continued deeper into the

building. Soon we entered a large room at the back. It extended for the length of the building and was illuminated by a number of large picture windows. Rays of sunshine glinted off particles of dust that floated in the air. A slight musty smell mixed with a number of other odors, which mostly reminded me of a new car smell. The cavernous room was jammed full of boxes, crates, and furniture.

"I stumbled on this last week. There are three more floors above us crammed full of the same sort of stuff."

"What is all of this?"

"Ass-Clown's bounty that he keeps off the books. Just look at it all!"

It was difficult to take in at once, and not unlike one of those old television reality shows about hoarders. Except this was on a far larger scale. There were only a couple of narrow pathways to navigate through the mess.

"There's a row of microwaves over there," Glenn continued as he pointed around, "an assortment of flat screen televisions toward the far end, camping equipment, toothbrushes, auto parts; it just goes on and on. I've only briefly looked it over and there's no sense of order to anything. It looks like it was just tossed in here as it was unloaded."

I took a couple of minutes to wander around, trying to process it all. Most of what I saw was an overwhelming mess of contradictions because many items I observed could no longer be used.

"Does he think the old world is coming back sometime soon?" I wondered. "Most of this stuff is useless."

"I'm sure it underscores the mental illness we always suspected he has, but I did find some things that can be used. It's enough to make you wonder what else is buried in here. It'll take weeks to go through it all."

"Useful? Like what?"

"There are cases of toilet paper over there we could liberate, sitting on top of those washing machines."

"You know we can't touch any of this."

"Why not? This place is a complete mess. He couldn't possibly notice if we took a few things here and there."

"Do you really want to play that game with Tony?" I cautioned.

What Glenn suggested was tempting, but it was also playing

with fire. Tony had a lot of laughable traits, but ultimately, he was ruthless when crossed. Both of us were keenly aware that neither of us was indispensable. I doubt Pat would've said anything if we suddenly disappeared at Tony's decree. Things like that already occurred with unsettling regularity.

"We just can't walk away without doing something about it," Glenn retorted. "All of this represents everything that's screwed up with the BSA. Don't you want to make things better?"

"Yeah, but we need to stay alive to make things better."

Glenn stewed silently. I understood his frustration. It was too easy to take rash action in those days. Many tried; most had failed.

"Look, let's just pull back and think about this for a while," I calmly suggested. "We have some time because I can't see how any of this stuff is going anywhere soon. There's no way Tony could move it all without a lot of people noticing."

"Yeah," Glenn reluctantly conceded. He drew in a deep breath and took one last look around. That's when I noticed a peculiar, crooked smile surface on his face. I'd never seen it before, but I have several times since. I had unknowingly planted a seed of resolve in him, which was funny because all I was trying to do was put him off from doing something rash. I thought he just needed some time to cool down so that whatever bold ideas that ran through his mind at that moment would melt away. I had no idea that I had supplied the first spark which would smolder for a while, but later igniting a firestorm of changes.

CHAPTER 4

As winter settled in, Glenn and I became closer friends. We often shared dinner at each other's homes and schemed about how we'd take Tony down. Most of it was benign brainstorming to blow off steam. Tony hadn't done much with his bounty, or *vault,* as we came to call it. We figured he couldn't do anything with it until the spring. It was nearing Christmas and several inches of snow had been dumped on us.

The cold and snow stopped just about everything. No longer were there fleets of snowplows and sanders to keep the roads open for the few vehicles that remained in operation. The weather also made it difficult for Pat to carry on his fight against the few remaining gangs. The push into new territories ground to a halt and the influx of supplies slowed as a result. Everyone just wanted to hunker down and keep warm.

Boston seldom experienced long stretches of severe, sub-zero temperatures, but I never realized how cold winter could feel without modern heating systems. My home was kept warm by a wood-burning stove that Glenn helped me install. On most cold nights, I climbed into bed dressed in thermal underwear with several blankets pulled over my head. It took me a while to get used to that; pre-pandemic, I had always slept in my boxers. My office was a little better. Several of us moved our desks into the same room and kept it warm with a portable heating unit powered by a generator. We arranged for the warehouse workers to cycle in for short breaks to get warm.

Glenn learned of my skimming arrangement with those in The Pit. It impressed him and he wanted to join. The winter brought on critical needs and we did our best to ease at least some of their burdens. We soon became known as the Robin Hoods of the BSA. Tony remained oblivious to our charitable deeds while he continued to stuff even more bounty into his secret vault.

* * *

About once a week, I received a visit from a designated messenger from The Pit. This messenger would bring me a list of items in critical demand. The person who carried out this role would change every so often in order to maintain our secrecy. Many in our plush Beacon Hill neighborhood hired people from The Pit to do small tasks, so it made it easy for my messenger contact to show up at my door. One day, an older man of Asian descent knocked on my door. He was supposed to fix a generator that didn't really need to be repaired. This signaled that he was the new messenger.

He introduced himself as Chung-Hee Kym. He had been born in South Korea and moved to America for his college education. He greeted me at my front door with a smile and a polite bow. I only gave him a dismissive nod as I closed the door. Once the outside world was safely shut out, I smiled and shook his hand.

"Please come in and warm up," I implored as I took his worn coat, certainly not heavy enough to keep him warm. All I could think of at that point was how to find him a better one. The more I saw these sorts of needs, the more I thought about Tony's vast vault of goodies. But Glenn and I still had a lot more work to do in order to deal with that.

"I'm happy to finally meet you. I've heard much about what you've been doing. Thank you so much for your kindness to our neighborhood."

"You're welcome. So, we're going to be working with each other for a little while."

"At least until I can get your generator working properly. I imagine we can make it an excuse for another three or four visits to get the repairs right. This assumes you don't mind being without your generator for those times."

"I don't use it very much. It's a terrible waste of gasoline."

"This is a very nice home. Do you have a wife? Children?"

"I live alone."

The fact that I was alone never caused me much sorrow. I could easily afford the company of a prostitute whenever I desired, but I never indulged. Besides the risk of contracting any number of rampant STI's, having a woman around was a dangerous luxury in that day. Finding one was easy. Many would be more than eager to pair off with someone like me to get what they really desired – wealth and comfort. It was a lousy premise for a relationship which became even more expensive as time went on.

It could even get you killed. I had heard that one of Pat's lieutenants disappeared with his new girl shortly after she thought she was entitled to anything she wanted. Apparently, this included helping herself to several bottles of rare wine that Pat had placed aside for himself. Despite having a whole warehouse full of liquor, it didn't take much to draw Pat's ire.

In all, it was too hard to find a good woman among the many who were adept at acting the part, and I already had enough complications in my life. I didn't need another Veronica around me.

Chung-Hee produced a wax-sealed envelope which contained the latest list of needed items. The wax-seal was important as it indicated that the contents weren't tampered with. The list inside requested most of the usual things Glenn or I could easily procure without drawing attention. I still liked to include a few extras whenever I could find something, but nothing too unique. I didn't want anything being traced back to me. I stayed away from bright colored clothing, expensive items, or anything that looked too new. Even something as simple as a cashmere scarf could draw too many questions. I had to hang on to the more extravagant items to have something to show to my occasional BSA crony visitors.

It always made me cringe when people like Chung-Hee came into my home. I could only imagine what he must have been thinking while sitting down on the expensive leather couch in my lavishly adorned living room.

"Can I get you anything?" I asked, noticing his careful gaze around the room as he sat.

"There is one thing." He hesitated as he reached into his pocket and drew out a small slip of paper. "I'm sorry to be so bold, but my daughter is quite ill with a serious infection. It's not the flu, but she needs antibiotics. I've written down several possibilities with the accompanying dosages."

"How old is she?" I asked as he handed me the paper.

"Four. She can swallow pills, so please don't worry about what

form you find the medication in. I'm sorry if this seems like a consid-
erable request from someone you have just met, but I don't know
where else to go. The hospital is not giving me the correct medication."

"How do you know it's not correct?"

"Because I'm a doctor and most of the hospital staff is incompe-
tent or unwilling to help me."

"Why do they have you fixing generators?"

Chung-Hee gave me a faint chuckle. "You didn't notice my
race?"

"I understand, but I figured you'd be assigned to something
associated with your medical background."

"I actually spend most of my time fixing or fine-tuning medical
equipment at the hospital. Repairing things like generators is something I do on the side for anything extra I can get for my family."

"What was your specialty?"

"Neurosurgery."

"A brain surgeon? Seriously?" His predicament underscored
what Glenn commonly complained about. I had never doubted that
he was right, but this was the first person I had interacted with whose
talents were being egregiously wasted.

"What can I say? Chung-Hee replied with a shrug of his shoulders."

I opened the note and read over his list. I'd seen a couple of the
medication names before, but most of it was gibberish to me.

"I have a friend who should be able to help me with this. If I succeed, I'll make sure my generator breaks again tomorrow and send
for you."

Tears welled up in his eyes. "Thank you."

"Not a problem. Oh, and before I forget, please tell your handler
the next drop will be made at C-6."

While messengers hand-delivered the lists to me, the deliveries
were dropped at varying locations. We only referred to them as codes
so the messengers had no idea where or when the drop would occur.
Only the coordinator at The Pit would know what the code meant
and dispatched a separate pick-up team. We found out the hard way
that some messengers were too tempted to skim some of the deliveries for themselves, so we compartmentalized our operation to

minimize that possibility.

"C-6, right."

"Are you sure you don't want anything to drink? I have a nice selection at my bar for when I entertain the BSA stooges."

"Thanks, but no. I really need to get to work on your generator. It should look like I've made an attempt to fix it in case anyone bothers to check."

"You're very thorough. Take as much time as you need and get warmed up. You can tell your wife that I'll try my best to get the meds for your little girl."

Chung-Hee gave me an awkward smile as he rose. I showed him the generator and he diligently went to work. It took me a while to understand why he had given me that awkward smile. I eventually learned his wife had been shot dead over the summer while they journeyed to Boston. Everyone seemed to have a tragic story but me.

* * *

The next morning, I walked to The Supermarket across the Longfellow Bridge. It was an icy trek because some of the snow had melted the previous day but refroze overnight. There were small teams of people trying to chip and shovel off the frozen slush. It seemed like a ridiculous effort. The roads were still mostly impassable and the crews were woefully understaffed. I would've slept over at The Supermarket like Glenn did, but I had had to meet with Chung-Hee to get the list.

I handed the list of meds to Glenn when I arrived, and he seemed confident he could score something satisfactory. By the end of the day, he paid me a short visit and discreetly handed me a brown plastic bottle of pills. He told me it was actually filled with two doses of possibilities from the list, in case Chung-Hee's daughter couldn't manage one of them. He seemed unusually motivated to go the extra mile and I figured it was because he had a soft spot for sick daughters.

I sent a messenger to call Chung-Hee back to repair my generator. To be honest, I wouldn't have known if it had actually been broken because I hardly used it. Gasoline supplies were quickly dwindling in the cold weather. We were incapable of producing any and the gas stations were starting to run dry. The recovery teams were also running out of cars to siphon. Instead of using candles, a privileged few recklessly wasted what little we had left to power their lights.

I left work early and walked back to keep my generator repair appointment. On my way back over the bridge, I noticed someone following at a discreet distance. I remembered seeing the same guy as I walked out my front door that morning. In fact, I also recalled seeing him a couple of days before. I came to call him Mr. Ordinary, mainly because he was failing so badly at trying to appear ordinary. He was young, lanky, and wore a weathered Red Sox cap.

My mind raced over who had a tail put on me and what I might have skimmed to draw such attention. It was probably Tony because Mr. Ordinary didn't seem good at what he did. If anyone else higher up in the BSA had me followed, they would've found someone more competent, and I wouldn't have noticed him.

I ignored Mr. Ordinary and walked on. There was nothing I could do about it other than to keep him thinking I didn't notice. I hoped he was just keeping an eye on me that afternoon and didn't plan to shake me down. On any other day, I wouldn't have minded if he did because Tony expected me to be smuggling things out. However, it would've been too difficult to explain the antibiotics. Medical supplies were generally considered off limits for skimming.

I made it back to my home and closed out the world behind me. I hid the brown bottle of pills in the best place I could think of in case my next visitor wasn't Chung-Hee. Occasionally, I peeked out the window, but Mr. Ordinary was gone.

A knock at my door an hour later announced the arrival of Chung-Hee. He entered and gave me his customary bow. I gave one quick glance around outside to see if Mr. Ordinary was still lurking. There was no sign of him.

"Good to see you again, Dr. Kym." I figured the poor guy at least deserved the respect to be called by his title. The affirming nod I received gave me a feeling of satisfaction. He later admitted to me how moved he was to be called *doctor* again. It never ceases to surprise me how the smallest gestures can be so important.

"I understand your generator isn't working again."

I smiled and walked to retrieve the bottle of pills. "Yes, you really need to do a better job at fixing these things. It's not like it's brain surgery."

His eyes widened as I handed him the bottle. Before he could open the bottle for a closer inspection, he sat down before his knees buckled.

"My friend wanted to be thorough, so he gave you two different doses. I hope they're what you need."

Chung-Hee carefully inspected the pills. His hands quivered and tears came to his eyes. "I can hardly believe this."

"Did we get it right?"

"Yes, both would've worked. Do you need to take one back?"

"They're both yours, Doctor. Maybe you can find someone else who needs what you don't use?"

Chung-Hee carefully closed the bottle and placed it in his pocket. Tears were running down his cheeks.

"May you be blessed, Walter. You're truly a saint in God's service."

To that point, I had not heard anyone talk about, or even refer to God, without its being part of an obscenity. I was convinced that the pandemic had completely driven religion from the world. The last time I had even thought about God was a few months back when I had been convinced He had taken a huge steaming dump on the world and moved on. So I was a bit curious how anyone could hang on to their beliefs after all that had happened.

"Would a saint resort to stealing?" I wondered to him.

"Have you broken any laws?" he carefully countered. He was actually right. I might have bent some guidelines, but there really were no laws anymore. There was only an understanding that you didn't take more than Tony or Pat thought you should. Thus far, I hadn't heard any complaints from either.

"Thanks for the good thought, but I think God turned His back on this hell-hole a while back."

"Maybe not," Chung-Hee politely rebutted with a smile. After a pause, he added, "I should get to work."

Once again he disassembled my generator. He didn't rush, either. I would've let him leave within five minutes so he could get the meds back to his sick daughter, but he was committed to making sure the generator fix looked legitimate. He didn't want to leave the slightest chance of anything coming back to implicate me.

* * *

"Damn, Walt. When do I get a turn at something like that?" Glenn asked me that evening. I had recounted to him what had happened as we sat eating dinner at my table. He seemed to take extraordinary joy from learning that he had supplied the right antibiotics.

The system we had developed for making delivery drops always kept us from experiencing the elation of the people we aided. We'd only occasionally hear something back through the messengers, which tended to blunt any satisfaction over what we were doing. It just had to be that way. Our identities had to be shielded.

"Are you sure the hospital pharmacist won't miss them?"

"Don't even worry about it. I sent on a batch of slightly expired substitutes, since they don't care about dates."

"Glenn, that man should be heading up the hospital," I griped. "He's a goddamn neurosurgeon!"

"Oh, please don't get me started on that again."

"By the way, I think I've picked up a tail."

"Seriously?"

"Yeah, some guy has been following me around over the past couple of days."

"You think it's one of Ass-Clown's lackeys?"

"This guy fits. He doesn't seem particularly good at what he's doing."

"Do you think Tony's onto us?"

"I doubt it. He's never shy about spewing accusations, so maybe he's just fishing around."

Glenn sighed. "Whatever the reason, it's going to complicate our deliveries to The Pit. I can't completely take over without eventually drawing too much attention. It's just the two of us, you know."

"I know. Maybe I should just confront this guy to see what it's all about?"

"Really bad idea. It'll just convince him you've got something to hide."

"What do we do, then?"

"We need to find ways to shake off the tail." Glenn paused and thought for minute. "Okay, how's this? If he's still following you, try leading-off with a visit to someone higher up in the BSA food chain. You know, make it look like a bribe or a gift. Your tail will probably let up and you can move on to other things."

An idea hit me. "Hey, Christmas is coming. Maybe it's time for us to reinstate the spirit of giving? I'm chummy with a couple of Pat's lieutenants who live in the neighborhood. You know a couple of BSA guys, too. I can try to lead off with a Christmas gift delivery, and then move on to the real drop point if the tail gets shaken off."

"Nice idea, Walt. I think it'll work, at least for a little while. We can only use it up until Christmas."

"What do we do after that? You know, if this guy keeps tailing me?"

Glenn sighed. "Then we'll need to make a move on Tony."

I got up from the table and paced. We had talked about it numerous times before, but it was always when we knew that we weren't in a position to follow through. Now it was getting too real for my comfort.

"You know how this will end for him," I said.

"Yeah," Glenn glumly replied.

We had never before openly acknowledged how it would play out. No matter how many times we schemed about it, we couldn't devise a way to get a guy like Tony into trouble without lethal repercussions. This wasn't a company you got fired from when the boss was displeased. You usually got executed. Tony was easy to dislike, but could we really hate someone so much as to hand him a death sentence? At that point, the only thing we could do was to come to a naive acceptance that the good simply outweighed the bad. I've heard it said that people tend to dehumanize their intended victim to make it easier, but I think we did the opposite. I can't ever remember us referring to him as Ass-Clown after that point.

"Now that we're clear on that," Glenn continued, "we're back to the same problem. How do we get him into trouble for stockpiling things like microwaves, televisions, and air conditioners? Nobody up the BSA food chain cares about shit like that."

"What if all the microwaves, televisions, and air conditioners are camouflaging something far more valuable? The place is a complete mess. He could be hiding almost anything in there."

"I know, but do we have time to dig through everything to find out? We'll probably get caught looking."

"Maybe we should just find a sniper rifle and shoot him from a safe distance." I tossed it out as a joke but found it ironic that it really wasn't far off from what we were planning. Still, something about my joke got Glenn thinking.

"Have you ever come across a sniper rifle?"

"Glenn, it was only a joke."

"I know, but think about it. What happens when recovered weapons or ammo comes into your sorting operation?"

"Tony jumps in with his goons and immediately takes them to the armory."

"Exactly. It's one of the few things he doesn't screw around with. It's the only time he gets off his lazy ass because it's something he has to do right."

"I agree, but how does that help us?"

"What if some of those weapons found their way into his secret vault?"

"He might as well take a shower with a hairdryer...well, if we still had electricity. It'd be a more merciful ending."

Glenn blurted a laugh. "Exactly. It would end him. Problem solved."

"But there's still no way to lift weapons from my operation. There are too many eyes on the process."

Glenn leaned forward. "Okay, let's think it through. Access to the armory is out of the question. It's closely guarded and everything is too well documented. If any of it ended up in Tony's vault, it would be obvious that he's being set up because even he wouldn't be so stupid to lift weapons from inventory. Whatever ends up in his vault would have to be off the books."

"I agree, and now we're back to our original problem."

"It's simple. We just need to uncover our own weapons cache."

"Simple?" I laughed. "Like guns are just lying around on the street waiting for us to come get them?"

"Can't you have someone lift a couple the next time your team finds some?"

"Make them disappear before they enter my operation? Maybe, but do you think we can find anyone in my pool of snitches to trust?"

Glenn sighed and nodded. "Point taken."

"What about police records?" I wondered.

"Records? What records?"

"Gun registration records. Pat found some nice hardware from former gun owners that way. We could use the same idea."

"Didn't you just say Pat's already thought of that?

"Yeah, but only around Boston. What about out in the burbs?"

"Way out there? Walt, buddy, I think it's time to call it a night. You're getting too tired to think straight."

"Yeah," I conceded and stretched my arms back. "What was I thinking? Probably best we sleep on it."

"Wait a minute," Glenn suddenly said. "I just remembered something Smitty told me."

"Smitty?"

"Yeah, it's the nickname for Pat's new lieutenant. You know, the guy from Southie."

"Oh, yeah. The tall, wiry, tough guy?"

"That's him. He mentioned a down-tick in refugees, and those who recently came in reported there are only a few people left out there."

"Out where?"

"West. That's why Smitty was telling me that. Because Pat's planning a push out that way this spring. They want to go out along Route 2. We've already got parts of Arlington, so he must be talking about Belmont, Lexington, and Concord."

I smiled. "Just the kinds of affluent towns I was talking about."

"Well, if we wanted to do a little recon, it sounds like it might not be as dangerous as we thought. If we go after dark, anyone still living out there will be inside trying to keep warm."

"How do we get out there?" I asked. "All the roads out of BSA territory are watched."

"We take another kind of road."

"Railroad?"

"Exactly. Maybe we could walk out along the old Fitchburg commuter rail?"

I had a really good idea. "There's a direct route that's far more pedestrian friendly: The Minuteman Bikeway. It runs right by the old Lexington police station and ends in Bedford, not too far from their police station. I doubt anyone would be watching that route, particularly if we go after dark."

"All the way out to Bedford? We're going to freeze our asses off. Then there's all the snow on the ground. Way too much noise."

"It's been warming up, so the snow should melt away in a couple of days. Let's at least make the walk to the Lexington police station and look for gun records."

"That might work."

"If we don't get another snowstorm, we can take a couple of days off around Christmas and check it out."

"Assuming someone hasn't already thought of it."

"Do you want to get rid of Tony or not?"

Glenn leaned back in his seat. A crooked smile emerged on his face; the same one I had last seen when we were in Tony's vault. "I'm up for it."

CHAPTER 5

Over the next two days, Mr. Ordinary followed me almost every-where I went. He didn't seem aware that I took notice of him, and he was so clumsy that I started to wonder if he truly cared about what he was doing. Perhaps I was supposed to notice him. It wasn't unusual for Tony to play mind games with people.

We decided to put our Christmas-gift idea into motion. The gifts weren't terribly elaborate and I easily found Christmas wrapping paper. There was plenty of it left behind in abandoned homes, but I had to act quickly before it was burned up. People were fueling their fireplaces with anything that burned.

To our surprise, our plan worked, but maybe a little too well. It stopped Mr. Ordinary from following me, but before long, Christmas gifts were being exchanged between all the BSA cronies out of fear that they would look stingy in the eyes of everyone else. Who would've known that Glenn and I would keep Christmas alive in a corrupt culture that was barely surviving around us?

A few days before Christmas, I informed Tony that we'd be taking a couple of days off. Tony didn't balk at it. He couldn't afford to. All the gift exchanging we'd started had earned us enough credit for some time off. The look on Tony's face when he agreed to the hol-iday break was comical. He had to have been pissed that his surveillance had been shaken off, but there was nothing he could do but wish me a merry Christmas through his phony smile.

Our plan was to walk to the Lexington police station and look for gun ownership records. It would be about a twelve mile round-trip walk, which seemed a reasonable goal to pull off in one night. We would also have some extra time to explore any nearby possibilities if an opportunity to look for guns presented itself. I had been through Lexington a few times in the past, so I was fairly familiar with the town.

The weather cooperated. It stayed above freezing, so the only storm we had before Christmas was a rainstorm. The ground was bare when we departed BSA territory on foot near the old Alewife T-station in North Cambridge. We caught a ride there with a trusted friend and had arranged another ride home with someone different. To them they thought we were just visiting some friends in the area for Christmas Eve. Theoretically, we could have walked directly to the Alewife station from Boston by following the old red-line subway, but that was out of the question. Nobody dared to explore the old subway tunnels. There were rumors about what was really down there – a hideout for black market thugs; deranged cannibalistic gangs; a home to any number of ferocious animals; a place were bodies were hidden. Maybe the truth was a little of each. Regardless of what actually resided in those long, dark tunnels, no sane person would ever venture down there. Besides, we had enough of a walk ahead of us to Lexington. We didn't need to add in a long trek out to North Cambridge.

We set out around eight o'clock in the evening on the paved former bike trail. The weather had become colder, but we had dressed for it. We took some empty nylon bags, just in case we got lucky and found something. We were only after files, but you still always had to plan for luck. We took our handguns with us. Both of us practiced on a firing range whenever we had some spare ammunition. I got to be a pretty good shot; Glenn, not so much.

Flashlights were the toughest things to get our hands on. Actually, they were easy to find. Working batteries were the scarce commodity. Out of all the things we brought with us that night, we spent the most time and effort acquiring those batteries.

The sky was clear, and fortunately there wasn't much moonlight. We needed the darkness to cover our trek up the trail. Some parts were obscured by fallen trees, but we managed to get by them with minimal use of our flashlights. There seemed to be no sign of life in the houses that were close to the trail, but we noticed an occasional flicker of light through a distant window or caught a whiff of smoke on the brisk gusts of wind. There was a little life left in Lexington and we tried our best to pass by unnoticed. It was dead quiet, and every time we stepped on a twig, the resulting crack seemed to shoot out and echo in all directions. We'd stop and listen, but there was never any sign that we were attracting unwanted attention.

It took a couple of hours to reach the police station. The front door had already been broken wide open, but there was no sign of life in the area. We carefully entered and had to climb past broken furniture and other debris strewn all over the hallways. A rainbow of spray paint decorated all the walls, put there by gang after gang. Eventually, we made our way to the basement records room and found it to be a complete disaster. File cabinets had been pushed over and beaten by who knows what. It looked hopeless.

Glenn shrugged his shoulders as he looked around at the mess. I started to wade deeper into the room to check over whatever file cabinet labels were left on the drawers. We spent almost an hour looking through the disorder to no avail. My hands were starting to get numb and I shivered in the cold. We were about to give up when I accidentally bumped into a file drawer while on my way out of the room. Like most of the other file cabinets, it had been beaten up and its integrity was undermined. It tipped over with a crash and spewed file folders all over the already cluttered floor. I cringed over the noise, hoping it was contained within the walls of the police station. Glenn gave me a frightful scowl, and I looked down to the new mess I had created. Then I saw it. I had to read the folder label twice to believe what it was. It was a master gun permit log, or at least a copy of it. I picked it up and waved it at Glenn with a satisfied grin.

"You lucky bastard," Glenn whispered with a smile.

We looked through it and quickly found the top gun owners in town. It was already nearing midnight and time to leave, but one address stood out. It was on Brandon Street. I remembered the street name because it was near a road that crossed the trail I'd memorized as a landmark. I found it on my map.

"It's right off the trail on our way back," I said, pointing to it.

"I think it's worth a look."

"Do you think we have enough time? We might not even find anything." I wanted to push on home. The frigid cold had drained my motivation.

"Come on, Walt. It's right along the way back. It's crazy not to stop and take a peek."

I relented with a reluctant nod.

After taking a few minutes to let our eyes readjust to the darkness, we started out of the station. When we neared the exit, I heard something shuffle outside. We pulled out the pistols that we had hoped we'd never have to use. I peered out the front door and saw a dark figure darting across the street toward us. That's when the first shot rang out. The muzzle flash came from an old church directly across the street. I heard the bullet impact in the doorway just above my head. The dark figure stopped and immediately reversed course, firing a handgun at us. I ducked back into the doorway as bullets seemed to streak everywhere from the panic shooting. The shooting stopped and I turned back out in time to see the figure still trying to run back to the old church. I quickly took aim and fired. After three rapid shots, the person fell into a stairway leading up to the old building. More shots cracked out from there and we ducked back into the entryway for cover. We were pinned.

"On three, I'll fire and you run out to the side of the building," Glenn whispered frantically. He counted to three and started firing at where the muzzle flashes originated. I darted out and soon reached safety at the side of the building. I really don't know if the shooter even saw me because he continued firing at Glenn. I quickly found a firing position and emptied my gun at the muzzle flashes. Glenn reached me just as I shot the last bullet from my magazine. We scampered back to the trail, which was well behind the police station and out of sight of the old church. We didn't hear any further shooting as we jogged down the trail. It was a treacherous run and we seemed to stumble over anything that lay in our way. When we reached a safe distance, after about a mile, we stopped jogging.

"I think you got the guy running back to the church," Glenn whispered through his panting. "But I got the one shooting at us."

"Seriously? You didn't notice him still shooting after you ran out of there?"

"He was?" Glenn replied. "All I heard was your gun."

"What do you think I was shooting at?"

"Damn, I was sure I hit him."

"Oh, come on, you have trouble hitting anything at twenty-five yards."

Glenn chuckled and started to reload his gun. "You're never going let me forget that, are you?"

We stood quietly for a minute and listened. There was no noise but an occasional gust of wind through the bare trees. I reached for a spare mag of bullets while ejecting my spent magazine. My pistol had been fired in anger for the first time, and I'm pretty sure I had scored kill number two, and maybe number three. Those were much easier to cope with. I hadn't had to look into their faces, but the thought of killing someone on Christmas still seemed tragically wrong.

After catching our breath, we continued at a more reasonable pace, stopping every so often to listen for signs of pursuit. Nobody seemed to be following. An uneasy feeling came over me. I wondered if they might have taken a short-cut and were waiting for us further down the trail. Blood had been spilled and revenge could be a powerful motivator.

Eventually, we reached the Brandon Street neighborhood and I again wondered if we should just settle for what we already found. It was tempting to keep moving on home, but the thought of having to come back to look for guns made Glenn press me to check out the house. Reluctantly, I agreed.

We worked our way around to the street and didn't notice any signs of life. With quick flashes from our flashlights, we found a street number on one of the houses and counted over to the address number we had found on the list. We gave the front door one quick flash to confirm the house number and immediately saw a familiar neon orange marking on the closed door.

"Infected," Glenn whispered in frustration, but I took far more encouragement from it.

"That means no one else would've wanted to go in."

"But I didn't get the right flu shot," Glenn protested.

"Everything's frozen. You won't get infected." I tried to open the door, but it was predictably locked. Noise was the last thing we wanted to make, so breaking it down or shattering a window was out of the question. I looked around the front porch for any place that I might think to stash a spare key. I turned over a couple of stubbornly frozen rocks nearby, but didn't find anything. Glenn felt under the window sills and eventually found a key holder taped in place.

"Good ol' duct tape," Glenn proclaimed quietly.

The key worked and we entered cautiously. A faint smell of

death was trapped inside. There was no doubt what was waiting for us somewhere deeper in the home. We went upstairs and eventually found a body lying in a bed. It was mostly decomposed but, thankfully, frozen. The floor was covered with the carcasses of dead flies. The right hand of the deceased was still clutching a handgun.

"That's only one," Glenn observed as he looked around. Our feet crunched over the thick layer of frozen flies and spider webs. "This guy is supposed to have a few more."

"Probably in the basement," I replied as I gingerly pried the gun from the frozen hand. We found two boxes of ammunition under the bed before going down into the basement. At the far end, we discovered a fireproof gun safe.

"This isn't going to be easy, is it?" Glenn sneered. "It's way too heavy to take with us."

"We can't do this with only one gun and a couple boxes of ammo." I looked closer and noticed that it would accept a key which would override the combination. "Where would this guy hide the key?"

"He likes duct tape."

We looked around the cluttered basement, but it was painfully obvious that it would take us hours to search it, assuming the key was even in the basement. We didn't have much more time to spend in there. We had to get back before daylight. Our ride wouldn't wait around for too long.

"Too bad neither of us is a safe-cracker," Glenn dryly remarked as he tugged on the safe lever. To our utter shock, the lever moved and the safe opened. The only explanation I could think of was that the owner had failed to fully lock the safe when he last closed it. Perhaps he was too sick to notice? Whatever the reason, we felt like kids on Christmas morning. I pulled out handgun after handgun, and several boxes of ammunition. We quickly packed them away in our nylon bags. There were a dozen guns in all, four more than were actually registered. I didn't care who this guy was, why he had unregistered guns, or why he had thought he needed so many of them. I was just thankful he had them.

The rest of our trek back was more difficult than we anticipated. We were now weighed down by our booty. The guns and ammunition were heavier than we expected. Our apprehension was also heightened, as though the guns gave off some sort of scent that would give us away. We were armed well enough to start a small war and desperately hoped we wouldn't encounter anyone. The closer we drew to the old Alewife T-station, the better I felt. Once we got back into BSA territory, we met up with our ride back home just as he was about to give up on us and leave. While our driver was someone we could trust, we still didn't give him any indication of what we were actually doing. The bags we carried could have easily been overnight bags, and we were returning from a visit with some of our Cambridge friends.

Around five o'clock, we shuffled our weary bodies through my front door. We carefully stashed everything in hiding places and crashed. Glenn dropped on my couch and I fell into my wonderfully soft, warm bed. We slept until noon, then had something to eat. While we weren't due back to work until the next day, there were still a lot of details to work out. The first part of our dangerous plan was thankfully over. Now came the exceptionally dangerous stage.

In all, what we found was a best case scenario. It had to be both guns and a list that was found in Tony's possession to show clear intent of finding weapons to keep for himself. Now we had to plant the guns and ammo somewhere in his secret vault, and at the same time hide the list somewhere in his office. Neither could be too easily found, or Pat would sense that Tony was being set up. We were baiting a former police detective with many years of experience, a man who could easily sniff out a frame-up. We had to made sure there were no fingerprints on the guns, ammo boxes, or file, just as Tony would do to cover himself. Our plan was clever, but we were careful not to be overly confident. Even if we perfectly planted all the evidence, any number of things could still go wrong.

I was the only one with enough credibility to tip Pat about something Tony was hiding. It had to be done in a convincing manner or it would blow up in our faces. We also needed to put it all into motion soon because a backlog of needed items for The Pit was quickly building. Too many were depending on us, and we couldn't let them go too long in the cold winter without a resupply.

If we succeeded, we would still need some luck that Pat would replace Tony with someone easier to deal with. Our chances actually looked good. Most of the replacement candidates we guessed at would suffice.

* * *

I kept Tony occupied the next morning with status updates, and he wasn't stingy with his complaints about how things hadn't worked smoothly in my absence. Our meeting gave Glenn plenty of time to sneak into Tony's vault and plant the guns and ammo. He was clever enough to hide them in boxes of air conditioners, something that would be unlikely to be used soon – if ever.

Glenn had his turn with Tony the next day. He conjured up a crisis that was sure to move Tony off his fat ass in a hurry. The only thing that could bring Tony nearly as much trouble as being caught hoarding weapons was knowingly distributing tainted medications. Pat didn't like it when too many people died in the hospital at once.

Getting access to Tony's office wasn't an easy task. The secretary keeping watch outside his door looked like she had been a mixed martial arts fighter in the UFC. Many thought Tony was a little whacked for choosing such a husky and unappealing secretary, but I thought it was one of the few smart things he had ever done. She was the perfect guard. Nobody wanted to flirt with her, or give challenge. I was on good enough terms with her to get access to his office, but she usually escorted me in and watched everything I did.

"Tony told me to update the daily food inventory list," I told her as I held up my file folder. "It's in his file cabinet."

She gave me a smirk, got up, and unlocked the door to his office.

I started to go in but stopped. "He also said something about checking over a supplemental list he left for you."

"Where?" she grunted.

"Not sure. He only told me he gave it to you yesterday."

She let out an exasperated sigh and turned back to her desk. I went in and opened his file cabinet while choosing a ceiling tile above. While positioning his chair, I grabbed one of Tony's red pens to check off the address where we had discovered the guns. After that was done, I peeked out to make sure the Amazon guardian was still occupied at her desk. She was still shuffling through papers as I quietly stepped up on his chair, quickly pushed open the ceiling tile, and slipped in the folder containing the police file. I had just stepped off the chair when she reentered the office.

"He didn't give me anything."

I pulled a file from his cabinet. "Probably because it's still in this folder."

She grunted and watched me check a few things off. I finished and put the folder away. She turned to exit as I noticed that a few flakes from the acoustic ceiling tile had fallen on his desk. I brushed them off as I walked by.

My stomach turned. It took me a few seconds to pull myself together after I left. It was only a folder, but it felt like I had planted a bomb.

* * *

I met Glenn back at his place for dinner. The next part of our plan was for me to tell Pat about Tony's vault the next evening, and the details needed to be planned out. Glenn was a lot like me. We always obsessed over the details.

"I wonder if Pat has anyone else coming over for dinner tomorrow," Glenn wondered.

"I'm never sure of the guest list. He tends to tell me it's a small gathering and ends up inviting a few more people. I'll just have to find a way to get him alone, particularly if Tony is there."

Glenn went pale. "You mean he could be there? I didn't consider the possibility."

"I'm not too worried. He's usually not invited because he tends to put down too much of Pat's fine liquor."

Glenn smiled and relaxed. "So what happens after this is over? You know, assuming it works and we get someone put in charge who we can deal with?"

"Life goes on, I suppose." I actually hadn't thought that far ahead. I was just looking forward to making supply drops without having to look over my shoulder so often.

Glenn nodded and reached for his glass of white wine. "You never told me much about your family."

I glanced to his half-empty glass. He wasn't a heavy drinker, but the abrupt change in subject made me think he had already had too much that evening.

"Nothing special. We were just an average middle-class family living in the burbs. My parents moved to Florida when they retired. I also had a younger sister living in Texas. I lost contact with all of them soon after the phones went out. I used to have a lot of friends living near my old apartment, but I haven't seen or heard from any of them. I suppose they're all dead."

"I'm sorry to hear that."

"What about you?"

"My parents died a few years ago. Highway accident. I had an older brother in California who caught the flu early on. He didn't last long. My in-laws were people I didn't like dealing with, anyway, so I have no idea what became of them. You know the rest."

I raised my glass for a toast. "It sucks to be us."

"Hopefully, pretty soon it won't suck as much," Glenn countered as he tapped his glass against mine. He gulped down the rest of his wine, looked at his empty glass, and set it down with a sigh. "How do we change things, I mean more than we already have?"

"Getting Tony ousted? I'd say that's going to be a major accomplishment in itself."

"But what does that really get us? Sure, we can continue to play Robin Hood, but what about all the other shit? What about getting good people, like your buddy Doctor Kym, back to doing what they do best? What about stopping the waste before we run out of everything? Where's the plan to rebuild? How do we get the fucking lights on again?"

The drinking and stress were getting to Glenn. The scent of pending victory over Tony increased his obsession over the bigger problems. He was right about it all, but he never seemed satisfied with the small victories. He had wanted it all back the way it was before the pandemic. Who didn't? It was a nice thought, but I just didn't see that happening.

* * *

The big dinner came the next night. The stage was set and it was up to me to light the fuse. I was nervous enough to puke. I had to make Pat think that I was acting in his best interest, and that I didn't have ulterior motives for ratting out Tony. I could only hope that Pat still saw in me the same guy who went out of his way to save his niece a few months back.

The guest list was light. Tony wasn't invited. It made my job a bit easier, but my nerves still tied my stomach in knots. That's when a familiar face greeted me. It took me a couple of seconds to recognize her. It was Pat's niece, Kathryn. I hadn't seen her since that day she'd quickly peered out from the back seat of the car to identify me. She looked like she'd aged a few years over the few months since I rescued her.

"Hello, Mr. Johnson," she said to me with a pleasant smile. "It's good to see you again."

"Wow. Sorry, but I hardly recognized you. How are you?"

"A little bit smarter now."

I heard Pat blurt out a laugh from behind me. "Gawd, we can only hope."

Kathryn snickered and tried to ignore him. "I'm sorry I never thanked you. I also feel bad for how bitchy I was over the whole thing."

"I'm just glad we can be here to have this conversation."

"So am I," Pat teased with a cynical chuckle. "Now can we all have some dinner?"

We all sat and enjoyed a fresh chicken meal. I couldn't remember the last time I had tasted chicken, but it was well before the pandemic. Small-talk initially dominated our time, then came war stories about recent conquests of the Smash-Five and Seven-One gangs in Dorchester. The top brass loved to brag about anything, and the more they drank, the more they embellished their exploits. My stomach was already soured by my pending task, and the graphic details of the stories only made it worse.

The evening was drawing to a close and I managed to linger while everyone else began to exit. Pat noticed me looking over his old family pictures as he said his goodbye to those who could barely walk straight.

"So Walt, something on your mind?" Pat asked as he stepped beside me.

"Was I that obvious?"

"You look like someone with some bad news to share."

"You're good."

"My old precinct buddies thought so. It's just too easy to read you. I think you sweated half your body weight away over dinner."

"Do you have a minute to talk?"

Pat chuckled. "Christ, do I dare not?"

Pat waved me over to his living room as I said goodnight to Kathryn. He closed the door and sat in a seat across from me.

"Kathryn looks like she's been doing some growing up," I commented to break the ice.

"I think that close call really shook her up. She's been a different person since, almost tolerable these days. I suppose that's another one I owe you for."

"How old is she, anyway?"

"Just turned twenty, and is finally acting more her age. But, Walt, I hope you didn't stick around to make small-talk about my niece. She's a real beauty, and a pain in the ass, but a little young for you, don't you think?"

I shook my head and let out a deep sigh. "I think something's up at The Supermarket."

Pat snickered. "Shouldn't you be telling Tony about this?"

"Not when it involves him."

Pat's expression quickly turned perturbed and leaned back in his high-backed chair. "Tread carefully, Walt."

"Look, Pat. I've never bothered you about anything before, but I just think something's very wrong. I've been seeing things that go way beyond the typical shit we deal with. I've also been hearing things about special deliveries to a building Tony's been using to stash his special finds."

Pat's eyebrows raised. "Can you be a little more specific?"

"Trucks that are supposed to drop at my building stop at his building first. I've heard whisperings of forays into places like Lexington and Bedford, when I know we haven't gone that far out yet. Look, I'd never turn on my boss unless something was really hinkey."

Pat smirked and leaned forward in his seat. The wheels seemed to be turning in his head. "You know, it was much harder keeping people honest before the pandemic. Now it's almost too fucking easy. You know why? I allow them to see just enough of the shit that surrounds us. Something like that has a powerful effect on people. It makes them much happier with what they have. Hell, they'd even be happy eating dog food after seeing what starving looks like. Tony is no different from anyone else, particularly about starving to death. So when I hear you tell me these things about him, I have to ask if you're really sure about this?"

"Absolutely. I wouldn't be here talking to you if I wasn't."

Pat smiled. "Okay, then. Tony and I go way back and I don't want to let him know I'm checking on him. You need to let me know what building he's been using and stay quiet. I'll have it checked out discreetly. Don't worry, none of it will ever come back on you even if you're wrong, and I hope you are wrong."

After disclosing which building Tony was using, I departed. I was sure I had succeeded. Walking home, the thought that I had just signed Tony's death certificate started to weigh on me. There was no going back. I kept trying to focus on the overall good Glenn and I were struggling to achieve, but my recent conversation with Chung-Hee kept nagging at me.

A real saint would never resort to plotting an execution.

* * *

The next day, Pat's team broke into Tony's vault. It took them a couple of hours to discover the guns. Glenn had left one of the air conditioner boxes unsealed, and that eventually drew the attention of the search party. The ensuing find was predictable.

A short time later, a trio of determined-looking thugs stormed into Tony's office. Tony was already on his way over to his vault after getting word that people were turning it inside out. One of his lackeys caught up with him and turned him back. By the time he got back to his office, Pat was waiting there for him. There was some yelling, and Tony ran out. He got to the end of the hall before he ran out of breath, took out his gun, put it in his mouth, and pulled the trigger.

I was called to Tony's office and passed the hall which had his blood spattered all over the floor and walls. Even though they had already removed his body, I really could have done without seeing that. I entered what was left of the office. All the ceiling tiles had been ripped out and paper was strewn all over the floor. Pat was sitting in his chair with a blank stare. I stood there for a minute and watched him glare out the window.

"Was it bad?" I finally asked.

"It was bad. He offed himself in the hall."

"I noticed. I'm sorry I was right about everything." For some reason, right then, I stopped feeling guilty about what had happened. I had spent a lot of time obsessing over the morality of our plan, but I didn't anticipate Tony's taking his own life. I was happy that Pat hadn't needed to kill him. Tony's death by suicide softened the blow for me.

"You keep handing me good things, Walt."

"I'm not really trying to," I attempted to joke.

"Now it's my turn to hand something good to you. I'd like you to take over The Supermarket."

I was in shock. Glenn and I had already put together a list of fifteen people that Pat should have chosen. Neither of us considered my name for that list.

"Me? Why?"

"Because I need someone I can trust here. I can't ever admit this to anyone else, but you're the most honest person I know."

I should have felt more guilt over the irony, but I felt fear above all. I had no desire to take on such a visible role with so much responsibility, but mostly I didn't want to report to Pat. He intimidated me too much. My mind raced and an idea quickly came to me.

"I appreciate it, but I think there's someone else who could do a much better job."

"Oh?"

"Glenn Bradshaw. He runs the medical sorting center."

"Yeah, I know who he is."

"I've gotten to know him pretty well. He used to be a VP in his old life, so he knows how to run an operation like this. I trust him, Pat. He's honest and will get this place back in shape."

"Are you sure you want to take a pass on this?"

"Yeah, I'm sure."

Pat thought for a while and smiled. "Okay. It's done. But there's one thing I do insist you accept. When I'm done with it, everything left behind in Tony's secret building is yours. Consider it a reward for your loyalty."

CHAPTER 6

"What in the hell did you get me into?" Glenn yelled at me that evening.

"I got you an opportunity."

"You--" Glenn started to say but stopped. He was too flustered to form a sentence. Instead, he paced around and began laughing.

"Pat surprised me with something neither of us saw coming," I continued to explain. "I didn't want the job because I knew you could do it better."

"Oh, please don't bullshit me. You didn't want the job because you're afraid of it."

"Okay, yeah, you're right," I confessed. "But think about it. Now you're in a position to make some changes. You can end some of the things we've been complaining about."

Glenn stopped his pacing and smirked. "Nice spin."

"Not spin. It's reality. You have the opportunity to put some things right."

Glenn sighed and smiled. I think it finally clicked. "Okay, okay, but I'm not going to let you continue slaving away with the village idiots."

"I don't mind it, as long as I can get some better idiots working for me."

"Absolutely not!"

"Seriously? You can't find me better people?"

"No, it's not that. I need you working beside me. We'll find someone else to babysit the day-shift."

"You really don't have to--"

"Hey, I'm not doing this alone. We both started this and now we both have to deal with how it turned out."

"Well, okay, I guess," I relented. "Just so you know, Pat gave me everything in Tony's vault."

"I heard. What do you want me to do with it?"

"Get some people in there to take inventory. Then you can take anything you need, so long as we prioritize The Pit."

"And if we find anything of exceptional value?"

"I doubt Pat's people will leave anything like that behind."

"We'll see."

"Just promise me you won't lose sight of the changes you've always wanted to make."

"Please feel free to kick me in the ass if I get off track," Glenn said with a grin. "Consider it part of your new job here."

"I'll be sure to find a nice pair of steel-toed boots."

"Seriously, Walt, thank you. It's a great thing you did for me. I'll never forget it"

* * *

Glenn wasted no time diving into his new responsibilities. I've never seen him so focused and full of life. The first thing he did was to completely reorganize the operation and hire in a number of people from The Pit to take over key positions. Chung-Hee took over Glenn's old position as head of the medical sorting facility. It still wasn't where I would've liked him to be, but it was a big step forward. The good doctor was quite pleased with his new duties.

Tony's vault yielded some surprising treasures. Most of it contained useless junk, but we still unearthed a significant amount of needed items that could be distributed. Glenn insisted that I hang onto a red Ferrari 458 Italia that was found in the back of the first floor. I have no idea where Tony found it or how he got it into the building without anyone's noticing. Of course, I had no use for it. I think Glenn wanted me to keep it so he could tease me. Now I can at least boast that I once owned a Ferrari, even though I never got a chance to drive it.

Glenn's personnel changes worked well. The skimming was put to an end. By February things in The Supermarket were running smoothly. Pat appreciated receiving far fewer complaints from those who normally didn't get all the things they needed. Such complaints had been a commonplace under Tony, who was always good at explaining them away.

I took advantage of our good standing and got approval to start opening up abandoned neighborhoods in Cambridge to relieve the overcrowding in The Pit. Pat acquiesced because he saw that someone was finally making good use of the people he had never really valued. For us, we were able to move all of our key personnel closer to their work. It was also a vast improvement over their former dismal living conditions.

During our time of secret supply drops, most living in The Pit had had no idea who their benefactors were. Only a few knew that Glenn and I were behind it, or that I had started the effort. Now that things had changed, supplies flowed more freely and secret supply drops were no longer necessary. Since Glenn made the changes, he became commonly identified as the mysterious Robin Hood behind the secret supplies. His popularity soared with just about everyone. I actually didn't mind that Glenn got the credit because it helped him do his job better. Things were improving and that's all I really cared about.

Glenn also took on a larger supply problem that loomed: food production. We were beginning to run low on even basic food staples like canned foods, pasta, and rice. It was doubtful that enough could be found to keep us going for much longer. So Glenn got the approval from Pat to form an agricultural team. They would find various seeds, tools, and open land to cultivate in the spring.

* * *

Spring came and life returned to the streets. Everyone seemed especially busy, particularly Pat. With the arrival of warm weather, he opened up several conquest campaigns to push deeper south and west. The armory was especially active. Ammunition and weapons flowed out at a brisk pace. Then came the requests for recovery teams to plunder newly captured areas. Smoke could often be seen rising in the distance as those few who had survived a harsh winter quickly succumbed to the BSA blitzkrieg.

By the end of May, most of the gangs south and west had been crushed. Executions of captured gang members were routinely carried out. There was no such thing as a prisoner of war during that time. Pat took a perverse pleasure in personally executing any suspected gang leaders. I heard that he would put an empty handgun to a leader's head and let them hear the firing hammer click. After days of torturing them with this, he would finally load a bullet in the magazine and shoot them.

Stories like that made me happy that I passed up the opportunity to run The Supermarket. Pat was someone I never wanted to directly report to. Glenn was far better at handling him.

In all, Pat lost two trusted lieutenants to the spring fighting. His wounded enforcers always received preferential treatment in the hospital, but too many died due to the numerous inadequacies in medical treatment. The territories were conquered and the bounty rolled in, but it came with a high price in life that seemed to erode morale in Pat's army. Most of them came back to the city, and those who weren't maimed turned their attention to eradicate another problem: wild dogs.

The flu hadn't affected the pet population, resulting in the abandonment of numerous dogs. They were set loose, formed packs, and eventually headed into the city seeking food when they ran out of smaller animals to eat in the suburbs. They were aggressive and started attacking people. Pat outlawed pets of any sort and ordered all dogs to be shot on sight. Thankfully, it kept Pat's bloodthirsty enforcers occupied, but it also became a running joke that they had more trouble killing dogs than gang-bangers.

The Italian gangs to the north of Boston became anxious because they were the only ones left standing. Pat had a treaty in place with them, but they always harbored deep suspicions about his true motives. They also secretly resented Pat's allowing himself to be called The Godfather. It was a title even they were reluctant to use among themselves.

* * *

"I heard Pat pushed out to Concord," Glenn said to me in my new office on a sunny day in early June.

"Why? What's out there?"

"Maybe he's after the old State Police barracks," Glenn wondered. "The prison is out there, too."

"Both places were probably looted a long time ago. There can't be that many gun caches worth the price to take the area."

Glenn sighed. "Whatever the reason, he's stretching us beyond what we can handle. We're barely covering his gasoline demands."

"Maybe it's just about an easy conquest?"

"Hardly easy. I heard most of the hicks left out there aren't shy about putting up a fight. I guess if they're crazy enough to stay out there, they're crazy enough to defend their homes no matter the cost."

"There's got to be something worthwhile out there. Pat's not stupid."

"Honestly, I think it's all he can do right now. He's not in a position to go up against the Italian gangs up north, but it could be a maneuver to put pressure on them."

"Seriously? I thought we were on good terms with them."

I remember being startled by Glenn's fist coming down on my desk. Before, it had been unusual for him to unleash his anger like that, but his new responsibilities seemed to draw more passion out of him. "That asshole should be more worried about building than conquering. We have more than enough territory to manage. We're wasting things we can't replace to keep his war machine going. And for what? All to inch the BSA flag a little further out on the map?"

"Hey, relax. We don't have any say in that. We're doing all we can."

Glenn relaxed himself and leaned in. "If he keeps pushing like this, one of his lieutenants is going to off him."

"You heard something?"

"Maybe." Looking back, what he said should have concerned me more than it did at the time. Glenn never hesitated to tell me who was feeding him information and only held back when he had made a rare promise to his source. Now he was in a position to hear all sorts of things and I was being shut out.

After a pause, Glenn smiled and shook his head. "Never mind, it's all just talk. I just get frustrated over what everyone's not talking about. We need to find ways to become more self-sufficient. We should be expanding our store inventories to include building materials, tools, and equipment. We need to find a way to get the utilities back. The only thing Pat sees is the next town he wants to plunder. It's all a fucking chess game to him. We've got to be more than an oversized gang of thugs if we're going to survive long-term. We need a better plan."

"I seem to remember this same speech sometime last fall."

"And look how far we've come since we sat on that bench and wondered how things could get better. Now we're running The Supermarket!"

"Are you suggesting we go further?"

Glenn laughed, but then that crooked smile surfaced on his face. "I don't think Pat has too much longer before he's going to deal with some fallout. Just keep your head down and eyes open."

An unsettling feeling enveloped me as Glenn left. I had never been good at politics or schmoozing up to the right people. Glenn was far better at that. He knew something was brewing. I could only hope it didn't upend our comfortable lives.

I went back to work and followed Glenn's advice. The thought of involving myself in another plot to change things was unappealing. I had had my fill when we ousted Tony. Things were going well in my world, and that's really all that mattered to me. I was content with the way life was at the time.

* * *

It was the second week in June when I received a surprise visit from Pat in my office. Never before had he made an appearance there. The last time I'd seen him was in Tony's old office after our plot was executed. Plus, I thought he was out in the boonies somewhere pressing forward to claim more territory.

"Walt," Pat greeted me with a big smile. "How have you been?"

"Pat? Hi. What brings you up here?"

Pat turned and closed my door. "I need to have a word with you."

That was something I never wanted to hear from him. Most who heard him say something similar usually ended up floating face-down in the Charles River the next morning. My heart skipped a beat as he sat.

"Is something wrong?" I feebly asked.

"I've got a little surprise to share with you."

"Good or bad?"

"Let me start from the beginning. Ever since we found that gun-owner list in Tony's office, I've wondered how and why he got it. I'd known him for a long time and it wasn't like him to step out of line like that. I had lots of other questions, like how in the hell did he get out to Lex-vegas (Lexington) without me knowing? But the one thing I'll never forget is the look in his eyes after I told him what we found. He knew he was totally fucked and didn't even try to talk his way out of it before he ran out and offed himself."

There was a dreadful pause as Pat held me in an uncomfortable gaze.

"So, what's the surprise?" I innocently asked. This only caused him to tighten his glare on me.

"Still working up to that. The Tony I knew wouldn't go so far off the rails. So I did a little investigating of my own. I started questioning his people and no one knew anything. This led to checking evidence, things like fingerprints. The guns and ammo boxes were clean. No surprise there. Tony knew better than to be careless about fingerprints. The file folder was clean, but I was able to lift a couple of prints off the page inside. Now that confused me. Why in the hell was the file folder clean but not the page inside? I expected at least one of those prints to match Tony's, since he had marked off the address in a red pen that came from his desk. They didn't match. I spent the next few weeks getting prints from every person that ever worked with him. No joy there. The mystery deepened, and how I miss the challenge of solving that kind of case. I eventually checked one remaining associate who I never would've suspected was involved, and that's where I got the fucking surprise of my life. Your fingerprints are on the address page. I guess you forgot to clean it after you marked that address with Tony's red pen."

I was caught and didn't know what to say. I had made a careless mistake and completely underestimated Pat's persistence.

"Tony was no saint, but he didn't deserve that," Pat continued. His eyes narrowed on me and his face turned beet red. "So, the only thing I want to know is why did the most honest man I know do this?"

"Because it made things better," I stuttered.

"Made things better? Are you fucking serious? I decide what's better! I trusted you, then you treat me like a dumb-ass to destroy Tony?"

I struggled to keep myself from trembling. "But things got better."

"I'll give you that, but you stupid sonofabitch, how am I not sup-posed to punish you? You made me look foolish and I can't afford to look weak."

"But we're the only ones who know about this, right?"

"You tell me," Pat said with raised eyebrows. "Glenn?"

I gulped and hesitated.

"Yeah, I thought so," he replied with a knowing grin. "I didn't think you could pull this off all by yourself."

Pat paused as he reached for his gun. As he pointed it at me, I couldn't stop my mind from racing over absurd thoughts of how I could have planned it better. I closed my eyes and waited for his gun to spray my brains across the back of my office.

In reality, I should have died a long time ago in my Waltham apartment; just another face among the millions who perished in the pandemic. Instead, I had survived so many close calls that it seemed ridiculous that life would end just as things were improving. I was about to become yet another victim of The Godfather's notorious temper.

Three shots fired. I flinched and my ears rang, but I felt nothing. I opened my eyes in time to see Pat fall to the floor. He was dead before his head glanced off my desk. I looked over to see Glenn standing in the doorway, smoke hovering around his pistol. He stepped in while holding aim on Pat's lifeless body. Blood pooled on the floor around his chest as another figure rushed into the office. It was Smitty, Pat's new lieutenant.

"What the hell?" Smitty gasped as he closed the door. He was a loyal lieutenant who often accompanied Pat, pulling double duty as his personal bodyguard. He could be hard to understand through his thick Southie (South Boston) accent.

"You okay?" Glenn asked me.

"Yeah," I mustered, my ears still ringing. I was also fighting off a dizzy spell.

Glenn turned to Smitty. "I came in just as Pat was going to shoot Walt. Sorry, but I couldn't let that happen. I had to put him down."

"Shoot Walt?" Smitty wondered. "No shit? He didn't say he was here to cap anyone."

"He thought I set up Tony with those guns," I added, trying not to hyperventilate.

"You?" Smitty incredulously asked.

"Smitty, honest," Glenn pleaded, "I just couldn't let him shoot my buddy."

Smitty squatted down and checked Pat for a pulse. He slowly stood up and shook his head. "He's gone."

"Shit," Glenn gasped. "I'm totally screwed."

"Look," Smitty started to explain to us in a surprisingly sympathetic tone, "Pat was always wicked shiesty about what went down with Tony. He's already offed two good shits he thought set Tony up with those guns. He found out he was wrong and kept at it. We always thought he was a little whacked, but I didn't think he was batshit crazy enough to come in here after Walt."

"What do we do about this?" Glenn asked.

Smitty paused and thought for a minute. "We tell everyone the truth. Pat finally lost it. Everyone's noticed the stress. All the fighting was gettin' to him. He snapped and had to be put down before he capped another good shit."

"So I guess this puts you in charge?" Glenn asked Smitty.

"No suh! The other guys will think I steered this to take over." Smitty paused and looked at Glenn with a wide smile. "You're goin' to take it."

"Me?" Glenn moaned.

"You're the shit these days. No one's going to want a skid like me in charge. I'll vouch for what happened here. The other lieutenants will fall in line. Most of them like you and won't fight it."

CHAPTER 7

Glenn and I sat in his living room that evening. After first talking to Smitty, one by one, Pat's lieutenants came over and asked their own questions. They seemed satisfied by what they heard, at least for the moment. None of them looked like they were going to shoot Glenn anytime soon. Smitty was the last to come in and he confirmed that the vote among the lieutenants had been unanimous. Despite some doubt expressed by a couple, Glenn would take over as leader of the BSA.

"What now?" I remember asking Glenn after a long period of silence. Smitty had left for the evening and we just sat, staring - almost catatonic.

"How the hell do I know? I never would've dreamed this would happen."

"You okay with, you know, having to kill Pat?"

"Seriously?" Glenn sighed and looked over to a picture of his wife. "He wasn't my first, if that's what you mean."

It was a shock to hear him admit that. I had always thought that Glenn had never killed anyone before.

"Sorry, I just assumed it was."

Glenn slowly rose and picked up the picture. He gazed at it with a profound look of anguish in his eyes. "It happened before I came here. My wife was sick and I got jumped by some punks on my way back from finding clean water. They were only armed with small kitchen knives. It turned out to be three kids, no older than thirteen. I completely lost it and didn't remember anything until I finally stopped myself from repeatedly bashing one of the kid's head into the pavement. He was already dead by the time I got control of myself. The other two had run off. Through the bloody mess I recognized him. I had coached him in little league a couple of years before."

"I'm sorry."

"I'm pretty sure they only wanted the water," Glenn muttered, showing no emotion. I wasn't used to seeing the distant stare from his eyes.

"Maybe I should go. It's getting late. We've had enough for one day."

"I want to stop the fighting," Glenn blurted as I rose. "The BSA needs to stop killing people."

"That's a good start."

"I also want to stop the corruption. We need a fair system of justice. No more bodies floating down the Charles."

"That would be, um, nice."

The more Glenn talked, the more energy and enthusiasm returned to him. "I want you right beside me. We're going to kick this into overdrive and build something better."

I hesitated. Glenn noticed. He knew me too well.

"I know that's a huge step up for you."

"Look," I tried to respond tactfully. "Helping you run The Supermarket is one thing; politics is something entirely different. You need people around you who are actually good at it."

Glenn smiled. "What do you want, then?"

"I'd rather stick to what I do best."

"Are you sure? Walt, I can give you whatever you want."

"The Supermarket is all I want."

Glenn chuckled. "It's yours, but I hope you're going to be up to expanding it. If the BSA is going to survive, we need to do more than just find things. We need to produce a wide range of items we can't find anymore. We've also got to end special treatment. Everyone's going to get equal consideration with the supplies."

"Isn't that a little risky? I mean, ending special treatment could piss off people you need on your side right now."

"I want to lead from the center, not from the special privileged. Equal consideration is what it should be about. Everyone has to share in ownership."

"That's going to lead to people crying Socialist."

"Maybe a few, but considering what we had before? I think people will see a difference."

"Why not start electing people to run things?"

"No, we're not ready for that yet. I've got to achieve stability first. No one's going to have confidence in anything until we show solid progress. Democracy will work far better after that happens."

"Okay, you're the boss." I started to leave but a question surfaced. I had wanted to ask it earlier, but at that moment I instead yielded to caution. It might have sounded accusatory. I decided to rephrase it. "I'm glad you had your gun on you today."

"So am I. I started carrying it after hearing some things from Pat's lieutenants. I guess I just felt safer keeping it on me."

"Lucky for me."

I left and walked back home. As usual, the streets were empty. I kept thinking about Glenn having his gun with him that day. He rarely carried it with him. I always teased him about barely hitting anything in target practice because he was always too timid with it.

As I approached my front door, I was startled by the sound of footsteps approaching me from behind. At that point I regretted not keeping my gun on me. My street was dimly illuminated by an occasional porch lamp, which was typically solar-powered. They tended to last a few hours into the night before their daily charge ran out. I turned and saw an outline of a slightly shorter figure walking towards me.

"Mr. Johnson?" a voice whispered. "It's me, Kathryn Donahue."

"Kathryn? What are you doing here?"

"We need to talk. Can we get off the street?"

The thought of her exacting revenge was the first thing that entered my mind. I glanced around to make sure we were alone. I couldn't tell if anyone else was lurking nearby, so there was nothing I could do except to invite her in.

"Please come in," I said as I opened my door. "Stay here while I light some candles. I don't want you to trip over anything."

Leaving her in the entryway, I went into my living room. I intended to keep her at a safe distance while I sought out something to defend myself with. I was able to grab a fireplace poker just before I reached a box of matches. As I lit the first candle, I slipped the poker beside the chair I would sit in.

"Okay, all lit now. You can see where you're going."

She came into the room and sat down on the couch. I noticed

that her mascara was smudged. My fireplace poker was out of her line of sight but well within my reach. It didn't look like she had a gun on her, but a knife was still a possibility.

"I'm sorry for what happened to your uncle," I said, wanting to appear comfortable.

"I was told that he was trying to kill you."

"Who told you that?"

"Smitty came by earlier to make sure I was okay. I still can't understand why Uncle Pat wanted to kill you. It doesn't make any sense to me."

It surprised me that she didn't know about what we had done to Tony. It hadn't occurred to me that Pat may not have told her every-thing. Neither did Smitty, which puzzled me.

"He thought I set up Tony with those guns."

"He was always suspicious about that. Did you, you know, do it?"

I hesitated, which only gave her the answer. I have always been rather clumsy at hiding the truth on the spot.

"I'm sorry, I really don't care if you did."

"That doesn't upset you?"

"No, it really doesn't. I never liked Tony. He was a total creep, always hitting on me."

"Did he do anything to you?" I asked as I glanced down and caught sight of the fireplace poker. A feeling of regret came over me. I felt stupid for being so paranoid.

"No, not really. I got pretty good at handling him before it went somewhere bad, but I had to put up with it. I don't think Uncle Pat would've believed me if I ever told him what was going on. I didn't exactly have a lot of credibility."

"I'm sorry. That must have been a terrible thing to deal with."

"It's okay, it wasn't that bad. Tony was usually drunk and easy to handle. I had a couple of boyfriends who were way worse."

"So what are you going to do now?"

"That's why I'm here. I need your help. I didn't know who else I could turn to."

"What's wrong?"

She gulped and grew anxious. "I'm really scared. A lot of people hated my uncle. Now he's gone and I'm on my own. Smitty said he'd look out for me, but I don't know if I can trust him. I can't think of any reason for him to protect me and every reason for him to give me up. There's really nobody I can trust, except you."

She started to quiver and tears began to flow.

"Hey, you don't need to be scared. I can help you, but it's not going to be easy."

"Please, I'll do whatever it takes."

"Even if it means walking away from everything you had?"

"I sort of thought it might come to that."

"Kathryn, I mean right here and right now: tonight. You're going to have to disappear. I can put you in a safe place and get you started in a new life, but you can never be Kathryn Donahue again, ever."

"I understand."

"I hope so. You can stay here tonight and I'll figure out what to do."

She smiled and breathed a heavy sigh of relief. "Oh, thank you."

I let her sleep on the couch while I stayed up to think out a plan. I had a number of options for her but had to carefully choose one that would allow her to stay hidden away indefinitely. It would have to be well outside of the city. The niece of Pat Donahue was likely going to be a tempting target for some time to come.

* * *

The next morning I got ready for my first day as the boss of The Supermarket. First, I had to arrange for a ride to work in order to take a detour deep into Cambridge. We were in the third phase of relocating people out of the overcrowded Boston neighborhoods to nicer homes closer to the Arlington line. It would be a perfect place to hide Kathryn away, far enough from Boston and amongst new neighbors who wouldn't pry into who she really was. In particular, I knew the neighbor who lived next door to the house I planned to move Kathryn into. She would be in good hands.

Earlier, I had sent for a car and saw a familiar black Mercedes sedan pull up our road. I typically walked or rode a bike to work, but on occasion I requested a car. Pat had set up a driving service for all his upper echelon to use. Most used them to stay protected behind the tinted windows while others just wanted the prestige of being chauffeured around.

I gave Kathryn a few things to get started in her new life, but she'd need a lot more to get established. She was walking away with only the clothes on her back. I had to admire her resolve. She had done some maturing and was different from the spoiled teen I had rescued.

Kathryn picked up a duffel bag full of items I packed for her and followed me to the front door. Just after I opened the door, I caught sight of someone ducking back into a doorway across the street. As Kathryn passed through the threshold, I pulled her back inside. I reached for my gun as the figure reemerged, pointing a gun at us. We ducked low as gunshots rang out. Several bullets chipped away at the exterior brick-faced wall. I took aim and fired three shots at the gunman who, inexplicably, had begun walking towards me. Two bullets struck him in the chest and he dropped. He couldn't have been an easier target to hit.

My driver opened his door and took cover on the other side of the car. That's when I realized that he must have seen something else, and I turned to catch sight of another gunman emerge further down the road. This guy had an automatic weapon. He opened fire as I fell back into my doorway. Fragments of brick flew everywhere as the bullets chewed up the exterior of the entryway. Once the firing stopped, I reengaged and fired several shots back. The second gunman ducked into a doorway to reload. By then my driver had opened the back car door and waved for me to come. I looked back at Kathryn and motioned her forward. She reluctantly came closer.

"Get to the car!" I yelled and pushed her out while keeping my gun aimed at the spot the gunman had disappeared. I figured he'd be back out any second, so I continued to fire at that doorway until Kathryn made it to the car. Once I expended my magazine, the gunman pivoted back out and started firing at me. I again fell back into my entryway to reload. I found it odd that he was firing at me and not at the car. He must not have seen Kathryn make her dash into the backseat.

Once the trigger-happy gunman emptied his gun, I bolted for the car, firing at his doorway as I ran. As soon as I was in, the driver sped away. By the time the gunman spun back out for another shot, we were skidding around the corner on our way to the Longfellow Bridge.

"Are you all right?" I asked Kathryn.

She quaked and reached for me. "I think so."

"What in the hell was that all about?" yelled the driver.

"What about you?" Kathryn asked as she started checking me over.

"I'm okay."

She stopped her inspection and broke down into tears.

"You want me to drop you somewhere safe?" my driver asked.

"Just keep going to that address in Cambridge."

Once clear of the bridge, my driver slowed to a normal speed. He was smart enough to know that a speeding car drew attention. We safely arrived at the Cambridge house without further drama. By then, Kathryn had settled herself down.

I first introduced her to her new neighbor, Alyssa, and then showed her around her new home. It was a spacious Greek revival style house that was probably bigger than she needed. Most of the other houses on the quiet street were still vacant, but they would soon be filled with families. I'd be sure to arrange for neighbors who would be eager to help protect her anonymity.

"I'll send you the first supply shipment soon," I said as we stood on her new front porch. "Let Alyssa know what else you'll need and she'll get word to me. It's important that you don't contact anyone you used to know, especially me. You can't ever reach out to me unless it's an emergency. Invent a new name for yourself and try to change your appearance. You're as far away from your old life as I can safely get you, and if you're careful, you'll be safe here for a long time. At some point, they'll give up looking for you."

Kathryn smiled and looked around her new neighborhood. "Are you going to be okay?"

"Yeah, I should be okay. It was probably one of Pat's enemies trying to get at you while they had a chance."

"Yeah, probably."

"Hey, they missed and their only chance is gone."

Kathryn sighed. "I suppose so."

I pulled out my pistol and handed it to her. "Do you know how to handle a gun?"

"My dad and Uncle Pat took me to firing ranges all the time."

"It's yours now. Please don't ever use it or show it to anyone unless you absolutely have to."

"Thank you. How can I, you know, repay you--"

"Don't worry about it. I owe you for what happened to your uncle. I never intended for it to turn out that way."

"I'm honestly surprised something like that didn't happen to him sooner." She looked the gun over and checked to see if the safety was on. They way she handled it gave me a good feeling. She was careful, deliberate, and clearly not intimidated.

"I've got to get going now, so this is probably goodbye for a long time. I'm not sure when it will be safe for us to talk again."

She gave me a hug and I walked back to my waiting car. As I got in, I saw her watching me leave and wondered if she'd really be able to adapt. I was afraid that she had lived too long in a lifestyle she couldn't do without. It was also probably unwise to have given my gun away like that, particularly not knowing what I was heading back into. I figured that if this had been part of an overall power-grab, Glenn was probably already dead and it wouldn't matter if I had a gun or not. I'd be dead soon, too. At least I had passed it off to someone who had better need of it.

* * *

I had my driver drop me in front of my Supermarket office. There was no point in running or hiding if things had gone to hell. After instructing him to forget what had happened that morning, my driver nodded and drove off. I don't think I had needed to ask him. He was going to ditch the car and forget about anything that happened anyway.

Everything around me seemed normal as I walked up to the building. When I entered, someone quickly approached me.

"Walt, are you all right?" Chung-Hee asked.

"I'm fine. You heard?"

"One of your neighbors got word to me. I think it would be best for you to come with me. Now."

"Why?"

Chung-Hee winced. "Because people are shooting at you?"

"Yeah, there's a story behind that."

"You can tell me all about it on our way to my office. No one will be looking for you there. We can wait there for news."

We took the back way out and quickly walked over to the side entrance of the medical sorting building. I explained what had happened to Kathryn along the way. No one seemed to take unusual notice of us. The Supermarket was business as usual. News traveled a lot slower in that time. Cell phones, texting, the internet, and even working land-lines were long gone.

"I'm very happy you were able to help her," Chung-Hee concluded as we entered his office.

"I owed her at least that."

"Owed her? Why? Didn't you already save her once before?"

I paused as I sat. I knew I could trust Chung-Hee with what had happened to Kathryn because I'd probably need his help to keep an eye on her. But sharing the truth behind why Pat had died would be far more difficult. I was afraid of what he'd think of me. I had stolen antibiotics so that his daughter could survive. I could easily justify that as an act to save someone. However, trying to justify what we had done to Tony was far more troublesome, even though Chung-Hee's new job had come as the result. The framing was a crime that would've sent me to prison under the old laws.

"Is there something you need to tell me?" Chung-Hee asked.

I again hesitated. My poker-face sucked. I wondered how I had ever been able to fool Pat with it the first time. Or maybe it was because I really wanted Chung-Hee to know. He was one of the few people I used as a moral compass when I thought mine wasn't working.

I decided to tell him everything. He sat and listened to my account of how we had ousted Tony with remarkable poise. At the end, he looked down and sighed deeply.

"It's a terrible world we live in now, isn't it?" he asked rhetorically.

"Did I really make it any better?"

A faint smile appeared on his face. "I would be most concerned if you had no desire to ask that question, nor felt any remorse over what happened."

I was speechless. Before either of us could speak further, we overheard someone abruptly announce that they had seen several gunmen walking around the campus. We rushed to the closest window and saw several heavily armed men who seemed to be searching, probably for me.

"Do you recognize any of them?" Chung-Hee asked.

"No, but they're probably looking for me."

"Let's move to another office down the hallway. It has a better vantage point."

I paused and sighed. "No, it's time to confront it."

"Are you sure? I'm confident that we can stay hidden. This building is a maze of rooms."

"Thanks, but I'd just be getting more people into trouble."

Chung-Hee reluctantly nodded. "I'll go with you."

"Absolutely not! You have a daughter to look after. I also need you to help Kathryn."

Chung-Hee paused and bowed. "You've tried to do more good than anyone I've ever met. May the Lord protect you."

I patted him on the shoulder and walked out. Frustration welled up inside me. It was the same feeling I'd had when Pat had aimed his gun at me. I was getting angry over the nonsense. Glenn's first day in power, and no matter how far I tried to distance myself from it, politics were already going to be the death of me.

The strangest things ran through my mind as I went to confront the armed search party. I was eying some scary-looking weapons, but all I could think of was how I hadn't had a chance to drive that damn Ferrari.

The men caught sight of me and shouting commenced. I thought it strange that they didn't point their guns at me. Instead, they turned and aimed away. As several more approached, one familiar face came into focus.

"Walt!" Smitty called out. "You okay?"

"What?"

"Simple question. Are you okay?"

I glanced around at a heavily armed contingent who suddenly seemed more concerned about everyone around us.

"Yeah, I guess so. What's going on?"

"What's going on?" Smitty asked bemusedly. "I thought you were fucking fish food! We came across the war zone back at your place and I thought they'd capped you. That must have been quite a shit-storm that came down around you."

"I barely got out."

"Yeah, I saw you dropped one of them. Nice work. We're looking for the guy who was hosing you from up the street. Don't worry, we'll find his sorry ass. We know who he is."

"What about Glenn?"

"He's fine. The lucky sonofabitch wasn't home when they broke in and shot up his bedroom."

"Who did this?"

"Fucking Jenkins. I thought he was okay with Glenn taking over, like all the other lieutenants. The slimy weasel gave us a head-fake and tried to make a play to take over. He's dead now. His guys are mostly dead or on the run. We've crushed his little coup. The rest of the lieutenants are solid with us."

"Where's Glenn?"

"Waiting for you in your office."

Smitty and a dozen men escorted me back to my office. Glenn was waiting in my chair with a wide smile.

"Jesus, Walt. You scared the hell out of me."

"How do you think I felt?"

"Seems that Walt knows how to handle himself," Smitty added with a big grin and a slap to my back. "You can ride with me any-time."

"Any other casualties?" I asked.

"Everyone else is fine," Glenn replied. "It was surgical. They only targeted you and me. But Pat's niece, Kathryn, disappeared."

"No sign of an execution at her place," Smitty added. "Nothing was taken, but I still think someone got to her. She's likely floating somewhere out in the harbor by now."

I did my best to appear shocked. "Why would anyone do that?"

"Pat pissed off a lot of people in his time," Smitty replied. "Too many are the type who would take it out on that girl."

"We'll find who did it," Glenn asserted.

"So you actually went out after I left last night?" I asked Glenn.

"I dropped in on a friend, lucky for me. Smitty was able to find me and keep me safe until everything was clear."

"I think all the shit's been flushed out of the system," Smitty con-cluded to Glenn. "We'll keep a couple of guys around you, just in case. Just don't screw up. I don't think we can keep putting this kind of bullshit down."

Glenn rose and gave Smitty a nod. "Relax, things are going to get better."

CHAPTER 8

To my amazement, Glenn's promise came true. Over the next three years, things did get better – a lot better. Almost immediately, Glenn managed to implement sweeping changes that were enormously popular with a majority of people. The special treatment to the privileged few rapidly ceased. If the rich had any notion of retaliation, their resolve quickly evaporated because of the strong outpouring of public elation over the changes.

Soon, Glenn reached out to the Italian gangs up north. In a stroke of genius, he offered them inclusion in the BSA. It was an easy decision for them, as they would have access to our robust resources, and several key Italian bosses would assume influential positions in Glenn's hierarchy. They were now part of the organization that had previously worried them most, and Glenn came out of the deal with several new friends. If any of the old lieutenants had a notion of making trouble for Glenn, their time ran out when the Italians joined the new regime.

Glenn drove a fundamental shift in priorities. Rebuilding was a focus and my recovery crews were busy finding supplies to quench the new thirst for building materials. Most were fairly easy to locate, but lumber was scarce. A lot of it had been burned up as firewood over the winter, so we needed to put a mill together to produce more. Fortunately, other things like bricks and cement didn't burn, and they weren't commodities people hoarded as a civilization fell apart. Whatever we didn't find in the many abandoned home improvement centers would be salvaged from tear-downs. The new BSA building inspector would rate questionable structures based on how much effort they would take to restore. Those requiring too much work were carefully torn down and any materials salvaged.

The next focus was energy. The Italians happened to be sitting on a healthy supply of gasoline and diesel, thanks to large storage facilities in their territory. More cars and trucks were put back on the road, but never near the point where traffic congestion became an issue. Supplies were carefully rationed. Propane and natural gas (LNG) turned out to be more plentiful than anyone anticipated. I suppose gasoline was easy for people to steal. They just didn't want to mess with natural gas.

Restoring electricity was a more difficult challenge. It was a tedious process, but partial power was eventually achieved in certain buildings, mainly done through solar and wind power. Solar panels in particular were easy to find and salvage. They were another of those specialty items that desperate people tended to overlook.

Probably the largest focus was agriculture. Glenn and I had already formed a number of agricultural teams under Pat's regime, but now Glenn stepped up the effort significantly. Any open land in the area became farmland. As soon as a tear-down was cleared, the open land was cultivated and planted. Old apple orchards were restored. Houses and garages were turned into barns. Many empty warehouses were converted into greenhouses so that food could be grown year-round. There was no shortage of laborers, as Glenn made major changes to the BSA selection boards. Very few refugees were turned away. We simply couldn't afford to lose the help.

My job grew much busier and I was content with it. I nearly tripled the number of people working in The Supermarket. We even branched out and opened several annexes to handle the increase in inventories. Our distribution processes were expanded, refined, and perfected. Very few people went without necessities.

Overall, exuberance blossomed the most over that period. You could easily see it in most people's eyes. Gone were the sullen expressions. After many dark days, the fighting finally stopped. Gunfire was rarely heard anymore. Corruption had receded to the point where it was hardly noticed. Bodies floating down the Charles were now rarely seen. People felt safer. They could walk from one neighborhood to another without feeling threatened because of their race or gender. Although nowhere near pre-pandemic levels, the quality of life was much better than it had been under the Godfather. The only people who weren't happy were those who had had the good life under Pat, but they were extremely reluctant to say anything against their wildly popular new leader.

Glenn eventually disbanded Pat's old circle of lieutenants. A couple were kept on as marshals in the new law enforcement organization. Former military officers were tasked to form a new BSA defense force. They consolidated all military-grade weapons and equipment. They also trained people and formed them into a cohesive unit. We even found a large cache of outdated battle dress uniforms (BDUs), so our new army actually looked like an organized and well-equipped fighting force.

Glenn also set out to map the boundaries of the BSA. It was actually a straight forward definition. Anything inside the old Route 95/128 highway, a twenty-mile semi-circle around Boston, was claimed by the BSA and fell under our protection. Everything between there and the old Route 495 highway, another semi-circle thirty-five miles from Boston, was technically under BSA control, but not to the point where any laws were strictly enforced. There were a few pockets of gangs in small areas who didn't want to join the BSA, and we didn't bother them. As long as they stayed out of our way, they were left alone.

Anything beyond that was no-man's land.

We made occasional raids into places where scouts uncovered important supplies. Our new military was second to none in the region. If we wanted something, no one dared stand in our way. The only area that Glenn was reluctant to venture into was Providence, Rhode Island. Reports from that area were grim. Major gang wars consumed the area like a cancer. Nobody saw any reason for us to meddle in their affairs. We already had plenty of territory to govern.

There was no news of any organized governance beyond our region. Our scouts ventured out as far as upstate New York but didn't find much of anything. New York City was rumored to be worse than Providence. We dared not send anyone to scope things out down there. The last thing we wanted was to reveal the existence of the BSA, or a tidal wave of refugees would be on our doorstep within a month. We simply didn't have the resources to cope with that.

We heard rumors of an alliance of some type up in Maine, but Glenn was never able to make contact or verify their existence. Everything north of Nashua, New Hampshire was a wasteland sparsely populated by survivalists, or *preppers* as many called them.

Glenn and I didn't see as much of each other during those first three years. He was intensely busy and I ran a sprawling operation that he didn't have to worry himself about. To be honest, I was content with that arrangement. The reason behind it was selfish. I had been his best friend, but that distinction also made me a target. The lower a profile I kept, the better it was for me. We'd try to have dinner together once in a while, but we were often joined by other big-wigs who felt they had more important matters to discuss. Then there was the heavy drinking which rendered any discussion of these supposed important matters a futile undertaking.

At one particular dinner, it was just Glenn and me. It was in the early spring of his third year of leadership and things had settled into a nice routine. Smitty joined us for the first part of the meal, but was called out for an impromptu meeting. He had assumed the role of Chief Marshal in the law enforcement division. Actually, I interacted with him far more than with Glenn. Smitty was always concerned about keeping the distribution channels at The Supermarket clear of corruption. He knew that if things began breaking down anywhere in my burgeoning operation, it could quickly undermine the confidence in Glenn's regime.

I got to know Smitty as a no-nonsense, tough guy from the South Boston projects. He projected an thuggish persona, but I suspected it was pretense. To me, he was a fairly intelligent person who always had a good sense of himself. He wasn't too patient with people he considered stupid, and had a short fuse with anyone he didn't like. I was always considered a *good shit* in his book, which meant that I was a tolerable, non-threatening person. His real name was Rich Smithfield, but everyone just called him Smitty. I never found out how he got his nickname but assumed it was a shortened version of his last name – if that was even his real name. He never talked about his past and was apt at changing the subject whenever it came up. It gave me the distinct feeling that he was hiding something. That was one of the few perks of that era. Almost anyone could leave the skeletons of their old lives behind and start over as someone new.

"So when are you going to settle down and find a nice woman?" Glenn asked me after Smitty left.

"Too busy, I guess," I replied as I finished off my last forkful of green peas. It was a feeble deflection but an honest enough answer.

The truth was, I couldn't find a woman I could trust. Despite trying to keep a low profile, I was known as the king of The Supermarket. It always surprised me how many women knew exactly who I was and would probably sleep with me if I ever offered. I was told that most men envied my position, but I tried my best to avoid women who showed too much interest. There was always something about them that made my skin crawl. Many were insanely beautiful, but the way they looked at me distressed me. It left me little doubt they were merely lining up their next pigeon - ready to suck the life and wealth out of me like a vampire. I had already had a turn with a smoking-hot girlfriend, and wanted no part of repeating that relationship fiasco. Trying to start a relationship with any woman I met during that time would've been Veronica all over again, but worse.

"I could easily arrange something short term," Glenn suggested with a wink. "It's not healthy for you to work so hard without any kind of a release."

His comment flabbergasted me. We had always agreed that using women like that was stepping out in front of a trainload of trouble. Blackmail, STIs, and drugs were only some of the pitfalls prostitutes brought along with them. In fact, one of our bets had been how long it would've taken for Pat to be done in by one of the many women he kept. Neither of us won that bet, but I'm pretty certain that in time one of us would have.

"That's okay," I politely replied. "I'm doing fine."

"Still reluctant to take advantage of the perks?"

"You know it's the baggage that comes with it. Remember?"

"Of course I remember, but now I have access to some nice, younger, clean ones. Trust me, you don't have to worry about all the trappings we used to fear. No strings attached anymore. Come on, Walt, it really helps."

I paused and attempted not to look displeased. I knew exactly what he was talking about and found it deplorable. Chung-Hee once told me how the pandemic had orphaned numerous children. He helped arrange many families in The Pit as unofficial foster homes, and I helped these families relocate into larger houses in Cambridge. Still, too many of these children were sold into sex slavery as they came of age, and sometimes sooner. Hearing Glenn tout this was the first distinct instance that shined a revealing light on the rift that had been growing between us. I wasn't ready to deal with it, so I changed the subject.

"So things seem to be working pretty smoothly in the BSA these days."

Glenn grinned and gave a slight shake of his head. "I have to admit, we've done a lot of good. We still have some pain-in-the-ass things to deal with, but I agree that things are working. People are generally happy."

"So any thought about shifting control over to an elected government?"

Glenn smirked. "Back on that again?"

"Just checking."

"Look, I know you've always frowned on the whole dictator-style of governing, but you have to admit that things got better a whole lot faster this way. There's no way we would've been able to make the same progress if we had left it all to a committee. They'd probably still be fighting over what color to paint the conference room."

"I'm happy with the progress we've made, but you're the one who wanted me to give you a kick in the ass to remind you of a promise you made."

Glenn chuckled. "Yeah, you're right. Consider me reminded."

"And?"

Glenn let out a deep sigh. "It's just a lot more complicated than I ever anticipated. It's too difficult to make those sorts of changes right now."

"So start small. Try holding a neighborhood election and see how it works."

"I already know how it's working. I'm trying it out with a neighborhood in the Kenmore district. I allowed them to form a governing board and they're driving me crazy."

"Seriously? Why didn't you tell me?"

"It's one of those things we agreed to keep on the down-low to see how it worked out. Otherwise, I'd have dozens of neighborhoods lining up for a turn at electing their own boards."

"You know something like that is going to be rocky at first," I attempted to reassure him.

Glenn threw down his spoon. "Are you shitting me? They've

been chewing my ear off about cleaning up the garbage dump at Fenway Park and turning it into something. But those chuckleheads can't decide if they want to make it a baseball museum, restore it to a ballpark, or just to make it a big carnival attraction. Like we have anywhere near the materials or manpower to do any of that! I couldn't give a shit about it, anyway. I'm trying to spend my time on trivial priorities like feeding everyone, clean running water, restoring ambulance service, or just clearing the blockages at the sewage plant so most of us can flush our goddamn toilets without them backing up. Oh, yeah, good ol' democracy in action."

I sat stunned and didn't know what to say. I had clearly hit a nerve that I didn't know was there.

"Walt," Glenn continued after calming himself, "I want to see democracy make a comeback as much as the next guy. Trust me, this job is wearing me down, but I just don't think we're there yet. We need at least a couple more years before starting something."

"And what if you get the same result then? Will you put it off again?"

"Walt, please understand that as far as any of us know, we're the only major civilized society that's standing. New York City is a disaster and nothing has been heard from anywhere else in the country. Boston could be once again ground zero for the start of a new nation, so we need to take it slow and make sure it all holds together. I don't want to be the guy who goes down in history for fucking it all up."

There wasn't much more I could say. Glenn had a valid point, and maybe the only one that really mattered at that time. The BSA wasn't an experiment that we could simply walk away from if it failed. There was nothing to fall back on or anywhere to run if everything fell apart again. The BSA had to succeed; there was no viable alternative.

* * *

A couple of days later, I had Chung-Hee over for dinner. We tried to connect regularly. His new job as chief of surgery at Boston General Hospital tied him up at odd hours, so it was always a challenge to get our schedules to sync up. Despite this, I managed to spend much more time with him than I did with Glenn. I also got to know his daughter, Soon-Yi, and it wasn't long before she started calling me Uncle Walt. She would usually tag along for these dinners, but a play-date kept her away that evening.

Our dinner discussion started with the usual subjects but soon meandered to the talk I'd had with Glenn a couple of nights before. Chung-Hee was always interested in my interactions with Glenn and I could also implicitly trust him to keep those discussions to himself. He never failed me in that regard. His quality of character was impeccable.

"He disappointed you, didn't he?" Chung-Hee asked after I finished.

"We're drifting apart. Leadership is changing him."

"I wonder."

"What do you mean by that?"

Chung-Hee smiled. "Have I ever told you how much I've admired the way you handle your position? You never seek attention or reward."

"Thanks, but I think you might be confusing my desire for self-preservation with something far more noble. The fewer people who know me, the less trouble I find myself in."

Chung-Hee laughed. "As I said, I admire the way you handle it."

"What does this have to do with what you're wondering about Glenn?"

"That your differences with him were always bigger than you thought. That perhaps who you're seeing now is the man Glenn always was."

I paused and put down my forkful of rice. "Are you saying that he really wants to keep running the BSA?"

"I can't say, but I don't think he's been completely honest with you."

"How so?"

"I would dispute his assertion that the BSA is the only viable society left."

"Why? What else is there?"

"Maine."

I chuckled as I chewed on a forkful of rice. "You're seriously giving credence to that fairytale?"

"Would a fairytale drive one of my best ER doctors to attempt a trek up there? He was convinced that there was truth to the stories."

"Trust me, I'm in the loop on that. None of our scouting reports have ever shown anything there."

"I'm not surprised."

"Why? Did your friend find anything?"

"One of our military units intercepted him before he got to Portsmouth. He was brought back and put into detention. I've been trying to plead for his release and was only allowed a brief visit with him. Now they won't allow him any visitors."

"I don't understand. Why would we send a unit up that far north after one person?"

Chung-Hee grinned. "Exactly."

"Do you think he saw something?"

"I think they want to discourage people from looking."

"That doesn't make sense."

"I agree. Why would anyone be concerned about people looking for something that's not supposed to be there? The answer is obvious. It's because we've all been deceived. Glenn knows something's up there and he's worried it will start luring our people away."

"I honestly don't think it's possible for him to hide something like that. My organization supports the scouting missions and I see all the reports."

"Reports can be altered."

"Look, let's assume for the sake of argument that something is up there. It can't be anything that big, and certainly not enough to justify a paranoia over people wanting to leave the BSA. Why would anyone want to leave the progress we've made here?"

Chung-Hee rolled his eyes. "Progress? Perhaps. Is everyone really happy? I think you need to get away from your Supermarket a bit more than you currently do."

"Why? What's wrong?"

"I'll just say that not everyone is quite as happy with Glenn and his organization as you seem to think they are."

I was bewildered. Chung-Hee had never hinted at anything like this before.

"Can you give me any details?"

Chung-Hee paused and smirked. "I advise you to get out and see for yourself. You might not have to look very hard."

I stopped pressing the issue. What he had said was confusing and unsettling.

Chung-Hee was always a bit frustrating when I tried to pry details from him. He was the type who wanted people to see and experience things for themselves. He was always reluctant to impose his opinion on anyone, and preferred to demonstrate rather than tell. I was reluctant to follow his advice. Looking back, I think I was just too afraid I'd find something to challenge my comfortable perception of reality.

CHAPTER 9

A week later, I was in my office looking over my morning recovery reports. My crowded schedule had quickly driven the unsettling conversation with Chung-Hee deep into the archives of my memory. I sat and checked major recoveries against inventory records on my laptop. The Supermarket was one of the first places to start using a computer network again. Up to that point, the absence of computers had been something that made my job a nightmare of paperwork. It was a game-changer to have them back.

Smitty came through my door and planted himself in one of my guest chairs. He would stop by at least once a week to check on any recent recoveries that might help his marshals. It was his way of trying to get first in line for any cool gadgets that came through before the defense force snapped them up. When he was looking for something, he was always extra nice to me, but he seemed politely tolerant in most other instances. I was glad to be on his good side because he could be awfully nasty to anyone he didn't like.

I always had a sense of what Smitty might be looking for and what General Anderson of our defense force wouldn't put up a fight to keep. The general was not nearly as easy to deal with, so I had to be very careful about what I let Smitty have.

"Morning, Walt."

"How's things, Smitty?"

"Not too bad today. Same old shit."

"I heard about Federal Street."

Smitty rolled his eyes. "Still too many idiots trying to make homes in the high-rises. Nobody seemed to learn anything after last year. It was only five floors, but we're lucky the whole goddamn building didn't burn to the ground."

"What keeps them trying?"

"It's all about the fucking views. They just don't care that most of those buildings were built to be offices, not homes. When it gets cold, they don't give a shit that there's no chimney to start a fire in. I swear to God, one of these days some dumb-fuck is going to burn down the old financial district."

"And you wonder why I'm not interested in any of the vacant spaces over there?"

Smitty laughed. "So, any cool shit come in this week?"

I checked my list. "Some handgun ammo that looks to be in pretty good shape. A couple more hand radios, the consumer version with a fifteen-mile range. I think they'll be compatible with the others I gave you last month."

"Batteries?"

"I'll be able to scratch up some."

"Please, none of that nickle cadmium shit."

"Okay, I might be able to dig up some nickle metal hydrides."

"Deal."

A messenger knocked on the door and stepped in to give Smitty a note. He waved him out and quickly read it over.

"I'm going to have to cut this short."

"Trouble?"

"There's a place out in Westford they think is hiding a large cache of specialized ammo. The defense guys are working it, but I want to take a peek at what they pull out of there."

"Ammo? What kind?"

"Supposedly armor-piercing. Haven't seen that stuff come around in a long time. I wouldn't mind a piece of that."

"If the General will let it go."

"No shit," Smitty replied with a laugh. "That's why I'm booking out there now."

I'm not sure what gave me the urge, but I suddenly wanted to go with him. "Hey, mind if I come with you?"

"Really?"

"Yeah, I've been cooped up in this office too long. I've got spring fever and I need some air."

"Wicked spooney. If it's a legit score, maybe you can help me get a piece of it."

"Deal."

I left my assistant to clear my schedule of the usual boring meetings for the rest of the day and went with Smitty. We fueled up his SUV and joined up with a deputy escort.

Throughout the BSA territory, the main highways and major secondary roads had been cleared and patched up. Everything outside the Route 95/128 belt was reasonably safe as long as you stuck to the highways or main roads. We had an additional advantage of having a two-vehicle convoy of marked BSA marshal SUV's that no one would mess with anyway.

Westford was located about thirty-five miles northwest. It was on the edge of quasi-controlled BSA territory, right on the Route 495 belt. Our defense force had an outpost two towns over in Lowell, but Westford remained an unsecured area for the few who still called it home.

I always enjoyed driving in those days, even if I had to be a passenger. Other than a few trucks and cars, we usually had the entire highway to ourselves. We could easily set our own speed limit, so long as the road was in good shape. Every time I went out for a drive like that, vivid memories of traffic jams from the old days came to mind. It was hard to believe that there had once been enough cars on the road to cause congestion.

Once outside of the Route 95/128 belt, we needed to keep a closer eye on road conditions and for red flags. These flags would be placed by those who encountered dangerous road hazards. These usually meant large potholes, downed trees, or sections of bridge decks that had crumbled away. Two red flags meant to stop, turn around, and find another route because the road ahead was impassable. While the BSA maintained all the roads in our territory, road crews rarely ventured out to the edge unless it was to fix a major issue.

Smitty blared his music while driving and I was surprised to discover that he was a big Oasis music fan. I had never had any strong preference for a particular band and didn't mind his taste in music. It was actually a nice opportunity to escape reality and think back to long-lost comforts for a little while. I was also thoroughly entertained listening to a tone-deaf, tough guy from Southie try to sing along.

"The defense guys have the building surrounded," Smitty said as he listened in on his police radio through an earpiece. "Some local hicks are putting up a fuss and they barricaded themselves in the building."

"Is it going to be safe?"

"Should be fine. There's a reinforced defense patrol on the scene. We can hang back and watch them do their thing."

"Those hicks have to be out of their minds to think they can defend that place."

"You think?" Smitty condescendingly retorted.

"Maybe there's something more valuable inside than we're being told?"

Smitty turned to me with a snide grin. "Well, light dawns on Marblehead."

"What?"

"That's why I'm the marshal and you're the Supermarket king."

We soon arrived to what used to be a chain restaurant near the highway. I counted six humvees and a couple of converted armored police personnel carriers sprinkled around the building. Smitty and our escort parked in the lot across the road, well out of range.

"Wicked overkill," Smitty commented after he got out and looked over the scene.

"Hey, isn't that General Anderson?" I asked after catching sight of him.

"Well, la-di-fucking-da, I feel safer already."

"What's he doing here?"

Smitty only snorted and rolled his eyes. We started to walk across the road but were stopped by a soldier dressed in full body armor.

"Sorry, girls. This is strictly a military operation."

"You bootin' us?" Smitty asked.

"You're quick. You can go back to your cars and bang a left back to the highway. We don't need any help."

"We heard there's ammo in there," I said.

"Who the hell are you?" the soldier snapped back at me.

"Well, well," came the mocking voice of the approaching General Anderson. He had been an army special forces team leader back in the day but got washed out due to some unnamed performance shortcoming. Once an enforcer in Pat's regime, he had never achieved anything of significance other than surviving the many conquests and killing a lot of gang-bangers along the way. Many wondered how he was able to pull off becoming general of the BSA defense force. Smitty had never liked him and probably knew far more about his story than he would tell me. I came to trust Smitty's judgment on those things. He was usually a reliable judge of character.

"If it isn't our esteemed Chief Marshal and the King of The Supermarket himself. Holy hell, I wonder what brought you two all the way out to the sticks."

"Real nice to see you too, General," Smitty greeted him.

"Now, let me take a wild guess," Anderson continued, "I'm thinking it's the same sort of thing that draws flies to a corpse."

"Armor-piercing ammo always gets my attention," I replied, trying to sound like I should be there.

"I'm just here to make sure it doesn't grow legs," Smitty added pointedly.

"Jesus, you guys are quite a pair. You just can't wait until the bodies get cold before you strip the place."

"What's going on now?" Smitty asked as he looked back to the scene.

"We've got an armed group of local hicks trapped in there. I gave them a hour to clear out, but they seem determined to stay. We're about ready to neutralize them."

"Any risk of touching off the ammo?" I asked.

"We have a way of dealing with it," Anderson replied with a cold, confident glare. The way he said it sent chills down my spine. I looked over to Smitty and knew he felt the same thing.

"Mind if we stick around and watch?" Smitty asked.

"Just hang back across the road and stay out of our way," Anderson concluded . He turned to walk back to his command vehicle.

"It's your show," Smitty retorted as we walked away. "And fuck you very much," he added in a low mumble that I barely heard.

We went back to our vehicles and kept watch. Smitty pulled out several pairs of binoculars so we could all see better. Nothing much happened for a few minutes. There was a lot of conferring and loitering, but there was no attempt to warn the people inside that their time was nearly up.

Then something strange happened. I saw one of the soldiers raise his hand and wave to everyone else. At once, they all put on gas masks. Two soldiers emerged from the back of a personnel carrier with oversized guns.

"Looks like they're pulling out the teargas launchers," Smitty noted to me. "It's showtime."

With another wave, several demolition charges blew out boarded up windows and gas canisters were fired into the building. It wasn't long before I could see brownish smoke start to leak out.

"Oh, pissa," Smitty mumbled.

"What?"

"Teargas is usually white."

"It's not teargas?"

Smitty sighed. "I don't know. At least we're upwind."

After a few minutes, several soldiers stormed into the building. We heard a couple of muffled gunshots, then everything went quiet. After about ten minutes, more soldiers went in. They opened up the place and set up gas-powered fans around the entrance.

We waited an hour as the smoke vented from the building. That's when the bodies were carried out the back. It was an obvious but lame attempt to keep a low profile on the cleanup. We had to reposition to a better vantage point in order to see any detail through our binoculars. A deputy soon gave us a short whistle to let us know that General Anderson was on his way out to give us an update.

"It's a bust," he announce with a grim face. "Nothing in there. The tip we got was bogus."

"You mind if we take a look-see?" Smitty asked.

"You'll have to wait a while longer for it to finish venting out. Then you can knock yourselves out looking around."

"What did you use in there?" I asked.

General Anderson grimaced. "Special lethal cocktail."

"Lethal?"

"Hey, if those assholes in there didn't want to come out, I wasn't risking my guys in a gun battle. You know how these goddamn hicks behave. We don't fuck around with them. I gave them plenty of warning."

There was nothing more to say and the general went back to his work.

Another half-hour passed before we were allowed anywhere near the building. The general had left the scene, and we started to make our way closer to the trucks they'd loaded the bodies into.

"Give it another fifteen minutes," a soldier told us as we approached.

"No problem," Smitty replied as he looked over to a pair of former National Guard trucks. "We want a peek at the bodies."

The soldier hesitated.

"Is there a problem?" Smitty pressed.

"Just make it quick and don't touch anything. There might be dangerous residue on them."

Smitty nodded and walked toward the trucks. I followed at a discreet distance, nervous about what poison we might be exposing ourselves to. It wasn't long before Smitty looked back at me and chuckled.

"Calm ya liwa, will ya? That soldier-boy would've been wearing a hazmat suit if it was really dangerous."

We reached the back of the trucks and looked inside. It was a grim sight. We counted a total of eighteen bodies. Half of them were children. Three were toddlers.

"What the hell?" Smitty snarled as we stood back and took it all in.

It was a horrifying image to see those kids clutched in a fetal position. A little blonde girl in a blue dress captivated my attention. I couldn't take my eyes off of her.

"Didn't they know there were children in there?" I fumed.

"Sweet Jesus," Smitty said as he turned to me with a dour expression. I'd never seen him show so much emotion before. "This is real sketchy."

"Why?"

"Christ, Sherlock, look at them. Do they look like backwoods hicks who would put up a fight?"

As we walked away, I turned to the soldier who was keeping an eye on us.

"Where you taking them?"

"To the morgue at Boston General."

We continued back to our vehicles. Smitty didn't say a thing. He was clearly upset, even though he tried not to let it show.

"So what now?" I asked.

"No fucking way that had anything to do with ammo," Smitty

grumbled to me in a low mumble. He turned to his deputies. "Make sure those chuckleheads don't sneak anything onto those trucks before they leave."

They nodded and moved off to seek out a better vantage point.

"What are you thinking?" I asked after they left.

"That we need a lookie inside."

We finally got the go-ahead to enter the building. A faint but pungent odor lingered in the air. We were assured it was safe, and the two soldiers who entered with us did so without their masks.

Daylight illuminated the areas around the windows and doors that had been broken in. Using flashlights, we looked over the darker areas closer to the center. There was the predictable mess caused by the brief skirmish, but aside from a lot of old spray-painted graffiti, nothing stood out to us. We spent a half-hour of careful inspection. If Smitty saw something that caught his attention, he didn't let it show.

Finally, to my relief, we exited the building.

"Did everyone behave out here?" Smitty asked his deputies as we arrived back at our vehicles.

"Seems like it. The trucks left and everyone else is just standing around scratching themselves."

"All right, wait around here another hour and keep an eye on things. Walt and I heading back."

* * *

Smitty was quiet for the first part of the drive back. He didn't even play his music. I patiently waited for him to start a conversation, but he was clearly lost in his thoughts. He even pulled out a cigarette and lit up. Up to that point, I never knew he smoked. I also had to warn him of a red flag he sped past. It marked a huge pothole that we barely avoided. It wasn't until we reached Route 95/128 when I finally broke the silence.

"So what was that massacre all about?"

"Not sure, but they weren't no hicks from the sticks. No way they were living there.

"How could you tell?"

"It didn't have that lived-in feeling. Too clean in some areas and too messy in others. They were just hiding there."

"Why?"

Smitty rolled his eyes. "Didn't I just say I had no fucking idea? I'm going to do some checking around to see if anyone knows something about it."

Smitty dropped me back at my office, but I couldn't concentrate for the rest of the day. It took a couple of days for me to flush the vivid images from my mind. To this day, I haven't been able to shake the image of that little girl in her blue dress lying lifeless on the dirty floor of the old army truck. She couldn't have been much older than five and was clutching her ears with both hands. That poor girl died frightened out of her mind.

* * *

A week or so after our trip to Westford, Smitty dropped by my office. I was anxious to hear if he had learned anything. He shut my door and sat with a solemn expression.

"So? What did you find out?" I asked.

"Enough," Smitty hesitantly replied. "Look, Walt. I'm going to ask you for a wicked big favor. I'll owe you for it, and someday a skid like me might be able to repay you."

"What do you need?"

"I need you to forget what happened in Westford. Put it out of your mind. Don't ever discuss it with anyone. It never happened."

"Can you at least throw me a bone?"

"Consider it good for our health. Is that enough for you?"

I've never seen Smitty so nervous over anything. If someone like him wanted me to forget about something, there was no doubt that it was in my best interest to forget about it. Period.

I could only nod to him in agreement. But I couldn't let it go.

* * *

A couple of days later, I ran some important items over to Boston General, giving me an excuse to drop in on Chung-Hee. He was finishing up with a consult. I walked with him to his next appointment.

"Is there a problem?" he asked as we waited for an elevator. Power had been restored to their elevators a few months earlier and I was surprised at how people around there didn't think twice about them anymore.

"I need a favor," I carefully replied as the elevator doors opened.

We were the only ones that entered before the doors closed. "There should have been eighteen bodies delivered to your morgue early last week. They were involved in an incident out in the boonies. I wonder if you could discreetly--"

"I'm not aware of any mass deliveries to our morgue."

"Is this something you'd be in the loop for?"

"Eighteen bodies? At once? This whole hospital would be talking about it."

"Could the delivery have been done in secret?"

"Trust me, Walt. You couldn't keep that big a secret around here. What happened?"

"The military gassed their way into a building that these people were occupying."

"Gassed? Are you serious?"

"I saw the bodies of several children among them. A soldier claimed the bodies were going to be delivered to your morgue."

"Children? I'll ask around, but I seriously doubt they came here."

"Be careful who you ask. Smitty was with me and tried to check into it. He asked me to stay quiet, which means someone got to him. It had to be something serious to put a scare like that into him."

"I'll be cautious. Are there any descriptions you can offer to help me locate these bodies?"

"Mostly Caucasian. One little girl was blonde and wearing a light blue dress. Smitty thought that they were all too well-dressed to be from the boonies."

"Dear Lord, I'm sorry you had to see that."

CHAPTER 10

I was surprised to receive an invitation to dinner with Glenn for the next evening. Its timing left me no doubt as to what had prompted it. It was yet another disappointing development in our friendship. Formerly, I would've just marched over there and directly talked to him about anything important. Times had clearly changed. We just didn't have that rapport any longer. My plan was to play dumb and let him bring up the subject.

We dined on pheasant. It was an extravagance which made me wonder if he was giving me my last meal. No one else joined us, which I thought was a bit odd. Glenn didn't seem preoccupied and acted like his normal self as we ate. We talked about the usual things, reminiscing about our time together in The Supermarket and the old days before the pandemic. When the liquor came out, he transitioned into more weighty subjects. I knew where the talk was leading when the fine whiskey started flowing. I was a lightweight drinker, so I nursed my drinks in order to keep a clear head. It wasn't long before he changed the subject.

"So I understand you came across a bad scene out in Westford."

"Yeah, it was bad."

"It must have been brutal to witness."

"Did you know there were children in there?"

"Yeah, I got the full report. We're all very upset about it."

"Who were they, really?" I figured if I didn't fire off such a direct question, Glenn would start to wonder why I didn't.

"Walt, I'm really sorry about what happened. Nobody wanted to see children killed. Our intelligence isn't as good as I'd like it to be. We still get things wrong too often. I've ordered a full review of our procedures so that something like this will never happen again."

He spoke in an authentic, concerned tone, and was acting like the old Glenn I used to know. It was nice to have him back, but I was still sober enough not to let my guard down.

"Have you talked to anyone about it?" he finally asked.

"I was told that I should forget about it and move on."

"Good advice. I don't want anything to get out there which could complicate our review."

I smiled the best I could. "You know me, I've got way too much to worry about already."

"So we're okay with this?"

Of course I wasn't. "Glenn, it's your business to handle. Glad I don't have to deal with it."

I left a short time later and kept a vigilant eye out for anything suspicious. I hated to think that Glenn would resort to methods that Pat had routinely used. Desperately hoping I wouldn't be fish food in the harbor by morning, my mind raced with each step I took. I started seeing threats in every shadow and quickened my pace.

I got home without any hint of trouble and hated myself for entertaining the preposterous thought that Glenn would resort to draconian methods. I felt ashamed that I had allowed paranoia to get to me.

* * *

A few days later, I got a message that Chung-Hee needed to meet with me to discuss a serious supply issue. Since I wasn't aware that any such problem existed, and because he had set up the meeting at a public cafe, I sensed it really had to be news about the missing bodies. I was both curious and reluctant to hear what he would report.

We sat down in a booth near a window and ordered a light lunch. He pulled out a number of folders from his briefcase and set out a touchscreen PC. To anyone observing us, we were all business.

"I discreetly checked around for those bodies," he spoke softly as he handed me a folder. I opened it and found random pharmaceutical inventory print-outs that had nothing to do with what we were talking about. I quickly understood what he was trying to do.

"Did you find them?" I asked as I lifted one of the papers out and pretended to look it over.

"I found no sign of them, so I pursued it further with certain people I know."

"Certain people?"

"It's best you don't know who they are, but they're trying to build an underground railroad to get people out of the BSA. Your description of the girl matched a member of a group they were trying to smuggle up north."

"Why?"

"As I told you, not everyone is happy with the way things are being run. The bigger question we need to ask is why our military would resort to such appalling extremes."

"I don't know," I replied with a shrug of my shoulders. "None of it makes sense."

"Really? Isn't it obvious?"

"Not to me."

"It's because they don't want us to know what's up there."

"By killing children like that?"

"At first, they were capturing anyone who attempted to flee. They brought them back and talked them into thinking they were foolish to consider leaving. That recently proved to be an ineffective strategy, so now they're just snuffing out refugees. To my knowledge, no one has been able to escape to the north."

"Are you sure that these *certain people* you know are telling you the truth?"

"I would never tell you this if I had any doubts about them." Chung-Hee paused and sighed. "Walt, I'm sorry to say that you have a distorted perception of our state of affairs. I know you have a strong friendship with Glenn, and I greatly respect how you've supported him, but the time has come to start facing the truth. He's no longer the person you knew, if he was ever the person you thought he was."

"Wait, what?"

"You heard me."

I sat dumfounded and had to reach for another folder so I could stay in character. I needed more time to process Chung-Hee's accusations. After a minute, I predictably grew defensive. The Glenn he was trying to portray couldn't be the same person I knew. However, what I was really struggling with was the possibility that I could have been that gullible.

"How can you say that I don't really know Glenn? Do you remember how much we've been through together?"

"Yes, you've told me many times."

"We've been through some tight scrapes. He saved my life as Pat was about to execute me in my office. I owe him more than I can fathom."

"I think he's well aware of that."

I gathered the folders and handed them back to him. "I think we're done here."

"Please take time to carefully consider what I've said."

I gave him a quick nod and got up to leave. My appetite was gone and I needed some air.

It took a week for me to get out of the funk that lunch meeting put me into. My mind raced over every little detail of my exploits with Glenn and I couldn't get it to stop. It was something that tempted me to start drinking. I had access to all the alcohol I wanted. Fortunately, drinking myself into forgetfulness wasn't something I was comfortable with. I'd seen too many people try and it rarely ended well. Work would be my outlet. I could easily bury myself in busyness.

* * *

Early in June, I got word about an unusual recovery. My vehicle reclamation department called me over to see the anomaly for myself. I entered a large garage bay full of trucks, cars, construction equipment, and anything motorized that was deemed salvageable. It was a busy place where vehicles were either restored or chopped up for parts. The site supervisor led me over to an armored personnel carrier that had been towed in that morning.

"Our defense patrol jumped this bad-boy near Groton."

"What is it?"

"You're looking at a Stryker model M1126. This sweetheart is fully equipped for front-line combat duty."

"Where did it come from?" I asked as I looked over the beat-up, slightly scorched vehicle.

"Not a clue. Our patrol killed everyone inside and left another vehicle, a Humvee, out there. It was too shot up to bring back."

"Any hope of restoring this?"

"It looks promising. We should have plenty of spare parts that can be adapted. I don't see much of a problem getting this thing up and running."

"I'd like to take a closer look."

"Not a problem if you don't mind the mess. My crew made a prelim sweep but hasn't had a chance to clean it out yet."

"Bad?"

"Yeah, a lot of blood left behind."

"Thanks for the warning."

"Oh, and just so you know, General Anderson told me he wants this to be his new command APC."

"I'm not surprised. Save it for him, the general always gets what he wants."

"No shit," the supervisor agreed with a laugh, and walked away.

I was left to inspect our new treasure. Most of the military vehicles we recovered were National Guard or law enforcement trucks and Humvees. This vehicle was entirely different. It was far more heavily armored, had a total of eight wheels, and looked like a small tank. The back door was open and I immediately saw a pool of blood on the floor. More blood was spattered around the interior. The recovery team obviously hadn't wasted any time towing it out, so nothing had been done to erase the grim aftermath of battle. It was a grisly scene and I pitied whoever had clean-up duty.

I went to the front and looked around. I was fascinated with the setup; I'd never seen anything like it before. I poked around a bit, looking over all the instruments and gauges. That's when I saw a handgun peeking out from underneath the seat. I reached down to pull it out. As I carefully removed it, I noticed that it was on top of a folded document. The way it was positioned gave me the impression that someone had quickly stuffed it there.

"Find something?" the supervisor asked from behind, startling me.

I inconspicuously slid the folded document into my pocket as I turned and held up the gun. "You guys need to do a better job of sweeping for things like this."

"Shit, sorry about that."

"You'd better log this in," I replied as I checked to make sure the gun was safe before handing it to him.

"I'll do it right now."

I lingered and talked a bit more with those who had performed the recovery. I wanted to learn more about the circumstances that had led up to the acquisition of our new treasure. There wasn't much to discover. A Stryker and Humvee were loitering at the side of Route 111 when one of our military patrols came upon them. There was a brief gun battle and despite having some heavy weapons at their disposal, whoever was inside the formidable Stryker were taken by surprise. They never stood a chance.

* * *

I waited until I got back to my office before I took out the document and carefully unfolded it. It was a map of Maine. There was a red circle around Auburn and a couple of routes were highlighted. Nothing else was written on either side. Regardless, it was a stunning piece of evidence that something important might be up there.

All my reports had shown Maine to be a fairly desolate territory. I pulled out a local map to study the area the Stryker had been pulled from. Groton wasn't too far outside of our territory, about forty-five miles west. I pulled up additional reports on my computer and saw that it was designated a low-risk zone. Our defense force regularly patrolled the area and reported a low instance of hostile contact. That's all I needed to see. I planned to visit the ambush site to find out for myself what this was all about.

CHAPTER 11

The next morning I signed out an SUV from the motor pool and headed west. It wasn't unusual for me to go on the road to inspect potential recoveries, but this trip would take me several miles beyond the Route 495 belt. Even though it was a low-risk zone, I wasn't sure I'd be allowed out that far. I had considered asking Smitty to take the trip with me, but something told me that it wouldn't be a good idea. I wasn't ready to have the conversation his questions would lead to.

The trip was uneventful. I easily found the exit to the secondary road that would take me to the location where the ambush occurred. I had traveled only a mile from the highway when I came across one of our military patrols parked at the side of the road. A soldier waved me to a stop. My SUV was clearly marked as an official BSA vehicle, which probably kept them from drawing their guns on me.

"What brings you all the way out here today?" a soldier asked.

"I'm here after a recovery."

"A what?"

"Recovery. Wasn't there a skirmish up the road the other day?"

"Yeah, we know. Didn't you guys already pull that APC out of there?"

"Yeah, but we left the Humvee behind."

"No shit. It was fucked up beyond repair."

"I heard, but I still need to check it over for salvageable parts."

"Are you serious?"

"Hey, there could be a goldmine of spare parts left behind."

The soldier looked over to his sergeant, who was listening nearby.

"How long will it take?" the sergeant asked.

"It depends on what I find. Is it safe out there?"

"We patrol around here all the time. There's nobody around. You should be okay, but you need to check in with us on radio and bug out before sunset."

"Works for me. What frequency are you on?"

The sergeant took a hand held radio off one of his soldiers and tossed it to me. "Call in if you see anything and we'll come in after you. If you stay past sunset, you're on your own. We're not waiting around for you."

"Fine, thanks."

I continued up the road for a few miles. The further I went, the more uneasy I felt, and the tighter I clutched the radio in my hand. Most of the road was clear, but I had to carefully skirt some fallen trees and an occasional branch. The last thing I needed to deal with was a flat tire.

I came across the wrecked Humvee on a secluded section of road. The soldier was right; it was totally burned out and looked to be a hopeless cause. I looked around, checked my handgun, and slowly got out. The country was peaceful and I could only hear an occasional call of a blackbird. I peeked into the Humvee wreck and saw the shriveled remains of a body still in one of the seats. I could only hope that the poor guy had been shot dead before the fire got to him.

I walked in a large circle looking for anything out of the ordinary. I saw an occasional bullet casing and spatters of dried blood. Then I came across drag marks in the gravel at the side of the road. They led to the grisly remains of four bodies well into the trees. They had been stripped of their clothes, and it looked like the local wildlife had already had their fill.

I crossed to the other side of the road and walked a bit into the woods. I'm not sure how it caught my attention, but I discovered a small pool of dried blood behind a tree. I looked further and found that it was part of a trail that led deeper into the woods. Clearly, a wounded survivor had attempted to flee the engagement. Perhaps someone had eluded our patrol. I stood for a minute and wondered if this was something wise to pursue.

I still don't understand what compelled me to follow that trail. Normally, I would've declined such a risky notion and driven off. My heart was in my throat with each step as I crunched through that patch of woods. I could have been lined up to be shot at any point; if whoever escaped the scene was still alive, he wouldn't hesitate to protect himself. I might as well have been holding up a big sign that said *Shoot the clueless idiot*.

After a half mile, the trail led into a subdivision of abandoned homes. I looked around and saw that the trail led to the back of a spacious colonial. The sliding back door was cracked open and I spied a smear of blood on the handle. There was no doubt that someone had escaped the skirmish. It was an insanely stupid thing to do, but I called out.

"Hello in there! I'm not here to hurt you. I saw your blood trail and wanted to see if you need help. I'm coming in, so please don't shoot me."

I slowly slid the door the rest of the way open. My handgun quivered in my sweaty grip as I entered what had once been somebody's family room.

"Are you in there?" I called out.

"Yes," I heard. It jolted me, and I pivoted to see someone lying on the couch. He was mostly obscured by shadows in a dark corner of the room, but the gun he pointed at me was in perfect view.

"Okay," I said as I held my gun up. "I'm not here to hurt you."

"You already said that," he grunted to me. "Now please prove it and put your gun down."

I slowly placed my gun on the floor. "Is that okay?"

"Take two steps away from it and keep your hands where I can see them."

I did exactly as instructed. "Okay, so now what?"

"Who are you?"

"I'm Walter Johnson."

"What are you doing here?"

"I was checking out the wrecked Humvee."

"Why?"

"I work for a recovery operation with the Bay State Alliance. I came to check for any salvageable parts. I found your blood trail and it led me here."

"You're not military?"

"No."

He lowered his gun. "Does anyone know you're out here?"

"There's a patrol stationed up the road. I'm supposed to call in on my radio if I need help."

"Why don't you put that radio on the table over there?"

I placed the radio on the table, wondering why I had even said anything about it. Thinking clearly on the fly has always been a weakness of mine. "Are you hurt?"

"What gave you that idea?"

"Right, sorry. Can I do anything to help?"

He struggled to prop himself up higher on the couch. "Probably not, and I'm sorry to say I don't have much for you to salvage after I'm gone."

"There has to be something I can do for you."

"It's been too long. I've lost too much blood and infection has already set in."

"What's your name?"

"I'm Major Joseph Paladin, United States Army."

"United States? Really? You're still around?"

"No, not anymore, and probably never again."

"Did you come from Maine?"

He paused and grunted. "Sorry, it's getting hard to stay focused. I really shouldn't say anything more until I know more about you. Tell me about yourself, Walter."

"How much do you want to know?"

"Be concise. I don't have a lot of time left."

"Well," I started to say as I sat down on a nearby chair, "I'm actually in charge of something we call The Supermarket. It's an operation that recovers, sorts, and distributes supplies to everyone in the Bay State Alliance. We've been able to bring back some of the old world to everyone. Have you heard of the BSA?"

"Yeah, I know who you guys are."

"Then you know we have good doctors and medical facilities that could save you. One of my best friends is Chief of Surgery at Boston General Hospital. Please let me take you there. I'll be more than happy to keep your identity on the down-low."

Paladin coughed for a bit. I think he had begun to laugh a little, which had set off the coughing. "I appreciate your offer, but I wouldn't survive the trip back. I'm going to die here."

"Can I get you anything?"

He paused and tried to reposition his bloodied leg. I could smell the gangrene, like rotting meat. I had smelled it several times at the hospital.

"How about some honesty? Why are you really here?"

"Okay, I found a map in the Stryker we took in. That's why I came out here. I was curious to find out what's up in Maine. All my reports say nothing's up there."

"Well, thanks for being honest with me, but I'm not supposed to tell you anything. I'll be dead soon, so there's no use trying to get anything out of me. I'm trained for that."

"I'm not here to interrogate you. I wouldn't know how and I suck at lying."

Joseph chuckled and coughed. "Lying is clearly not one of your strengths."

"What were you trying to find in this area? I'm not aware of anything important around here."

Joseph didn't answer but instead reached into his shirt. I could hear him sniffle as he pulled out a gold cross necklace. He held it tightly in his closed fist as he whispered something to himself. I watched as a tear rolled down his cheek.

"Were you trying to find someone?"

He continued to whisper to himself.

"You're praying, right? My friend, the surgeon, is also religious. You're one of the few others I've met who is, too."

He stopped his whispering. "Do you believe in God?"

"I don't know. I went through Sunday School growing up, but it mostly put me to sleep. It's hard to think there's really a God after all that's happened."

He looked intently at me for a minute before a faint smile came to his pale face. "Thanks for being frank with me. Maybe you can help, after all."

"With what?"

"I need you to finish my task."

"I thought you just said you weren't supposed to--."

"Yeah, it goes against my orders, but I just can't let my mission die here. It's too important. I need to trust you. You need to know the story."

"Story?"

"Do you have something to take notes on? I'm going to explain everything, but I'm not going to last long. You'll probably only hear it once and it's important to get the information right."

I nodded and got up to search. All I could quickly find was a blank school composition notebook with a cartoon character plastered on the front. It looked like a square yellow piece of cheese wearing pants and a goofy grin.

"I'm ready."

Joseph took in a deep breath. He was fighting to stay focused. "Walter, I'm going to tell you a story for the ages. First, I'm not from Maine. I was actually heading there. I'm taking something very important to them."

"Them?"

"The Maine Republic."

At that point I thought he was slipping into a hallucination. I handed him a bottle of water I had with me.

"You've never heard of them?" he asked as he drank. The water seemed to sharpen his focus.

"No, not exactly. The BSA denies anything is up there, but they've also been real cagey about the subject."

"The Maine Republic is real. Not quite as far along as what you have in the BSA, but they met most of our criteria."

"Criteria?"

"Let me tell you my story and you'll understand."

He took in a deep breath and shifted to a more comfortable position. He explained to me that he was the surviving senior officer of a secret Department of Defense project called *Phoenix*. Four military facilities scheduled to be closed in the 1990s had been converted into vast secret underground warehouse vaults. They would remain mostly empty until a special order was issued. This order would only be given when a national emergency occurred which fit a specific set of criteria. The pandemic met the criteria and the *go* order was issued. It took priority over everything. All military units recalled specific equipment and supplies, consolidating them at predesignated staging areas. From there, trainloads of weapons, equipment, food, medicine, and anything else that could reconstitute a military force were stored away in these huge vaults. Major Paladin's group was part of the Phoenix command bunker. Their responsibility was to wait, listen, and evaluate in the aftermath. When the dust settled, and under a specific set of directives, it was up to them to find a starting point to rebuild the country.

During the time his team was locked away, they broke quarantine and most of the senior staff eventually succumbed to the flu. It fell on the next senior officer to make the big decision; that was Major Paladin. Unable to establish contact with any surviving U.S. leadership, he decided to start rebuilding with The Maine Republic. He was on his way to meet up with their leadership in Auburn and then to open up one of the vaults located at the old Loring Air Force base in northern Maine.

I was a little indignant that the BSA had been passed over. It seemed that we would be the logical choice since we had already made so much progress.

"Why not the BSA?" I asked.

"Because The Maine Republic is a democracy."

"That's it? The BSA wasn't chosen because we don't vote?"

"There were several other factors. Maine also has an acting general who's a former Air Force brigadier general, not some washed-out special forces reject."

"Yeah, I'll give you points for that one."

"I made radio contact with General Osgood of the Maine Militia a month ago and set out to make the journey up there. We were on the last leg of our trip when we got ambushed by your forces. It was my fault. The trip was going much faster than I anticipated. I got lax and shouldn't have come so far east before turning north. I didn't think you'd have patrols out this far west."

"How did they overwhelm you so easily?"

"Hey, we all have to stop and take a piss at some point."

"Seriously?"

He paused and a look of dejection came over him. "They were on top of us before I knew it. I was taking a leak in the woods when I caught a bullet in my leg. One of my men shot the soldier who wounded me but got shot down a second later. I stayed down and I guess they lost track of me in the skirmish. Four of my men surrendered and your general showed up a little while later. He had them beaten to get information and shot each in the head after they wouldn't talk. Your thugs stripped them, dragged them off, burned our Humvee, and took the APC. I stayed hidden and watched until they left. Is this giving you a better picture of why we didn't choose the BSA?"

I let out a deep sigh. "Yeah."

"Walter, I'm going to ask you to do something that violates all my mission guidelines. I want you to make the trip to Maine for me."

"Oh, I don't think that's a good idea at all. I'm not the right guy for something like this, and the BSA has the border all locked up. Besides, are you really sure you want to trust me with all of that? You should know that our leader is a personal friend of mine. I helped him to get where he is."

"You'd take this to Glenn Bradshaw?"

"What if I did?"

"I'm under a strict directive to fulfill my mission or die to keep the contents of the vaults from getting to the wrong people. I'm pushing that aside because I just can't let this critical opportunity die so easily. I can't stop you from taking it to the BSA, but I have faith that no matter what choice you make, it'll work out for the best."

"For the best? That's an awful lot of faith you're placing in someone you just met, and especially after my telling you that Glenn's my friend."

"Do you think he would put this to good use?"

I hesitated to answer. It surprised me that I did. "I don't know."

"I thought he was your friend."

"Ever since he took over, we've been drifting apart. We're not as close as we used to be. He's not the same person I used to know. I hate to admit it, but you might be right about keeping something like this away from him."

Paladin snorted a chuckle and smiled. "I've never believed in coincidences. Now I'm certain that you were led here to take over this task."

"Now you're sounding just like my friend, the surgeon."

"He sounds like a good man."

"He's the best man I know." I paused and breathed a heavy sigh. "Maybe it's best that all this should die with you."

"If you think it's the best course of action, then bury it or maybe sit on it for a while. Just don't wait too long because some of the benefits are time-sensitive."

"What do you mean?"

"Some of the supplies will go bad after a while. There's also access to a dormant satellite communication network. It'll open up a special priority channel to any remaining U.S. military overseas bases. It'll let them know that you're up and running and you can tell them where to come home."

"There are still military bases out there?"

"You'll have to find out. I'm not sure who's still out there because our access to the communication network failed a year after Phoenix was initiated. The system reverted to an automatic mode, which sends out a ping every day. It tells anyone listening that the system is still active and to stay tuned. It's sort of like listening to music while on hold."

"Do you really think anyone's still listening after all this time?"

"When we first initiated the Phoenix directive, we were able to make contact with several foreign U.S. bases. The directive ordered them to hold fast and defend their facilities until things stabilized here. If they didn't receive instructions after a period of five years, it would be up to their local commanders to decide what to do. We're still in that five-year window, but you'll have to get into the vault in order to find out who's still out there. There could be thousands of our military waiting for a recall order and direction. There could also be no one left."

"Okay," I reluctantly said. "What do I need to do?"

Paladin carefully detailed how the vault could be accessed and I scribbled away. The first step was to assume his identity. I would take his uniform, dog tags, and ID card. General Osgood wasn't aware of what Paladin looked like, but they had set up a simple verification process that involved a short identification phrase. All I needed to say to him was *I am Nehemiah*. I really didn't understand that obscure name, but I'd heard it somewhere before. I'm sure they kept it unique so it would be hard to duplicate.

The second step was accessing the vault. He handed me a special key to open the first door, then dictated three sets of combinations to open the main door. There was no room for error, and if I was under duress, I could enter certain combination variations which would lock everyone out for a set amount of time.

The third step was problematic. There was a special USB flash drive which contained an encrypted key to activate and operate the vault's automated inventory management system. This was not in his possession. It had been left in the Stryker vehicle. Paladin told me where it was hidden, and it seemed likely that it would still be there, at least for a little while. My crew would soon be cleaning out the inside and might find it, so I had to recover it quickly.

Paladin was fading fast. He struggled to give me a couple of last details before he started to slip in and out of delusions. Fever was consuming him and he started talking to people who weren't there. In his last lucid moments, he reassured me that he was at peace and was looking forward to being reunited with his wife and children. I've encountered many Christians since that day, but I've never seen such confidence about what was waiting after death. There was no doubt in my mind that Major Joseph Paladin was an extraordinary man. I stayed with him until he took his last labored breath.

* * *

It was a long, melancholic walk back to my SUV, carrying his bloodied uniform. I didn't even have time to bury his body. He had urged me not to worry about burial because it meant nothing to him. My task became the most important thing in his dying thoughts.

I hid the items in my SUV and started driving back. The radio hadn't called out to me during the whole time. I ran across the same patrol as I neared the highway.

"Find anything worthwhile?" the sergeant asked as I gave his radio back.

"It was a total loss."

"Told you so. What took so long?"

"Once I gave up on the Humvee, I scouted around for anything else. Didn't want to waste the trip out here."

"Find anything interesting?" he asked as he started to look into the back seat. I anticipated his curiosity and pulled out a can of powdered sports drink mix that I found in the house. It wasn't as valuable as a bottle of liquor, but on that hot day it was something that ran a close second.

"Thought you guys could use something to sweeten up your canteens," I said as I tossed the can to him.

"Sweet Jesus, thanks!"

"Thank you for the radio and watching my back," I replied as I

shifted into drive. "Be safe."
    "You too, buddy."

CHAPTER 12

That evening, I went to the garage to retrieve the USB flash drive. A few workers were still busy finishing up when I walked in. The Stryker vehicle was right where I had left it the day before. Paladin had told me the flash drive was in a special nook toward the front, right hand side of the main cabin. The rear door was still down and the blood had been cleaned out. Some items had been taken out and piled nearby, but the crew only removed things that needed to be cleaned.

I entered the main cabin, turned on a work light, and quickly located the nook. It contained an unmarked, black USB flash drive. I gave it a quick inspection; there was nothing remarkable about it. With a smile I turned off the light and exited the vehicle.

"I wouldn't get your heart set on anything," a stern voice said as I exited. I turned to see General Anderson.

"Sorry?"

"The APC. It's mine."

"Oh, yeah. I heard you claimed it. I already talked with my people, so they know it's going to you."

"Good, because I can't see how your buddy from the projects would need something like this for law enforcement." Anderson had never liked Smitty and wasn't shy about taking sly jabs at him. Smitty usually did the same, but I always tried my best to stay neutral. They despised each other and fought like dogs over bones if they desired the same equipment. Fortunately for me, this particular bone was too big for Smitty.

"I agree. Something like this is way out of his league."

"Good," he replied with a smug grin and looked to my hand. "Did you find something in there?"

I held up the flash drive while summoning all my strength to keep it from shaking. "This? No, it's mine. It dropped out of my pocket when I was looking around."

"Looking for what?"

"Oh, nothing specifically. Just curious. I've never seen anything like this before."

"Impressive, isn't it?" he asked as he looked at it with a proud expression.

"I'd like to find more."

"And I'd like you to find more, too, but they're rare around these parts. I need you to make sure it's prioritized for refurbishing. I'll have a list of things that I'd like done to the inside. I should have it to you sometime tomorrow. I just need to take a couple of more measurements."

"Well, I'll leave you to that," I said with the most relaxed smile I could fake.

"Oh, I'll also need a list of anything that's been taken out of this. Consider its contents sensitive and off limits."

"I'll make sure the supervisor understands."

* * *

I went over to Chung-Hee's home the next evening for dinner. He had recently moved into a nice apartment a couple of blocks over from mine. It was a corner unit above a former retail store on Cambridge street and located much closer to his work at Boston General. I had always encouraged him to seek out something better than the dank two-bedroom flat he was shoved into at The Pit. I thought he had stayed there far too long, but he never seemed to mind. I once had a nice house lined up for him in Cambridge when he started working at The Supermarket, but he had politely turned it down. To him, people were more important than places. Although I would've gladly found him any luxury home he wanted, I think the main reason he took that new apartment was because it allowed him to spend more time at work. I was just happy he had finally found the type of home that he deserved.

Unable to get my mind off the previous day's events, I hadn't slept well. Apparently it showed and Soon-Yi greeted me with a much needed hug.

"Hi, Uncle Walt. Are you sad about something?"

"I had a tough day today."

She immediately gave me an extra hug and I had a hard time staying composed in her arms. Something about that little girl's embrace could boil the harshness out of any day. Chung-Hee quickly picked up on my melancholic demeanor and ushered Soon-Yi out to start her homework.

I told him everything that had happened. It was a relief to finally tell someone. I had kept more bottled up in me than I realized because I was trembling by the end.

"That was an amazing day. Would you like a drink?"

"No thanks. The last thing I need right now is to start a bad habit."

"Wise."

"So are you going to say it?"

"Say what?"

"That you told me so. You were right about Maine."

"I'm only happy that you found the truth."

"You know, every time I deserve a good dope-slap, you're always too kind to me."

"A good doctor treats the cause, not the symptoms. When do you plan to leave?"

"I'm still not sure what I'm going to do. I need some time to think about it."

"Understandable. This is an enormous decision."

"What would you do?"

Chung-Hee smiled and put his hand on my shoulder. "Walter, something like this will certainly change many lives. It's going to have a profound effect on our region, but I also think those changes could have global ramifications. Whatever comes of it, I think it's obvious that you were chosen to continue and finish Major Paladin's work."

I let out a sigh. "What is it about religious people and being chosen? You'd think God would have a better handle on that because I feel like I'm the least qualified person to be doing this."

"Didn't you wonder the same thing when you took over The Supermarket?"

I chuckled. "That wasn't exactly a decision with global ramifications."

Chung-Hee didn't reply, but only offered an expression that he gave me on occasion. It was one of those *you're so much better than that* looks he liked to gently scold me with.

"I was sort of hoping you'd have something more discouraging to say. You know, anything to help me to feel better about taking a pass on this."

"You should know me better than that. What about Major Paladin's uniform?"

"It's bloodstained and I'm soaking it now. I wish I could take it to a professional cleaner."

"I might know someone who can help. I'll check and let you know."

"Great. You just keep making this task sound more plausible by the minute."

* * *

Over the next couple of weeks, I tried to return to a normal work schedule while I thought over my dilemma. There were plenty of things to do which distracted me for short periods of time, but my thoughts would quickly return to that unremarkable black flash drive I had hidden away. The implications of whatever I would decide were overwhelming. The more I pondered, the more I resented being the person who ended up with the responsibility to carry the burden. I was torn over what to do. The fact that I hesitated to bring it to Glenn only reinforced my notion that he shouldn't get his hands on it. I struggled with that notion because my Supermarket operation supported a lot of good people who could potentially prosper from the contents of the vault.

Taking it to the Maine Republic had its own daunting set of issues. I had no idea who these people were or if they deserved to have this find. However, Major Paladin and his team had spent years evaluating the situation in the outside world. He probably had a whole room full of brilliant people working on it. Who was I to wantonly disregard all of their analysis?

The more I thought it over, the more I grew comfortable with the idea that no one should get access to the vault. That way, no one could abuse the abundance of what was locked inside. It was an easier and safer choice to make. I was already quite comfortable with my life and I didn't have any desire to upset the status quo. After all, the BSA probably didn't really need this stuff because we seemed to be doing just fine on our own.

I had everything I needed to open the Loring vault except any resolve to do so. I locked away the uniform, key, composition book, and the flash drive so I could forget about them for a while. While I felt good about my choice that no one should be given access, I still wasn't one-hundred percent sure. I needed more time to let it simmer in the back of my mind.

* * *

A few days after putting everything off to think, I was surprised to receive a message from a long forgotten acquaintance: Alyssa in Cambridge. She left me a request to re-establish contact with Kathryn Donahue. It wasn't urgent, but important enough to break the long-standing code of silence. I had not seen or heard from Kathryn since I left her at her new Cambridge home over three years ago.

That evening I visited one of our annexes which handled clothing reclamation. Almost everyone had gone home for the day, so it was a perfect spot to arrange a meeting with Kathryn. If I was being watched, a visit to this annex wouldn't raise any suspicions. The location also had a number of ways to enter that wouldn't draw any undue attention. Kathryn's instructions were to arrive before me and wait in the manager's office posing as a job seeker.

I walked in and made my way past piles of clothing that were being sorted. Only a couple of late workers remained on the job. The office was upstairs and I could see the lights as I climbed the staircase.

I opened the office door and found Kathryn patiently waiting. For a couple of seconds, I wondered if it was really her. She stood up with her now short brown hair and slender frame to greet me. Her freckles had faded a bit and she wore less makeup. In all, she was now a grown woman with a warm and confident smile.

"Is that really you?" I asked as she greeted me with a hug.

"It's me."

"It's great to finally see you again. I wasn't sure if this day would ever come."

"Me either."

"I hardly recognized you. Good to see that you took me seriously about changing your appearance."

"I've had a lot of practice since you left me at my new house."

"You look good."

"Thanks. So do you. You've lost some weight."

"Too busy to eat, I suppose," I replied as I gestured for her to sit. "How have you been?"

"Doing well. I've been living a quiet life. I love the house. It's a real gem. Wonderful neighborhood. I've been working at a greenhouse that grows all sorts of things."

"I'm really happy to hear it all worked out."

"It was hard at first, but Alyssa helped me. I've been able to build a nice life, thanks to you. I hear stories about you from time to time."

"Really? Because I try awfully hard to stay out of stories."

"That would explain why it was only time to time."

"So you're Molly Donnelly these days?"

"Yeah, I just had to keep something Irish about my name."

"Good for you, Molly. Now down to business. Is there anything wrong?"

"I'm not sure. I overheard a coworker say that a deputy was asking around the library for someone who looked like I used to. My old name wasn't used, but it's the first time I've ever come across something like this. I'm sorry if I'm being an alarmist, but I just wanted to resurface to see if something was going on."

"You did the right thing. I haven't heard of anything, and no offense, I had sort of put you out of my mind. But I know the chief marshal. You remember Smitty?"

"Oh, yes."

"We see each other at least once a week. I'll try to make a discreet inquiry. Other than hearing about your description, have you noticed anything else unusual?"

"No, and I've been paying more attention lately."

"Anyone new in your life?

"No, I keep to the same small group of friends."

"Have you told any of them something a little more personal about your past recently?"

"No, but I'd trust them anyway."

"Sorry to get personal, but has there been any pillow-talk with a boyfriend lately?"

She smiled and looked down. "I've been careful to stay unattached."

"Oh?"

Her expression faded. "Yeah, celibacy. It's the downside to keeping a low profile. I had to turn away a few guys. A couple were nice, but most were total creeps. It got to the point where people started thinking I was a lesbian. I didn't say much about it until women started hitting on me."

"Oh, awkward much?"

She laughed. "Oh, yes. Nothing like being surprised by a coworker copping a feel."

"Ouch. How did--""

"Not something I like talking about. Only happened once, but it left a bad memory."

"Fair enough. Have you been anywhere new recently?"

"Not really. I did stop by Waltham last fall. It took me a while to find it, but I walked by the place you found me in. There are a lot of farms around there these days. The whole area is pretty wide open."

"I know. I went there last summer to look over the new farm initiatives. Your uncle was right; the gangs nearly burned it all to the ground that year. I tried to find my old apartment but it had been torn down. Nothing but a field of corn growing there now."

"Times have changed."

"For the better," I said, probably to convince myself of it.

"For the better," she politely echoed.

"Well, it doesn't sound like we need to do much right away. Just ask Alyssa to help keep an eye out for any strangers in the neighborhood. I'll get word to you if I hear anything from Smitty. You might want to come up with a quick exit plan, just in case."

"I've had one in place since you dropped me there."

"Good. Well, I've got to get going now. I'll leave here first. Hang around for another twenty minutes or so before leaving. It's just to make sure you're not seen by anyone who might be following me around."

"People are following you around?"

"There's always that possibility. If they're good at what they do, I probably wouldn't be able to notice them."

"Who would do that?"

I hesitated. "Well, since I'm in charge of The Supermarket, it could be people who want to make sure I'm not doing something I shouldn't. Not that I'm doing anything wrong. I've always run a clean operation."

"So you're saying Glenn is watching you?"

"Well, yeah, I suppose."

"I thought you were good friends with him. Is anything wrong?"

"Oh, everything's fine. Nothing really to worry about. Just the new realities of the day."

"Well, please be careful."

"Thanks. It was really nice to see you. We should try to arrange to do something, you know, to give us more time to talk and catch up. Somewhere safe and a little, uh, nicer."

Kathryn laughed. "I hope we can, someday."

I left her sitting in the office. My spirits were lifted. For the first time in days, I had been taken completely out of the dilemma that consumed my world.

That feeling wouldn't last long.

As I walked past piles of clothes on my way to the exit, somebody sorting through one of them stopped me in my tracks. It was his weathered Red Sox cap and lanky frame that caught my attention. I watched him for a few seconds before he noticed I was there. He looked up at me and his expression shifted. Mr. Ordinary stood before me, stupefied.

"I've seen you before, haven't I?" I asked.

He looked around, probably to see if anyone else was there. As far as I could tell, he was the only person left working.

"It was three years back, around Christmas. You were following me."

He stood and said nothing, but the worried look in his eyes was all I needed to see.

"I'm not going to do anything to you. I'm sure you were just following orders. I'd just like to know one thing. What was Tony looking for?"

His expression changed. He looked confused.

"Don't worry, it's all in the past. It's just something I've always been curious about."

He sighed and looked down to his shoes. "I shouldn't say anything about it."

"Why? It's ancient history."

He looked up and I saw fear in his eyes. "It could get me into trouble."

"How? Tony's long gone."

He smirked and shrugged his shoulders. "Hey, look. I don't want any trouble."

"The way I see it, as your boss I could cause you a lot of trouble. If you still want a job after this shift is over, you'll answer my questions. Does that help make it easier?"

He sighed. "I wasn't supposed to watch you. I was only supposed to get you to notice me watching you."

"Okay, so why would that get you into trouble today?"

"Because Tony didn't hire me."

"Who did?"

"Glenn Bradshaw. Now do you understand better?"

I felt a jolt like an electrical shock. "Okay, fine. We didn't have this conversation. We never saw each other."

He nodded and went back to work. I rushed out to my car. After driving only a couple of blocks, I had to pull over. My thoughts ran rampant and I could feel my heart beating too fast. A distressing realization started to come into a sharper focus. Anger surfaced as I reluctantly came to an acceptance that I had been played. Any doubt about why Glenn had his gun conveniently with him on the day he shot Pat were laid to rest. My mind couldn't let go of the vivid memory of Pat's gun pointing at my face. Frustration boiled over and I wanted to get back at Glenn. I thought about the Loring vault and knew it would be a fitting payback for all he had done to me. But my intensity cooled as my mind tried to ponder on the logistics of making such a trek north. It was a daunting task, and while my motivation to undertake it was at an all-time high, I still needed one last push. Revenge alone wasn't quite enough to dislodge me from my comfortable life.

CHAPTER 13

"You look like shit," Smitty said to me the next morning in my office. "Have a wicked ripper last night?"

"No, I just didn't sleep well."

"I'd make a Dunkies run if they were still around."

"Oh," I groaned. "I'd give almost anything just to smell a doughnut shop again."

"Aren't your guys trying to grow coffee beans?"

"*Trying* is a good word to use right now. Are you here to annoy me, or to get a line on your weekly list of goodies?"

"Are you up for it?" Smitty asked with a chuckle.

"Yeah, just bear with me." I rummaged through some folders for the list I had made for him the day before.

"I heard we're growing some tea that gives you a wicked kick like coffee."

"I'm sure you hear a lot of things."

"Got that right. And you won't believe what I was asked to look into the other day."

"What's that?" I asked, still rummaging.

"Glenn actually wants me to canvass for Pat Donahue's niece, Kathryn."

I accidentally dropped the files. "Seriously? I thought you said she got capped after Pat was killed."

"Yeah, but Glenn seems to have his own ideas about it."

"What makes him think she's alive?"

"I have no goddamn idea. If she is, I'm sure she's probably turning tricks somewhere down in Provi (Providence), or maybe making babies with the preppers up in Cow Hampshire."

"It's been, what, a little over three years? What's so important about her now?"

"Oh, don't get me started. Somebody in his circle probably needs appeasing. I honestly couldn't give a shit what happened to that spoiled little bitch. Looking around for her is just a waste of time. I'm putting a couple of my dip-shit deputies on it because I can't afford to put any real talent into it right now. They'll putter around with it for a while and I'll probably get to report that I haven't found a trace of her. Hopefully, it'll be enough to satisfy everyone. Find that list yet?"

I picked up the folders I had dropped and found the list. We spent the rest of the meeting going over the latest treasures he might be interested in, but I found it difficult to concentrate. I had received the one last push that I needed.

* * *

"I'm going to Maine and I'm taking Kathryn with me," I abruptly declared to Chung-Hee over dinner the next evening. We had avoided discussing the subject for the first half of our meal. He didn't bring it up, probably to avoid putting pressure on me. However, I was already on the cusp of settling the issue in my mind. It all came together while he was explaining how Soon-Yi was staying over at a new friend's home that night. It was almost comical because he was in mid-sentence when I blurted out my declaration.

Chung-Hee leaned back in his chair with a surprised look on his face. I'd say it was more a happy kind of surprised than a confused one. "Wow. What made up your mind?"

I hesitated. "I know what it should be."

"And what's that?"

"Because I can't continue to live out a comfortable life while hiding something away that could change everything."

"But it's not?"

"Sorry, but my real motivation isn't nearly as noble. It has more to do with something I recently discovered about Glenn. I don't want to get into it, but it proved to me that you were right all along. He was never the person I thought I knew. I can't let him get his hands on that vault."

"I'm sorry about that. The truth can be quite difficult to face."

"I don't know for sure what's waiting for me in Maine, but at this point I'd rather put my trust in Major Paladin's judgment."

"And Kathryn?"

"Smitty told me yesterday that Glenn wants to find her. I'm not sure what Glenn wants with her or why anyone thinks she's still alive after all this time. There's just no way I can leave her behind on her own."

"I thought you had her hidden away safely."

"Not safe enough. Smitty's not taking Glenn's request too seriously right now, but that could easily change. Kathryn's in danger and can't stay."

"Are you certain she'll want to go with you?"

"I can't see why not. I'm going to talk to her about it in a couple of days, but the way I see it, taking her with me will finally solve her fugitive dilemma. She can start a new life without having to look over her shoulder."

"Are you going to tell her why you're really going?"

"I think it's best she doesn't know anything about the vault. What do you think?"

"I agree. Telling her everything would only put both of you in more danger. It's very important that the secret of your true mission is maintained. You'll have enough trouble just planning your escape. Because you're a high-level manager in the BSA, your disappearance will represent a major security breach. Just as soon as Glenn discovers that you're missing, he'll search for you with all his resources."

"I'm expecting that."

"The people I know would be willing to help you."

"Thanks, but no thanks. No offense, but they're batting zero. Not something that inspires any confidence."

"Success going north continues to elude them, but I'm certain they could help in some way. Perhaps just sharing their experiences with you could help plan your route?"

"I doubt it. My escape plan has to anticipate a number of factors they wouldn't normally deal with. Like you said, once I'm gone, Glenn's going to go nuclear and turn everything upside-down looking for me. I'm going to have to contend with resources that normally wouldn't be used to find people. Just thinking about it makes my head spin. I also don't want to involve more people than necessary. The less who know what I'm doing, the better."

"I know," Chung-Hee replied with a frown.

That's when it hit me. I was never very fast at putting things together, as Smitty always teased me. "Oh, no. I'm so sorry, I just didn't realize it until now. You know too much. You're going to have to come with me."

Chung-Hee smiled. "And how would a fifty-four-year-old man and an eight-year-old girl factor into your chances of success?"

"I can't leave you guys behind. You're one of the first people they'll interrogate."

"You're correct. I can't hope to resist the violent interrogation methods they'd use on me, so they'll eventually learn what I know. That can't happen because it'll profoundly change the situation. Glenn will be aware of the vault and is sure to lash out against the Maine Republic to prevent them from accessing it. It's certain to start a war that could destroy both sides."

"Which means you'll need to come with me."

"Not necessarily. You're correct that I can't stay, but instead of going with you, I'll take Soon-Yi south to Providence. It'll be easier and safer for us that way. The underground railroad has successfully helped many people get there. I know of a church in that area which could help us to get resettled. The reverend is an old friend of mine. He even shares your first name."

"I feel terrible that you'll be displaced. All the work that you've done at the hospital, your new home, all the--"

"Material things matter little to me and I'm confident I'll be useful wherever I end up. Your task is far more important. You must reach Maine without anyone in the BSA knowing where you went and what you really have with you. That way, the Maine Republic can access the vault and have time to empty its contents without any interference."

"How long will it take for you to set up your escape?"

"I'll make sure we're ready to go at the same time you do. It's important that our departures coincide. Otherwise, either of our disappearances will draw undue attention to the one who remains. It's equally important that we don't know the details of the other's escape plan."

"I agree. Once I'm done up in Maine, I'll find you as soon as it becomes possible."

"We'll look forward to it."

* * *

It took a few days to set up a meeting with Kathryn, especially since I wanted to have it in a nicer place while being discreet. I timed it to coincide with a recovery site visit I had at the old Hanscom Airfield in Bedford. We met in the next town over, Lexington, just off the old Battle Green. Not too many people had resettled there yet, so it made it easy to keep an eye out for anyone who could have been following me.

I found her sitting on the steps of an old church just across the street from what was left of the Minuteman statue. It had been pulled down years before and lay in several pieces in the overgrown weeds. Looking back, I think that was a perfect symbol of what remained of our old civilization. It's what moved me to lead the effort to restore the Battle Green many years later. That neglected patch of tall weeds would finally be reclaimed as a historic site. But I'm getting ahead of myself.

It took some effort for Kathryn to free up some time and bike out to Lexington, but seeing her there in such a relaxed scene made it worth the trouble. It was a beautiful, early summer day on a peaceful stoop in front of that old stone church. Despite nobody being around, overgrown bushes kept us out of view.

We sat and talked about what we'd both been up to over the years, all the little things we hadn't had time to discuss at our first meeting. She enjoyed my story about the late-night search of the police station just up the road. It was especially funny to her because she had biked up that same trail.

Overall, she seemed content with her life as it was, making sharing my news of Glenn's investigation even more difficult. She was stoic as I told her what I learned from Smitty.

"The decision's yours," I finished. "I don't know how Glenn got the notion that you're still alive, or why it even matters at this point, but I think the safest thing for you to do is leave the BSA."

She frowned and looked out over the tall weeds. "Well, I always figured this could happen. Where would I go?"

"North, to The Maine Republic."

"Maine? Really? So, there's really something up there?"

"Yes, and I've learned there's a lot of good people living there. It may not be as comfortable as it is around here, but it'll be a place you won't have to be looking over your shoulder all the time. You can settle there and stay. No need to keep an exit plan handy."

"How do I get there?"

"I'll take you."

"Wait, does that mean you're planning to leave, too?"

"Yes."

"Why? I thought that--"

"Things aren't as good as I want to think they are."

There was a pause. She gazed at me, perplexed. "What's happened?"

"Long story. I guess I woke up and began seeing all the things that Glenn's really been doing. I realized how caught up I was in my own world, and how I refused to look around at what was actually going on. As if not seeing the truth would allow me to stay in my comfort zone. I suppose I didn't learn much from the pandemic."

"What's been going on?"

"Nothing that's going to lead us to anything good. I think it best that I don't get into any details. You'll have to trust me. We need to get out while there's still time."

"Okay, but won't they notice right away that you've disappeared?"

"It's going to make it interesting, but I have access to resources that will help us to make a clean escape. Right now it's nearly impossible to go north. Our defense force has cut off access to keep anyone from leaving. They're killing anyone who tries."

"Killing?" Kathryn recoiled. "Now this is sounding insanely dangerous."

"Don't worry, I'm not going to let that happen to us. I'll find a way past it all."

"How?"

"I'm still working on the details, but I know we'll be hiking our way up there."

"Why can't we just drive?"

"I've already considered driving, boating, and flying up there. None of them will work."

"How about just taking bicycles?"

"I also thought about that, including motorcycles, dirt bikes, ATVs, and even motor scooters. The roads aren't in great shape, so we need to travel through rough terrain, if required, and do it quietly. Going on foot gives us the flexibility we need."

"I don't get it. Wouldn't it be better if we got up there fast, you know, before anyone notices we're gone?"

"It's more complicated than that."

"Explain complicated, please."

"Look, once someone notices that I'm gone, Glenn is going to have a conniption. He'll hit the panic button and get everyone out looking for me. So when we depart, we can't leave any trace of where we might be heading. This especially rules out a dash up to Maine before the BSA catches us. Besides, I don't think we'd be very welcome there if I came charging in as Walter Johnson, former BSA Supermarket boss, wanted by the BSA, and with half our military giving chase."

"So you need to walk away and disappear."

"Sound familiar?"

Kathryn laughed. "Yeah, sorry, I should have known better. When do you think we should leave?"

"You're okay with doing this?"

"I've always had to be okay with leaving on a moment's notice. It's been part of my life since my uncle died. I have to admit, though, the thought of settling somewhere I don't have to be so careful sounds awfully appealing."

"Good. I'm thinking we'll depart sometime in August. It'll give me time to carefully plan this out."

"Am I going to be safe until then?"

"You should be fine. Smitty isn't taking Glenn very seriously, so you should be safe as long as you stick to your routines. It's very important that you don't do anything that draws unusual attention to yourself. Just keep doing what you've always done. You're obviously very good at it."

Kathryn smiled.

"After today, we can't see each other until we leave. Until then, I'll pass you messages through Alyssa."

"What should I be doing to prepare?"

"Absolutely nothing. Remember, you can't risk being seen doing anything out of the ordinary. I'll take care of the details. When the time comes, I'll set it up so you just simply walk away."

"It won't take long for people to notice I'm gone."

"I'll still be missed much sooner than you. I can hopefully plan it well enough to squeeze out a few hours before the alarm is sounded."

"Only a few hours?"

"It should give us enough of a head start."

Kathryn sighed and looked down. Her concern was impossible to miss.

"Look, I know the BSA has a lot of soldiers and equipment. If we do this right, they won't know where to start looking, and they'll have way too much territory to cover. I like our chances."

"There's got to be something I can do to help besides acting like I'm doing nothing."

"There is one thing. I'll need all your sizes. I've got to get you the right clothes, shoes, et cetera."

"That's it?"

"Yeah, that's it. You're already doing enough just staying under the radar."

Kathryn offered me a warm smile, leaned in, and gave me a quick kiss on my cheek. "Thank you. Again you're risking so much to keep me safe."

"You deserve it. Please remember one important thing about this: absolutely no one can know about our escape. Not your close friends, neighbors, or even Alyssa."

"Even Alyssa?"

"Especially her. She needs to be as surprised as anyone else. She'll understand it's all to keep everyone safe."

We soon parted ways. She rode her bike back to the Minuteman Bikeway and I decided to take a stroll up Massachusetts Avenue to the old police station. I wanted to take one last look at it before I left. On the way, I couldn't stop thinking about Kathryn. Our clandestine escape planning caused me to regard her far differently than before. It was no longer possible to see her as that young, spoiled dra-ma-queen whose rape I prevented a few years ago. She had matured and now possessed a depth of beauty that invoked new thoughts. I wondered if Pat would've recognized her.

I arrived at the old police station. It looked much different in the daylight and had been restored as a BSA Marshal outpost. I looked

across the road to the church that Glenn and I had shot at on that cold
Christmas Eve. Through the tall weeds, I caught sight of a makeshift
cross stuck in the ground. It had to be a grave, probably a few years
old. It took me a minute to realize that it was positioned near the spot
where I had shot the fleeing gunman on that night. There was no
name on it and the white paint had faded away. I stood there and
wondered if that would be my fate while going to Maine - gunned
down and forgotten in a lonely patch of weeds.

* * *

Throughout July, I dedicated every spare moment of time planning our escape. I even went back over possibilities which I had
earlier rejected. Flying was completely out of the question. The BSA
Air Corps had a few operating aircraft. Most of them were single
engine Cessnas for survey work. There were also a couple of helicopters that the defense force utilized. In all, flying wasn't nearly as
common as it was before, and I didn't know the pilots well enough.
Even if one agreed to fly us up there, or anywhere else nearby, it
would mean that someone else knew too much about our plans. That
kind of trust was out of the question.

Boating was the next logical choice. I had my pick of countless
yachts or large boats to use. Many had been shrink-wrapped and
stored for winter before the pandemic started. However, despite a
resurgence of fishing vessels that went to sea every day, they were
carefully watched by several restored police and coast guard boats
that patrolled the harbor. There was also an intimidating 110-foot
island-class cutter that was able to escort the larger fishing boats into
deeper waters. There might have been a chance to slip by, but I just
didn't know enough about boating and I couldn't afford to show a
sudden interest; too many would notice.

Driving seemed to be the obvious choice, but it was still the most
dangerous. All major roads leading north were closely watched.
While I might have had a chance to find a back road through the
embargo, an observation airplane or any number of patrols would
almost certainly spot us. There just weren't enough cleared back
roads with adequate tree coverage all the way up to Maine.

My plan remained to make the journey on foot. It would be
easier to stay out of sight and the additional time it would take to

make the journey would help throw off any pursuit. Search parties would be left guessing which direction we took, and that would allow us to enter Maine without a posse on our heels. Regardless, there were still a number of details that needed to be fleshed out.

My intention was to pick Kathryn up on my way out to a recovery site inspection I'd fake somewhere south. We would instead head west toward Lunenberg, where we would hide the vehicle and set out on foot. There were a number of back roads through uninhabited areas which would allow us to easily pass unseen into southwestern New Hampshire. From there we'd continue north through the lakes region, turn east past the White Mountains, and then into Maine. It was taking a long way around, but I was confident it was a route that would allow us to slip under the BSA radar. It also allowed us to journey through mostly uninhabited regions, avoiding entanglements with any locals. My goal was to travel completely unnoticed by anyone.

Part of my Supermarket duties involved supporting intelligence operations that took place outside of our territory. Before scouting missions took place, extensive aerial observations were conducted to gauge the climate and determine concentrations of local inhabitants. I had access to numerous observation reports of New Hampshire, which helped me to determine our best route. Everything I studied showed that the areas I intended to travel through were sparsely populated. Most areas north of Manchester, New Hampshire were sketchy, but all indications pointed to few or no inhabitants in areas that had had small populations before the pandemic.

I wanted to travel as lightly as possible. August weather in the area was still on the warm side, so clothing could be light. A good deal of weight in our backpacks would come from food and water. Depending on what we encountered, I estimated that our trip would take no longer than two weeks. Carrying enough supplies for a two-week period was simply too burdensome. However, thanks to a decisive advantage I could exploit, we'd only have to carry enough food and water to last two to three days at a time.

What was that advantage? Before the BSA sent scouts into remote areas, special aerial supply containers were parachuted into predesignated coordinates. This is what my Supermarket operation managed. We stocked the containers, determined where they should be dropped, and kept track of the disposition of each one. Airplanes made low-level drops to avoid being seen, and the containers had a special homing signal device installed. Once a scout neared the supply drop coordinate, a special tracking device sent out a signal to trigger the homing device, leading the scout right to it. There were very few instances where a supply container was swiped before the scout could find it, but several containers were always dropped to offset that possibility.

My plan was to coordinate sporadic supply drops throughout areas along the planned route. This was a crucial part of our escape plan, as it would pre-position the rest of our needed supplies so we wouldn't have to carry them with us. Once I came up with the drop sites, I'd relay them to the BSA Air Corps. They just did what they were told, so I could request a set of drops and make any record of them disappear. It would be as though they had never occurred. Pre-supply drops were frequently made, and pilots wouldn't remember them all.

* * *

I set the departure date for August 17th. It was a day I could schedule a visit to a recovery site, but in reality I would never arrive there, and I would make my other key personnel think I was else-where. We would have a few precious hours before my absence would be noticed, and maybe a couple more out of the confusion that would follow. I sent word to Kathryn to schedule a vacation day. She would tell her coworkers that she was taking time off to get projects done around her house. Chung-Hee was notified so that he could start his escape to the south on the night before we left. This would assure that he and his daughter would be in Providence by the time Katheryn and I started out.

The supply drops were already underway for scouting missions that would never take place. I started to assemble the supplies we'd walk out with and made sure they could be easily hidden in my BSA SUV. I kept to a normal schedule to head off any suspicion of what I was planning. Everyone seemed completely unaware of what I was doing.

CHAPTER 14

A couple of weeks before my departure date, I received an invitation to dinner with Glenn. I suppose it was overdue, but I had hoped he'd be far too busy to schedule anything until after I was gone. I couldn't risk postponing because I'd never put off a dinner with him before. In order to avoid suspicion, I had no choice but to attend.

I dreaded going because the damage potential made my head spin. Memories resurfaced of the dinner I had had with Pat in order to set Tony up. Only Glenn could read me better than Pat ever could. There was no doubt that this dinner would require a serious upgrade in my acting skills.

My mood lightened as I entered his home because a few self-important BSA managers had invited themselves over. They would typically use the opportunity to lobby Glenn for whatever they needed at the time, and it was a bonus to have me there to help arrange what Glenn granted them. At any other dinner I would've loathed having them around. That night I was more than happy to share in their company.

The evening was going so well that I abandoned a plan to come up with an excuse to leave early. However, I probably should have quit while I was ahead. After dinner, Glenn served up the cheap hard liquor and those bozos weren't shy about putting it down. I always stayed away from it and noticed that Glenn was nursing his drink. He clearly wanted some time with me and knew how to end things early with the smooth-talking big-wigs. Predictably, they quickly faded and said their goodbyes by ten o'clock. I didn't have much choice but to sit and watch them leave. They were so blitzed that they hardly made it to their chauffeured cars without help from their drivers.

"Lightweight leeches," Glenn joked as he shut the door behind the last to exit.

"So I'm guessing they won't remember all the crap they pried out of us," I joked. Actually, it was probably not far from the truth.

"Especially the duck-boat," Glenn replied with a chuckle. He sat down in his recliner. "So my friend, we finally get some time. How's things with you?"

"Pretty busy."

"I hear you've been getting out more lately."

"You hear correctly. The weather warmed up and I wanted to see more of our territory. It also helps if the boss shows up on site once in a while."

Glenn laughed. "You're learning."

"I try."

"Hey, are you aware that I'm looking for Pat's niece? You know, the brat you saved back in Waltham?"

And so it began. Glenn hadn't wasted much time cutting to the real subject, which meant he was anxious about something.

"Smitty mentioned something about that a while back. What's up?"

"Oh, I just heard something recently that she might still be around."

"Seriously? I thought she got capped."

"So did I, but nobody ever confirmed it."

I leaned back in my chair, trying to appear relaxed. "Why do you want to find her now?"

"I'm just trying to reach out. If that poor girl has been hiding out since Pat died, I owe her for what I did."

"Sounds reasonable to me. Any leads?"

"Nope, and I'm about to turn up the heat on Smitty. I get the feeling I'm being stonewalled."

"By Smitty?"

"Yeah, even Smitty can act up once in a while. But that's my problem." Glenn paused and leaned forward. "What I really wanted to talk to you about is holding elections. Now before you faint on me, I'm thinking it's time to try out your idea, starting small."

"I thought you already had enough of elected boards."

"You caught me on a bad day. I've had a change of heart since then."

"What did you have in mind?"

"I want to start somewhere new, maybe over in Chelsea."

"What about Brookline?"

Glenn grimaced. "Brookline?"

"It might go smoother there."

"I'm thinking it needs to be a little more north."

"North? Why? Something up with the Italians?"

"Just trying to mend some fences. I need to prioritize some building materials up that way, too. They want framing lumber and plywood."

"We don't have much left, and it's already committed to Roxbury."

"I don't give a fuck about *Glocksbury*," Glenn seethed, using an old derogatory nickname for the town. "I want it redirected to Chelsea."

"Okay, whatever you want."

"Just get it done. Are you being honest with me about Pat's niece?"

The abrupt shift in subject was jarring, and unlike the Glenn I knew. "What do you mean?"

"Simple question."

"Glenn, if I knew anything, don't you think I'd would've said something to you by now?"

He sat and looked at me with a suspicious gaze. I desperately tried to hold my composure.

"Never mind," he finally said.

"Are you okay?"

"Yeah," he replied as he rubbed his eyes. "I'm just, er, tired. Long day. I should cut you loose so I can get some sleep."

* * *

"Of course I'm fucking stonewalling him," Smitty exclaimed to me in my office the next morning. "He's looking for her because one of the old Greastie bosses is convinced she's still around. This sick bastard wants to carry out some psycho revenge shit for something Pat supposedly did to him. It's all because Glenn's on the skids with the Italians. We've been burning up a lot of their gas and they don't feel they're getting enough in return for it. There's not much left and they're pressing Glenn for all sorts of ridiculous things."

"I guess that puts you in a bad position."

"No shit, Sherlock. You figure that out all by yourself?"

"What are you going to do?"

"What do you think? I've got to step it up and find this girl. I'll get my best guys on it soon."

"How do you even start to look for her?"

"If she's still in the area, I'm thinkin' I'll start looking south. Probably Deathchester (Dorchester) or Murderpan (Mattapan). Pat did a lot of damage down there and she probably thinks it's a good hiding place. Then there's always the Irish Riviera a little further south."

"That's a lot of territory."

"It's times like this when I think Glenn's losing his touch."

"Really? He also talked about holding elections and redirecting building supplies."

"Where?"

"Chelsea."

Smitty blurted out a laugh. "Chelsea? Now that's more the Glenn I know. Trying to work around the old bosses by winning over the people in their neighborhood. He did it before over in Kenmore. Got them all juiced up on democracy to shut out the old order, then let 'em all fall apart fighting with each other. After they're all at each others throats, he'll go right back in and save them from themselves. He knows how to work the system."

* * *

"I'm not sure how much time she's got left," I explained to Chung-Hee the next evening. It was our last dinner together before our departures. "Do you think we should try to move up the timetable?"

"That's going to be difficult for my people. They aren't that flexible. It's going to be a challenge just to get us to Providence by morning."

"Yeah, you're right. I suppose I'm even less flexible. There's too many things in motion that would have to be changed. Let's keep the original schedule."

"I agree. Perhaps you can have her temporarily relocated?"

"I'd like to, but doing that could draw too much attention. I suppose we'll just have to hope that Smitty's people will be tied up looking around down south long enough so we can get away."

Chung-Hee rose from his seat and sat beside me on the couch. He did something that he'd never done before and I'll never forget. He grabbed my hand and prayed. It was awkward, but I understood that he was just doing something he thought would help. I figured we could use all the help we could get.

* * *

"We're getting close," Smitty reported in my office during his weekly visit. I already reviewed the latest finds with him, and he surprised me with an abrupt update on his hunt for Kathryn. "We flushed out a strong suspect in Cambridge."

My heart sunk and I desperately tried not to react. "What do you mean?"

"A person of interest fled before we got to her house. The neighbors are a little too tight lipped about her, so we're thinking she's the one. Or she's at least someone with something to hide. We're all on the lookout for Molly Donnelly."

It was less than forty-eight hours before we started our escape, and now Kathryn was in the wind. Smitty left and I sat with the most god-awful helpless feeling. I had no idea of how to help her. The original plan was to pick her up at the old Alewife T-station on my way out to the recovery site that I was scheduled for. I wondered if it would be best to bypass the rendezvous point and just carry out my escape alone. I quickly dismissed that notion. It would be extremely risky to show up there with so many people looking for her, but I just couldn't leave without trying.

* * *

I stuck to the original plan, hoping that Kathryn would do the same if she could. She always had a quick exit plan in place, so I trusted that she'd be able to stay out of sight for a couple of days. I also assumed that Smitty would be the first in line to tell me if she was caught, and there had been no such report.

I loaded the items we'd be starting out with in my SUV the night before. The thought that I was leaving for good had finally sunk in. I had been too busy obsessing over escape details and the fate of Kathryn to dwell on the reality that I was leaving everything. I slowly walked through my Beacon Hill brownstone that evening and many memories surfaced. It was going to be harder to leave than I had thought. I spent my last night in my warm, comfortable bed, but I hardly slept. My thoughts swirled around what I was doing. A few times I wanted to cancel the whole thing. Each time I came back to the same sobering reality that too much was already in place, and it would be impossible to explain away everything I had arranged for my escape. I had no choice. I was totally committed. I had to go. It was simply too late to change my mind.

The next morning, I departed for work at my usual time. Everything had to look like it was just another workday. I left the inside of my home just as I would on any other day, with a few dishes in the sink. I was tempted to find an obscure corner to sign my name, but I was always paranoid that yielding to such a small indulgence could come back to haunt me. My office knew that I was heading directly out to a recovery site in Weymouth, and the recovery site foreman had no idea I was scheduled to come.

I drove over the Longfellow Bridge for the last time and took Memorial Drive past the Supermarket campus. It would be the last time I'd ever see it. Walter Johnson would need to disappear forever.

I made my way to the Alewife Brook Parkway, which led past the old T-station where I was supposed to pick up Kathryn. As I approached the intersection by the parking garage, I caught sight of a BSA deputy car parked across the road. I almost panicked and made a U-turn but calmed myself as I saw that the deputy was busy talking to someone leaning into his passenger window. I drove past unnoticed and turned into the parking garage access road. I slowed and scanned around for Kathryn.

The transit station was in the process of being restored, so there was a lot of construction equipment around the garage structure. I had driven more than halfway down the access road and wondered if it was wise to backtrack to take another pass. That's when a construction worker in a worn yellow hardhat stepped out from behind an excavator and reached for my passenger door. I stopped, wondering if this guy knew something or maybe wanted to pass a message. I started to lower the window when the door opened and he got in.

The hardhat came off to reveal Kathryn.

I continued on at a casual pace and got on the highway.

"You okay?" I finally asked, looking in my rear-view mirror to make sure we weren't being followed.

She let out a deep sigh, trying to slow her panting. "I am now."

"Do you think you were followed?"

"No, I got to the station clean," she replied as her panting faded. "Almost didn't make it in time."

After a mile, I started to relax. I reached for a container of water and held it up. "Thirsty?"

She nodded, took the container, and gulped down the water. I could see her posture relax as she handed the empty container back to me. She didn't say anything, but she sniffled a couple of times before falling asleep. Five minutes later, she was soundly sleeping.

* * *

It took nearly two hours to weave through back roads before we arrived in Lunenberg, forty-five miles west of Boston. Kathryn slept the whole way. I easily found the building I had scouted in aerial photos to hide our vehicle. There was a garage at the back that I expected to be empty, and I was able to park the SUV inside. It was my hope that it would take searchers months to find it, if they ever did. It was now a needle in a large haystack.

The area was completely deserted, so we could relax while getting dressed and assembling our backpacks. We wore camouflaged lightweight hunting clothing that I had acquired from a former outdoor sporting warehouse. Only one change of clothes would be taken with us to help keep our backpacks light. I put on a holster with the 9-mm semi-automatic handgun that had belonged to Major Paladin but put his uniform in my backpack. I didn't plan to wear it until we were closer to Maine. I had also made up a fake military identification card and put on his dog tags. There was one other thing I needed to put around my neck.

"What's that?" Kathryn asked as I finished putting on Paladin's cross necklace.

"Part of my new identity."

"Who are you supposed to be now?"

"Major Joseph Paladin, former United States Army Intelligence."

"That's awfully specific."

"It's someone who died recently. I got access to his personal possessions. It'll help sell my new identity."

"Should I call you Joe?"

"Joe will do, once we get into Maine."

"And I stay Molly?"

"Probably best. I'm not sure how much they'll know about the BSA, but Donahue may not be a safe name to have."

"Too bad. Hoped I'd be able to use my real name again."

"Sorry."

"No problem. Molly's been working well for me."

Kathryn surprised me by pulling out the handgun I had given her when I left her in Cambridge. It was one of the few things in her emergency exit bag. We only armed ourselves with one handgun each. I had considered bringing rifles, but they were difficult to obtain and too heavy to carry over distance. My goal was to avoid situations that required the use of heavier weapons.

I had also brought a mini-tablet loaded with maps, aerial photos, and the supply-container homing beacon codes. Fresh batteries were stocked in the supply containers. As a backup, I had printed several maps on waterproof paper. I spent some time going over the route with Kathryn. Our first goal was to get over the state line into New Hampshire, via Route 13 into Brookline. We would be far enough west to be outside of normal BSA patrol routes. When planning that approach, I had often thought of how different life would be if Major Paladin had taken that road instead.

"Ready to go?" I asked.

"I guess," Kathryn replied as she pulled on her backpack. "Are you sure we'll get a good head start?"

"We'll find out."

Kathryn didn't reply, but I could see the apprehension on her face. I suppose I should have said something a little more reassuring, but I was just as worried as she was. I was concerned that saying anything more would've revealed how frightened I really was. We needed bravery, and it took every ounce of courage I could scrape up to take those first few steps forward.

I was also thinking about Chung-Hee. If all went as planned, he and his daughter would already be in Providence.

So we officially started our long journey on a warm, cloudy afternoon in August.

CHAPTER 15

Kathryn and I barely spoke to each other during that first afternoon. Our minds were preoccupied with thoughts of when my absence would be noticed and the search would be launched. I suddenly felt like a fox desperately trying to gain some distance before the hounds were set loose on us. While we didn't expect to see any search activity until the next day, it was difficult not to dwell on dire scenarios involving something going wrong.

Even from the absence of conversation, it was a quiet walk. It helped us to maintain a keen situational awareness: watching, listening, and even smelling for any sign of life around us. The region was void of people as I had anticipated. There was nothing but pleasant scenery. The terrain was easy and we kept up a good pace. We would easily get into New Hampshire by nightfall.

I was right, and we stopped for the night near Potanipo Pond in Brookline, New Hampshire. It was an hour before dark when I found an area of brush. We set our tent there. It had taken some effort, but I had been able to acquire a two-person dome tent in a green color that would blend in with the foliage. We had enough room to stretch out but no privacy. Our first night was awkward, but we grew used to having little personal space while sleeping. It eventually became comforting to be close to each other during what always felt like our most vulnerable period: nighttime.

We couldn't have a fire, and our food was prepackaged or military MREs. Bathing would be a luxury, so I had brought along a lightweight portable solar shower. It hardly took up any space in a backpack, but it required us to stay in one place long enough to allow the sun to heat the water. Loitering wasn't an option during the first part of our journey. We needed to gain as much distance from the BSA as possible before we could ease up. We'd just have to endure each other's stench.

I had rarely gone camping as a kid, and even less often as an adult. Kathryn had much more experience and seemed to know about all the little things I was otherwise clueless about. She knew how to stow food to keep the wildlife away and that made me feel a lot less helpless. We were particularly concerned about wolves, bears, and wild dogs. Wild dogs especially worried me because of the problems we had with them in the BSA. It had taken a couple of years to get them under control. I had hunted and shot dogs on a few occasions, so it didn't bother me. It was the noise from shooting our guns that I wanted to avoid.

Kathryn still hadn't said anything about her two days in hiding before our rendezvous. She seemed solemn and didn't want to talk, so I didn't bring it up. We had enough on our minds.

* * *

We woke up the next morning, ate, and packed up. After taking trips behind the nearest tree with a shovel and toilet paper, we were ready to roll.

It was late afternoon when we heard the first airplane. We stopped and scrambled under the nearest tree. The single-engine Cessna passed south of us.

"Looks like they're right on time," I said after the plane's engine faded in the distance. "Still too far away to see us."

"How bad is this going to get?"

"I expect to see one every once in a while, and probably more often in a couple of days. They have to be spread pretty thin searching in all directions. It's a lot of territory for them to cover, and we should be hard to spot. We'll be fine walking at the edge of the road. Just keep listening."

"What about at night? My uncle told me that search and rescue teams used thermal imaging cameras."

"I think they have a couple, but we should be okay as long as we camp under a thick umbrella of trees. Besides, most pilots I've talked with don't like flying at night these days. There's nothing lit up on the ground they can use to navigate with, like roads or towns. There's also nothing to mark any tall obstructions. That's what scares them the most."

Kathryn smiled for the first time since I picked her up the day before. "You really thought this out."

"Every important detail, I hope. I like to think it'll give us the advantage."

We started walking again and I thought it was a good time to inquire about her escape.

"So what happened to you after you fled your house?"

"Not much. I blended in crowded places and slept under bridges at night. I felt like a homeless person. I had a close call on the second night. I woke up just in time to pull my gun on some guy who thought he was going to have a good time with me."

"I'm so sorry you had to go through all that. I wish I could have helped, but it was too late by the time I found out."

"I'm really surprised you came for me at Alewife. I thought you would've given up and left without me."

"I'd never do that."

She turned and gave me a gracious smile. "Thank you."

* * *

We camped that night near the Piscataquog River outside of New Boston. It was another quiet evening as we settled down to sleep. Twice we thought we heard an airplane pass in the distance before the sun went down but couldn't really tell. The search seemed to be happening far away from us, which gave us a boost of confidence. However, our progress was going to slow down soon. The price to keep up a brisk pace was paid in the form of blisters on our feet. Despite finding a nice pair of hiking shoes, my sedentary life-style yielded thin callouses. It surprised me to see that Kathryn experienced the same blistering. She liked to jog, so I figured she'd have tougher feet. We went through a lot of tape and bandages that second night.

"How did Glenn find out I was still alive?" Kathryn asked as we lay in the darkness.

"He wasn't sure you were. Smitty told me one of the old Italian bosses wanted you found. It was over something your uncle did."

Kathryn sighed. "Not surprised. Oh gawd, they all hated Uncle Pat, but he loved it. They were especially pissed at how he let everyone call him The Godfather. I always thought it was crazy stupid, but he just loved finding ways to taunt them without it blowing up. It always worried me because I heard they held long grudges. Now I get to deal with all the shit he pulled."

"Was your uncle good to you?"

"He was hardly around and never said much to me when he was. When he opened his mouth, he was usually yelling at me for something I did." Kathryn paused and chuckled. "Most of the time I was a pain in the ass. Oh, the utterly obnoxious things I did to piss him off. I wasn't very nice, but neither was he."

"What about your dad?"

There was a pause before she drew in a deep breath. "I'd rather not get into that right now."

"Sorry, I'm prying too much."

"No, it's okay. It's got nothing to do with my dad. It's just me. I'm not proud of who I was."

"I think we all have things we're not proud of."

Kathryn laughed. "I bet you weren't an insufferable bitch who chewed through boyfriends like gum. I'd spit them out as soon as they lost their flavor. Honestly, if it weren't for the world coming to an end, I hate to think of what I'd be like now."

I was about to say something but stopped. I heard something coming up the nearby road. We were situated in a spot that over-looked the road, but set back and well concealed in the brush.

"It sounds like trucks," Kathryn whispered.

I reached for my gun as the vehicles neared. We heard the snaps of branches and the crackle of the dried leaves they ran over. Soon we saw their headlights and other beams of brighter lights reaching out to both sides of the road.

I placed my hand on Kathryn's back. "Just stay calm and quiet. We should be okay, but keep your gun nearby."

A pair of BSA Humvees crept up the road while powerful searchlights scanned around. The noise was unnerving. I suddenly felt my confidence wane as I wondered if our cover would be ade-quate. As they started to get close, I felt Kathryn bury her face into my shoulder. A spotlight beam swept past us a couple of times, but there was no change to the pitch of engines. They passed without seeing us. It took a few minutes before the hum of their engines faded into the distance.

"We're in the clear," I whispered as Kathryn came up for air.

"That was too close."

"They must be trying to get us to panic and do something stupid because they really can't see much of anything."

"It almost worked."

"Well, get ready. They're going to be back this way soon for the return trip home."

Kathryn sighed. "I don't know if I can take--"

"Sure you can. It'll be just like the first time. They'll pass right by and not see us."

We waited for what seemed like hours for the Humvee duo to make their return trip. Just as we thought they might not come, we heard the hum of their engines. Their lights once again lit up the darkness. However, they passed by at a higher rate of speed, probably satisfied that the route was clear.

"See? Much easier this time. They've gone home."

* * *

Sleep eluded us until the early morning hours, and we woke up groggy after sunrise. We quickly ate, relieved ourselves, packed up, and scoured the area to make sure we didn't leave any trace. By the time we got out onto the road, it was raining. We broke out our ponchos and forged ahead. The rainfall proved to be helpful because it kept the search aircraft grounded. It also likely drove anyone who might have resided in the area inside. We still felt uneasy as we walked, and the occasional rumble of thunder set us on edge.

The rain tapered off by afternoon and we took a break. My shoes were soaked and the bandages protecting my blisters were failing. I took off my poncho and flung the water from it. Kathryn took off her shoes and looked over her waterlogged feet, which didn't look much better than mine. I retrieved the first aid kit and started to replace the bandages on her toes. That's when an amusing observation hit me.

I thought about all the movies and television shows I used to watch about small groups of people in similar situations, on the run or fighting to survive in the wilderness. I hardly noticed that underneath all the makeup, the characters still managed to look glamorous. They never seemed to trouble themselves over details like rancid body odor, where to go to the bathroom, or how to deal with chafing.

They also seemed to have plenty of time for romance before overcoming their dramatic circumstance.

By contrast, Kathryn and I looked like a couple of rejects from a rehab clinic. Our backs hurt, our legs ached, and our blisters tormented us with each step we took. We smelled ripe and the mosquitoes never left us alone. We were always on edge and approached each bend in the road with trepidation as if that duo of BSA Humvees would be waiting for us. Kathryn was a strikingly beautiful young woman, but to be honest, right then I didn't find her at all physically appealing. Unlike those movies, there wasn't anything close to a glimmer of romance in our situation; reality drove out any such thought. It also didn't help that she had had to flee her home without the chance to pack any specialty items, and the timing of her menstrual cycle wasn't cooperating. I felt pretty stupid for not anticipating something like that, especially after living with Veronica for five years.

I didn't care how she looked or smelled. I was glad she was there with me because I couldn't imagine attempting that trek without a partner.

Bound up with fresh bandages, we pressed on. We were closing in on the first supply container drop point, and it was important for us to restock. The rainy morning had slowed our progress, so we didn't have much time to locate it before dark. After a couple of attempts, my tablet successfully triggered the container's homing device. It steered us in the right direction, a couple of miles off the road we were following.

"Are you good at climbing trees?" Kathryn asked as we looked up to the supply container hanging from a tall pine tree. "I'm not too good with heights."

"Not a problem," I replied as I got out my knife. It wasn't terribly high up, and most of the parachute lines had already been severed in its fall into the tree. I cut the last few lines away and the container fell to the ground with a thud.

"I hope there was nothing breakable inside."

"They pack these things to take a beating," I replied as I climbed down, "because they usually do. Even the homing transmitter is designed to endure a lot of punishment."

"Hey, so, about that transmitter," Kathryn said as she looked over the four-foot canister. "I was just thinking, can anyone else trigger the homing signal?"

"Don't worry, I set up a special encryption code that only I have," I said as I lifted up one side and turned off the homing transmitter. "There's no way anyone else could set one of our container signals off."

"Good, because that would've been a, well--"

"A silly oversight?"

"I was actually going to say a monumental fuck-up. Sorry, I used to have a bad habit of blurting out unfiltered thoughts. I'll shut up now."

"Don't worry about it. I sort of thought the same thing."

Kathryn gave me a perplexed look.

"What did I say?"

"I'm just not used to someone being so polite about my snarky bullshit. My uncle would've ripped me a new one if I ever said something like that."

"Sounds like you blurted out a lot of unfiltered thoughts to him."

Kathryn smiled. "Oh, if you only knew."

We dragged the container about halfway back to the road. It was getting dark, so we found a good spot to set up our campsite. We enjoyed opening the container, like it was a birthday present. Food, water, fresh batteries, and even a new first aid kit were inside. We restocked and managed to relax a little for the first time since we had set out.

We lay down to sleep and I remember hearing only a distant howl of a coyote as I drifted off. We were situated pretty far off the road. I thought it was unwise to stray too far from our route to set up camp, but in the wake of the Humvee patrol, we did have an improved feeling of security. What we couldn't hear couldn't frighten us. From then on, I made it a point to put a little more distance between our campsites and whatever road we followed. It proved to be a comforting strategy.

* * *

We didn't hear any aircraft as we walked the next day, which I found peculiar. I expected to be ducking aircraft more often at that point, but the search didn't seem focused on where we were. I didn't know what to make of it. We'd occasionally stop for a break under a tree and I'd take out my binoculars to scan the sky. There was nothing to be seen but a couple of towering cumulonimbus clouds to the north. All we could do was to accept our good fortune and cautiously press on.

Kathryn and I hardly talked to each other while we walked. We were concerned about making too much noise. We even developed a simple hand signal system to silently warn each other of possible threats. The lack of conversation didn't bother me very much. I wasn't the chatty type when anxious. Neither was Kathryn. Our primary focus was conquering the journey, and to that goal we made a very good team.

The days seemed to blur together. It was just the two of us in a vast, picturesque wilderness. We were imperceptible spirits passing through beautiful, lush landscapes and an occasional vacant town. We'd sometimes come across a nice view of a mountain, but out of concern that we might be spied by anyone with a decent pair of binoculars, we never lingered. Traversing large, open areas unnerved us. I had always been fond of the wondrous vistas they offered, but having to walk across them tied my stomach in knots. My worst fear was encountering a search aircraft while we were in the middle, exposed with nowhere to hide. We always felt safest when our route had plenty of trees.

We saw no signs of human habitation, but we never went out of our way to look for any. The scouting reports I had studied grossly underestimated the situation in New Hampshire. Our reality showed a region completely absent of human presence. The pandemic was typically harsh on rural areas and small towns. It either killed everyone or drove them away in the aftermath. It was rare to find a small community that remained intact. Most survivors opted to migrate to larger population centers for a better chance of survival.

We passed by plenty of vacant houses, but we didn't sleep in them. We could have become trapped in a place we didn't have much control over. Mostly though, just the sight of those barren homes bothered me. It felt as though each house was a tomb that shouldn't be desecrated. As we walked by them, I always got the uneasy feeling that we were being watched. It wasn't by anyone still breathing, but by phantoms of a not so distant past. I had never been superstitious or believed in ghosts, but a stroll past those rundown, desolate homes was enough to make anyone reconsider. I'm sure the whole thing was caused by nothing more than fatigue, but even Kathryn never uttered an objection to passing up those houses. I knew she was feeling the same thing.

Once we left these areas, our thoughts returned to the usual concerns. Of these was encounters with wild animals. We actually hadn't seen much wildlife, which was comforting. I suppose the wolves and coyotes were just too shy to come close, and Kathryn helped us to take the necessary precautions to minimize food scents. We had our handguns if needed, but firing them off presented an even greater concern: making too much noise. That's why I had a small can of pepper-spray tucked away.

The only instance of an animal confrontation was while we were near New Hampton. It was a vacant town, like all the others. As we were walking down a road, I heard rustling coming from my left side. It was soon followed by low growling. Eventually, a ferocious, gaunt rottweiler came into the open just ahead of us, snarling as it slowly approached. The rest of the pack stayed back and concealed. I stopped and froze, yielding to common advice when confronting a vicious dog. I looked around and wondered how we could scare it off without making too much noise, but then remembered my can of pepper spray. Before I could reach for it, Kathryn walked ahead of me and directly at the dog. She drew her gun and shot it without hesitation. The bullet hit the rottweiler's hindquarter and it let out a screeching yelp. It staggered and limped away while whimpering.

"You can't hesitate," Kathryn said to me as she safetied her gun and put it away. "I wounded it so he'll go back to his friends and suffer. They won't bother us again."

"You've done this before?" I asked as I slipped my can of pepper spray back into place.

"We had a big dog problem back in my neighborhood. It gave me a lot of practice with the gun you left me."

"We'd better keep moving in case that gunshot got anyone's attention."

"What were you reaching for?"

"Pepper spray."

Kathryn smirked. "You've lived in the city too long."

We continued on with no sign of pursuit, animal or human. I would've expected to run into more animals than we did, particularly dogs. I can only guess that they had run out of food and followed the human migration to populated centers. The same thing had occurred in BSA territory. Only the truly wild animals could survive without humans around.

Every second or third day, we'd locate the closest supply container. In all, only one failed to activate its homing transmitter, but I had arranged redundancies to counter the possibility of a compromised drop site. My plan was working far better than I had anticipated. I was feeling pretty proud of myself.

With each passing day, hope grew that we would actually make it into Maine. There continued to be no sign of pursuit, but we were careful to maintain our vigilance. Our blisters were bothering us less, so our pace was steady and strong. However, we were careful not to push too far each day. There was always the temptation to get ahead of our schedule to arrive sooner. If we rushed, we risked being thrown off of our resupply regimen. The last thing we could afford was to find ourselves out of supplies without a supply container nearby.

By the end of the first week, we had made it up to Sandwich, just north of Lake Winnipesaukee. On the way, we had been forced to take a couple of detours because bridges had failed or a route showed signs that people might be around. It didn't take much to motivate us to seek an alternative route - usually a whiff of smoke, an unusual sound, or a stretch of road that looked a little too clean. We didn't take any chances, particularly with the populated town of Conway close by. A year before, one of our scouts never returned from investigating that area. It had been deemed hostile.

* * *

I triggered another homing device which led us to a supply container just short of Eaton, New Hampshire. It was close to the Maine border and our plan was to cross over the next morning. Whatever was in Conway thankfully hadn't come further south. Like everywhere else we had trekked through, we found the region vacated of people. We had enough time to restock our backpacks and put out the solar shower to heat in the afternoon sun. The showers we took were brief, but it washed away days of sweat and grime. We felt human again and were in much better spirits that evening.

The night was uneventful and we slept soundly. I was awakened the next morning by a strange noise. It had been faint when I heard it in my sleep and was gone by the time I fully woke. It was a distant but deep thumping sound. I dismissed it as a waking dream. As I crawled out of our tent, I heard nothing but birds chirping and the occasional screech of a hawk. It was another beautiful summer morning. After breakfast, we packed up and continued our journey. The terrain was typical of what we had been dealing with, but our steps showed more enthusiasm. The Maine border was finally within reach.

We walked along the side of Brownfield Road outside of Eaton, New Hampshire. It would lead us right across the border into Maine. As we came around a bend to a lengthy straightaway, the morning sun was in our eyes. It didn't take long before Kathryn raised her arm, which was a signal that she had spotted something suspicious. Quickly, we retreated into the woods at the side of the road. Once safely hidden, I took out my binoculars for a closer look. The road ahead cut through a marshy pond with a small bridge at the center. At the front of the bridge, a person was standing in the middle of the road. I gasped and tried to get a better focus.

"What is it?" Kathryn quietly asked.

"I must be seeing things." The figure was just loitering with what looked like a white flag in hand, dressed in what appeared to be casual clothing, not like those of a soldier or survivalist.

"What's that supposed to mean?"

"Take a look," I whispered as I handed Kathryn the binoculars.

"That's bizarre," she replied after a short inspection.

"I think we can get closer without being seen."

"Why? We should just back off and find another way around."

"I just want to take a closer look. This is the first person we've seen the whole trip."

"Standing out in the middle of nowhere like that? It's probably someone we don't want to meet."

"We'll be fine. Just move slowly and stay quiet."

She followed me reluctantly as I stealthily made my way forward. I stopped at a point where I could get a better look through my binoculars. Once I focused, a jolting recognition came to me.

"It's Glenn."

"What?" Katheryn grabbed my binoculars and looked for herself. "What in the hell is he doing here?"

My heart sank. "We've been caught."

"No, not yet. He doesn't know we're here. We can go back and take another way around."

"He knew this was the place we were going to cross over," I thought aloud. "It's why he's waiting here."

"Fine, let him wait. Let's get going."

I took another look at him through my binoculars. "That noise I heard this morning. It was a helicopter, one of the Hueys we salvaged. That's how he got up here. It's not going to matter which way we take, he'll be able to get ahead of us."

"Walt, listen to me. There's still too much ground for them to search. We'll have a chance if we leave now."

I sighed. "I don't know. I think it's best if I go and see what he wants."

"What? Have you lost your goddamn mind?"

"What's the harm in talking?"

Kathryn clinched her teeth. "Don't be a fucking idiot. It's a trap. He's not here to let you go."

"Maybe."

"Maybe? Jesus, how can you think there's a maybe in this?"

"Then he'll be satisfied that he found what he came looking for. Because he's not going to stop until he does. He doesn't know that you're with me. You'll stand a far better chance of slipping away."

Kathryn's stern expression faded. "Walt, please don't do this. You've come too far to give up."

I took off my backpack and handed it to her. "Stay hidden and try to work in closer. Keep me covered if you can, but don't do anything stupid."

"Oh, sure, like the example you're setting?"

"If anything bad happens, stay low and find another way into Maine. Be sure to give my backpack to General Osgood when you get there, okay? It's very important."

The anguished look on her face was heartbreaking. "Please don't leave me."

I smiled and gently patted her on the shoulder before I rose and walked out onto the road.

I knew Kathryn was right: it was likely a trap. We might have had a chance to slip into Maine if we had turned back and tried to find another route, but I knew Glenn wouldn't give up so easily. My primary motivation was to keep Kathryn safe and get the vault instructions to Maine, but there was also something about how Glenn put himself out there all alone in his street clothes with a white flag in his hand. I'm sure he had snipers covering him, but I doubted he was setting me up to be shot. That would've been easier to achieve without his standing out in the middle of the road like that.

He caught sight of me as I walked towards him and started walking to me with a sorrowful expression on his face. Soon, a faint smile emerged as he got a better look at me.

"Jesus, Walt, you look like a complete mess. Hiking doesn't suit you."

"How did you find me?"

"The thought of you surviving off the land seemed too ridiculous to consider, so I figured you'd need some help. You did a nice job erasing your tracks with those pre-supply drops, but the Air Corps keeps better records than you think."

"I sprinkled those things all over the place and I'm the only one who had the codes. How did you know to come here?"

"I didn't need to have your codes. All I had to do was keep my airplanes orbiting near the border while listening for any signals that you triggered. The homing signals have a five mile range which works in all directions, including up. You triggered one in the area yesterday and the rest was easy to figure out. I just looked at a map."

I felt like a complete idiot. "So what now?"

Glenn paused and looked at me with a pained expression. "Walt, what happened? What did I do to drive you up here?"

I was caught off guard by the questions, or maybe I was still reeling over how easily he had found me. Regardless, I wasn't in any frame of mind to have a long discussion with him. After what he had done to me, I didn't feel like I owed him an explanation.

"I didn't like where it was all heading."

"Why didn't you just say something? You know I would've listened. We can still work this out."

"You actually want me to come back with you?"

"Of course! I need you. We can fix what's wrong."

"Do I have a choice?" I asked as I looked around. There was no doubt several BSA soldiers were hiding nearby.

Glenn paused and grimaced. "I'm not here to force you to come back."

"If I decide to continue on, you'll just let me go?"

"What can you possibly find in Maine?" Glenn snapped as he pointed down the road.

"Why did you lie about them? Why did you lie about Tony? Pat? You manipulated everything we went through so you could get what you wanted."

Glenn frowned. "I did it for everyone who suffered under that bastard. The Godfather? Really? The guy was out of his mind. He needed to be ended and I'm sorry if I had to bend the truth to do that. I always had your back. I've had people watching out for you in ways you've never noticed."

"And yet Pat pointed his gun in *my* face."

"I was right there, outside your door the whole time. I would've never let him hurt you. Smitty made sure his gun was loaded with blanks."

"Those weren't blanks chewing up my brownstone the next morning!"

"Yeah, I know. That one got away from me."

"Got away from you?"

"Look, I'm sorry for the deceptions, but I thought it best that you didn't know. You've done so much and I didn't want to put all of that on you."

"It still wasn't the right thing to do."

"I know. I'm sorry. I just wanted to make it easier for you."

"Well, you've got your kingdom. You don't really need me around anymore."

"Walt, please. You need to think this over. You're leaving more behind than you'll ever be able to find in Maine. Come on, we've always done great things together, and there's so much ahead of us that needs to be accomplished. Think of all we've been through together."

"I'm sorry, it's time for me to move on."

Tears welled up in his eyes. "All right then, if that's what you really want."

"That's it? I can just walk away?"

Glenn fought to maintain his composure. "I said it was your choice."

"My choice is to keep going," I said. I figured if anything went wrong, continuing to walk down the road would give everyone there the impression I was alone. It would give Kathryn a chance to slip away.

"Goodbye, Glenn. Best of luck."

Glenn stood there as I walked by him. He shook his head and a tear ran down his cheek. It seemed inconceivable that I'd be allowed to leave. I looked around as I slowly approached the small bridge, wondering where the snipers were hidden. The thought came to me that I'd probably be dead before I heard the shot anyway. With each step I took, nothing happened. I wondered if my executioner was teasing me or if he just needed more time to line up his shot.

I was on my tenth step when three rapid gunshots cracked out from behind me. I flinched, stopped, but felt no pain. I turned in time to see Glenn fall to his knees and drop a handgun in front of him. I ran back and caught him before he fell to the ground. There were two large bullet wounds in his back. He looked up at me as I steadied him on his knees. He coughed and focused on something below my neck. His hand reached up and grasped Major Paladin's cross necklace that hung out of my shirt.

"What's this?" he softly asked before the last bit of life drained from him. He died in my arms and I gently laid him on the pavement.

A figure appeared from the other side of the bridge and started jogging toward me with his arms raised. It was Smitty. Kathryn also appeared and walked toward me with her gun aimed squarely at Smitty as he crossed the bridge.

"Calm ya liwa, girl," Smitty pleaded as he reached us. "I'm not here to start any trouble. You don't need to shoot me too."

Kathryn lowered her gun and turned to me. "Glenn was going to shoot you."

I looked at his gun on the ground and gave her an affirming nod.

"Is he gone?" Smitty asked as he knelt down to get a closer look.

"Yeah."

"She's right, he was going to shoot you," Smitty said as he looked up to Kathryn. "Miss Donahue, I presume? Or is it Molly Donnelly?"

Kathryn only smirked at him.

"Well, well," Smitty continued, "Just look at you. I would've never recognized you. You're all grown up now."

We rose back to our feet as I looked around. It was only the three of us standing around Glenn. Nobody else was in sight.

"What did I do?" I wondered, the reality of the moment pressing on me.

Smitty looked down to Glenn's lifeless body with a scowl. "I don't think he deserves any grief. He was never the friend you thought he was."

"Who was he, then?"

"Someone with one hell of a personality disorder," Smitty quipped.

I offered him a confused grimace in reply.

"Oh, come on, Walt, get a fucking grip. He told you what you wanted to hear so he could get what he wanted. He did that to everyone he met. I think we all saw the signs but didn't really want to do a damned thing about it."

"He just wanted to make things better," I mumbled.

"In his own dysfunctional way, yeah, he did make things better."

I shook my head. "So what are you going to do now?"

Smitty shrugged his shoulders. "I'm going home."

"What about Glenn?"

"No suh, I'm not taking him back with us. People are going to think I put those bullets in his back. I'd rather try to tell them he fell into a river and got swept away."

"We can't just leave him lying here."

"You're right." Smitty turned back and waved. Three BSA soldiers appeared and started walking to the bridge. "Get out your shovels!"

* * *

It took us an hour to dig a grave at the side of the road. I placed

Glenn's body in it and watched as everyone else filled it in. Kathryn fastened two sticks together to form a cross. After standing it in a pile of stones, we stood and gazed at the fresh grave.

"If it wasn't here, he was going to get capped back home, probably soon," Smitty explained. "Everyone was wicked shiesty around him. I think too many people were getting wise to his bullshit. I'm sure the Greasties would've been first in line to cap him after we got back."

"Was it really that bad?" I asked.

Smitty glared at me. "Aren't you the one who bolted?"

"I was protecting Kathryn."

Smitty turned to Kathryn. "Nice shooting, by the way. You capped the guy who offed your uncle."

"Oh, bite me."

Smitty chuckled. "I like her, Walt. Glad you were listening to my hints even though it took you so goddamn long enough to move her."

I could only offer Smitty a perplexed look.

"Jesus, Walt. Do you think I didn't know you hid her away?"

"I guess not."

Smitty snickered and clucked his tongue. "Walt, there are times I think you're fifty shades of fucking stupid, but you've always been a good shit. I hope you two find a good home in Maine. Settle down and have lots of babies. Just don't ever show your faces in the BSA again, ever. Consider us even for keeping quiet about that day in Westford."

He nodded to his soldiers and they all walked back across the bridge. I continued to stand with Kathryn beside Glenn's stark grave.

"Are you okay?" she asked me.

"I don't care what Smitty thinks, I believe Glenn really tried to make things better for everyone. He just lost his way."

"I'm so sorry, I didn't mean to shoot him. He pulled a gun while you were walking away and I just reacted."

"It's okay," I reassured as I put my arm around her. "Now you understand what happened back in Waltham."

To this day, I'm still deeply conflicted about what happened to Glenn. It's just too easy to conclude that he simply deserved his fate. When he died in my arms, I was struck with an oddly distressing thought. Despite all he had done to me, I felt an unsettling sense of responsibility for what had befallen him.

Smitty was always good at sizing people up and spent a lot more time around Glenn during those last three years, but I can't bring myself to categorically place all the blame on a personality defect. I've pondered this for years and have come to a sad acceptance that Smitty was right about my naivete. Despite all the deceptions Glenn resorted to, I had been put in a position to help a leader in desperate need of a conscience. Instead of asserting myself more in Glenn's life, I chose to close myself off in my own small, comfortable world. I chose to ignore all the questionable things he did. I was too quick to dismiss my suspicion about why he had his gun on him on the day he shot Pat as well as his timing to save me. I was also too quick to ignore Chung-Hee's warnings. All I wanted to do was to kick back and let Glenn figure out how to get things done.

Many will probably disagree, but during his time as leader, I believe Glenn had been a better friend to me than I was to him. Despite his shortcomings, he created a protective bubble around The Supermarket to shelter me from the unsavory people and vile things that I lacked the capacity to cope with. He wanted to shield me from the dysfunction, egotism, and sordidness which surrounded him. It's all the stuff I didn't want to see.

In the end, the evils that Glenn routinely contended with wore him down because he faced them alone. The power he wielded corrupted him, and I had failed to help him resist it. I don't condone Glenn's methods and behaviors, but I often wonder how different things could have been if I'd only paid more attention.

Glenn Bradshaw died on a lonely road and was thoughtlessly discarded by those who had no genuine interest to help him. In many ways, Walter Johnson died with him that morning.

CHAPTER 16

We heard the helicopter take off as we started up the road to the border. Its plangent, chopping rotors soon faded away. I could only imagine the excuses that Smitty was conjuring up in order to appease anyone who cared about why Glenn didn't come back with him. Kathryn and I might have been walking into a situation we knew little about, but I was far more relieved not to be back in the BSA. The power vacuum was sure to cause trouble and I hoped the many good people I had left behind wouldn't get caught in it.

In less than a mile, we passed a faded blue sign welcoming us to Maine. The landscape didn't change. We faced at least three more days of hiking. Our goal was to reach the Sebago Lake area and find a populated center. From there we needed to get to Camp Keyes, Augusta, where Major Paladin had told me I could find General Osgood.

Despite our tragic encounter with Glenn, our enthusiasm was bolstered. We only had one more resupply container ahead of us, but we still took our time. We showered regularly and took more rest breaks. However, there was something I struggled with. While Kathryn knew I was going to take on a new identity, she didn't know why I chose Joseph Paladin. I had made a wise choice to keep her in the dark in case something went wrong. Now we were nearing the finish line of our trek, and I wondered if she should be told the truth.

* * *

We were gathering items from the final supply container when the shooting of Glenn finally caught up with Kathryn. She had been stoic up to that point, which seemed normal because we usually didn't talk much while we walked. However, as we sat down and opened the container, the sight of the first-aid kit inside triggered a response.

Kathryn had been toughened by her life in hiding, but killing someone was an entirely new and morbid experience. Her resiliency had been used up, and she broke down and cried on my shoulder for a while. Her reaction caused my dreadful memories to resurface of that terrible night back in Waltham after I killed Reaper. I wanted so badly to help her more, but it was part of a process she needed to go through. I could only offer her some comfort and the company that I had never had.

After a while, she fell asleep in my arms. I carried her into our tent and gently laid her in her sleeping bag. As I sat in the darkness and listened to the serenade of crickets, my thoughts were consumed by what happened to Glenn. Guilt was slowly burrowing into my conscience, but then something occurred to me. I had been so caught up in wrestling with blame that I had failed to realize that something remarkable happened that day. Without a second thought, I had walked into almost certain death in order to keep Kathryn's presence hidden. I had never done something like that for anyone before. Up to that point, the closest I had ever come to disregarding my own safety to help another was for, well, Kathryn.

Right then it struck me that Kathryn had become more valuable to me than what I was carrying to Maine. I decided that I wanted to tell her everything about why I was on the trek. I figured she had earned the right to know the truth, and not telling her would disrespect everything she had endured. She needed to know what we really protected.

The next morning, we sat down for breakfast and I recounted everything to her. As I explained it all, it was hard to not make it sound like a wild fairytale. As if I were a modern day Ali-Baba who had to say *open sesame* to access a magical treasure cave. She took it well and fittingly capped it off by noting the irony of Smitty's thinking that I was the stupid one.

* * *

We were walking along a road outside of Baldwin, Maine when we heard an approaching vehicle. I had earlier decided to put on Major Paladin's uniform with the expectation that we'd run into someone soon. The road was noticeably cleaner here, lacking the layer of leaves and branches that we had routinely seen in New Hampshire. Civilization had to be close. I was surprised we hadn't run across someone sooner.

"Car," Kathryn said with a smile. We made no effort to hide, and it was an unusually pleasing experience. Our days of invisibility were finally over.

"Yup. Too quiet for a truck."

A light blue sedan with a light bar on its roof came into sight.

"A police car," Kathryn said as it approached. "Really?"

"I hope."

The blue strobe lights turned on and it pulled up beside us. The window opened to reveal a state police officer in full uniform. He was clearly flabbergasted as he looked us over.

"And just who might you two be?"

"I'm Major Joseph Paladin, United States Army, sir."

"Really?"

"Could we trouble you for a ride? We've had a really long hike into Maine. I'm trying to get to General Osgood in Augusta. He's expecting me."

His eyes widened. "You bet you can. Please get in."

We got into the police cruiser of Officer Tommy James, and he pulled a fast U-turn while turning on his siren. "You're the first United States anything to come through here in a long time. So what's going on in the world? What ever happened to Uncle Sam?"

I sat in the front seat and shared a smile with Kathryn in the back. "I'd love to tell you, sir, but I'm instructed to talk only with the General about that."

"Well, I'll get you back to our station in Gorham where there's a radio," Officer James enthusiastically replied. "We can get a hold of the militia and get you to the General."

Officer James was a nice guy, but I found it odd how he freely accepted our story. There was no hint of suspicion from him. We could have been lying about who we really were, despite the fact that we actually were lying. He never even checked us for weapons, even though we had put our handguns away in our backpacks. It just wasn't the type of greeting we expected.

We reached the police station and found that the police officers there weren't quite as easy to impress. I was asked for identification and we were separated for questioning. They were polite and professional. My assigned officer carefully took notes and respected my wishes to exercise care with my backpack. We were given water and a hot meal, our first since we left the BSA.

We were put in a hotel for the night, which was watched by the police to make sure we didn't disappear. It was hardly necessary as there was no way either of us was going to pass up a night in a real bed. After many days of sharing a small tent, we didn't give it a second thought to share a room. We were both asleep as soon as our heads hit those wonderfully soft pillows. Even though there were two double beds in the room, we still slept in the same bed. It's hard to explain why, but I suppose we had become so accustomed to sleeping close to one another that it would've felt strange not to.

The next morning we were served breakfast in our room. We savored every bite of those potato pancakes smothered in pure maple syrup. Things in Maine seemed a bit better than I had been led to believe.

Long, hot showers came next. I let Kathryn go first and didn't mind the twenty-minute shower she took. She deserved every second of it. She exited the steamy bathroom with only a towel around her, which made me pause. It wasn't so much the enticing sight of her in a skimpy towel but what she had come to mean to me. I had seen many attractive women back in the BSA, and I remembered how meaningless and shallow they really were. No matter how alluring they appeared, I knew I couldn't trust them because their ulterior motives were always too obvious. Now a woman stood in front of me who had walked every arduous step at my side through a dangerous journey. I had quickly come to trust that she'd always have my back. I would do anything to protect her, and she hadn't hesitated to kill someone to save me.

Kathryn displayed a remarkable quality of character that I thought was impossible to find in that deeply dysfunctional world. She was far from the spoiled princess I had first encountered in Waltham. Her smile as I passed her on my way into the shower left me with a profound sense of accomplishment over keeping her safe. That's why I married her a couple of years later; but sorry, I'm getting ahead of myself again.

After I was able to shave and look human again, I put Major Paladin's uniform back on and Kathryn helped to make sure all the details were just right. She had had some experience making sure her uncle was polished in his police uniform back in the day. We were escorted back to the police station, and was greeted by a military officer.

"Major, I'm Colonel Schmidt of the Maine Militia," he declared with a salute.

I hesitantly returned his salute, never having stopped to think about how an officer needed to act around other officers. Major Paladin had never had the chance to coach me on that. "Sorry, Colonel, I'm not even sure how to approach our respective ranks."

"Not a problem. I'm here to take you to Augusta. General Osgood is anxious to meet you."

"I'd like my companion, Molly, to come with us."

"Can do, Major. Shall we go?"

We walked out back and I was surprised by a row of six heavily armed Humvees and a Stryker armored personnel carrier that waited for us. I stopped and marveled. The convoy looked every bit as formidable as anything in the BSA defense force. Maine clearly had a well-equipped and organized military.

"We're getting into the fourth Humvee in line," Colonel Schmidt said as he led us to the vehicle.

The trip lasted about ninety minutes, and the Colonel remained quiet for the entire trip. He was clearly a professional who knew how to keep his mouth shut, something I had rarely experienced with the BSA defense officers. I was actually relieved not to enter into a conversation with anyone. The less I talked, the less I risked saying something that would've given me away as a fraud.

I looked out the window and didn't see much. We were traveling north on Route 295, which was then a sparsely-traveled two lane divided highway. It wasn't too much different from driving around the BSA, except there were a lot more trees in Maine. I didn't see much activity until we neared Augusta.

We pulled into Camp Keyes and were greeted by a contingent of heavily armed soldiers. After exchanging a few salutes, I was led to the office of General Brendan Osgood, former Brigadier General in the United States Air Force. Kathryn was led to a reception area to wait for me.

"Welcome to Maine, Major," General Osgood greeted with a deep, commanding voice. He was in his early sixties, tall, bald, and had a serious demeanor. His nondescript blue uniform lacked any U.S. insignia.

"Thank you, sir," I replied nervously as I looked around. Two other soldiers were in the office with us. They watched intently with their hands on their holstered handguns.

"So?" General Osgood asked, shooting a glance to one of the soldiers.

It was clearly time for the authentication code. "I am Nehemiah."

General Osgood relaxed his posture and nodded at the soldiers. They immediately saluted and left the office.

"Now that we have that out of the way, how was your trip?"

"Long and eventful."

"Please sit and tell me about it."

I sat and took in a deep breath. "There's a lot that you need to know."

* * *

I spent close to an hour recounting every detail of who I really was, how I had come to meet the real Major Paladin, and my journey into Maine. He didn't say much at first, but then had a number of questions about the BSA, which I freely answered. I showed him the key, the USB flash drive, and my notes on accessing the vault. The cartoon character on the composition notebook cover drew a smile from him.

"I can walk anyone you want through the processes and password sequences," I concluded.

General Osgood leaned back in his chair and chuckled. "Son, do you think I'd let someone else have the honor of opening that vault after everything you've gone through to get here?"

"But how can you trust me? There's no way to verify my story."

"Why would you lie about something like this?"

"You believe me?"

"Honestly, I'll believe you when you open the vault. You're going to remain Major Joseph Paladin until that happens. Understand?"

"Yes, sir."

"Good." He picked up his phone receiver and pressed the

intercom button. "Please send in Lieutenant Hoffman."

A few seconds later, a young officer entered and saluted the General.

"At ease, Lieutenant. This is Major Paladin, U.S. Army Intelligence. Major, Lieutenant Hoffman is my best special ops team leader."

Instead of salutes, handshakes were exchanged. It then struck me that we were technically not part of the same army and probably didn't have a reason to salute each other. Or maybe he just didn't have much respect for anyone in Army Intelligence. I eventually found out it was the latter.

Lieutenant Bill Hoffman was almost thirty, but he looked younger. He was a former Green Beret who had a determined but soft spoken personality. He'd seen a lot of action while deployed in Afghanistan and was well respected. Despite this, he didn't carry himself with as much conceit as I would've imagined.

"Where to, General?" Lieutenant Hoffman asked.

General Osgood looked at a large map of Maine on his wall. "Loring. Shit, it just had to be all the way up there."

"Still in range for a helicopter insertion," Lieutenant Hoffman said.

"Yeah, but still way out in unsecured territory."

"Unsecured?" I asked.

"Most of Maine is," General Osgood replied.

"We'll need a drone pass to get a current read on what's going on around that area," Bill said as he rose and made a closer inspection of the map.

"Whatever you need, Lieutenant."

"I'll probably need a reinforced insertion team. If it's all clear, a couple of Blackhawks should get us all up there, and back if needed."

"You have all these things?" I asked.

"One of our best kept secrets is how many ex-military fled up here after everything collapsed," General Osgood replied. "We've got a lot of good personnel and equipment, but not a lot of gas and spare parts to keep it all going."

"Our reports showed that the BSA never understood how much was here in Maine," I carefully said, trying to keep awareness that Lieutenant Hoffman wasn't going to be told about my true identity.

"Probably why we kicked their asses," Lieutenant Hoffman said with a smirk.

"There were some skirmishes down near Kittery a couple of years back," General Osgood explained to me. "It didn't go well for them and they haven't tried again since."

"Having a fucking idiot for a general didn't help them, either," Lieutenant Hoffman added.

"Okay, Lieutenant, why don't you form your team and start reviewing intel. Dismissed."

"Yes, sir." Lieutenant Hoffman saluted and exited.

"I never heard about an attack on Maine," I said after Lieutenant Hoffman left.

"What did you hear about us?"

"Nothing, other than rumors. The BSA always denied you existed. I was kept out of the loop, even though I helped to supply scouting missions up here."

"Yeah, and most of those scouts ended up staying with us. How certain are you that no one in the BSA leadership knows what you brought up here?"

"I shared this with only one other person, and he escaped with his daughter to Providence on the night before I set out. There's absolutely no way anyone else could know about the vault. If Smitty suspected anything, he wouldn't have let me go at the border."

"And your wife?"

"Kathryn's not my wife, at least not yet. I told her everything a couple of days ago. My plan was not to, but, well, I think she earned it."

General Osgood smiled. "We'll get you situated until we figure out mission logistics. I'd say be ready for a trip up to Loring in the next day or so."

"I'll be ready. Can I ask a favor?"

"Sure."

"I'm supposed to be an army officer, but I have no idea how to act like one. Paladin didn't get a chance to cover it."

General Osgood chuckled. "Don't worry, I'll bring you up to speed. I also haven't said anything to our President about all of this because, well, it still sounds too good to be true. I'm trying not to get too enthusiastic about it just yet. No offense."

"None taken."

* * *

Kathryn and I were set up in small, separate apartments nearby. She had insisted that we didn't share a place. I was a little confused by that, but she later explained to me that it was important to her that we didn't move in together. There was something special between us and she wanted to take it slow. She didn't want me to be another stick of gum that lost its flavor after a short while.

I found it hard to sleep that night. Thoughts of opening the vault swirled around my mind. I also think I had grown too accustomed to having Kathryn sleeping next to me. She mentioned to me the next morning that she had slept very well. Go figure.

The electricity was rationed and turned off promptly at ten o'clock every evening. The food was good but lacked the selection I was used to seeing in the BSA. It was clear that our first night at that hotel had been a special treat that few in The Maine Republic regularly enjoyed. We were kept under guard and I was occasionally consulted for details that were needed to plan the mission. I was told to prepare to depart sometime the next day.

* * *

The next morning I was woken early and led to a special ops planning center on the base. A group of eighteen soldiers waited for their team commander to start the briefing. Lieutenant Hoffman came into the room and started laying out the details of the mission. The presentation was serious and delivered with a professional polish, until Lieutenant Hoffman began using terms like *heist* and *bank job* to describe my part of the mission. I saw the snickers and contained chuckles. It didn't help that he gave me the codename: *Oceans Eleven*.

Although it was pretty straight-forward, there were a lot of details and considerations to review. This was a highly trained team of former special forces and navy SEALs who were deadly serious about every detail of the mission. Aerial footage from drones was reviewed and scoured for any potential hazards. It seemed that the old Loring base, which had been converted to a civilian airport, was uninhabited. However, any settlement or sign of human activity within a twenty-mile radius was carefully examined and evaluated.

The vault access point was completely hidden, which didn't sit well with this team. They disliked unknown factors. Since the whole mission could be considered an unknown factor, I quickly got the impression that I wasn't the most popular person in the room.

The plan was to take two UH-60 Blackhawk helicopters and land in the southeast corner of the airfield. The team would then establish a defensive perimeter and secure the helicopters. Because fuel was an issue, they would have to be shut down until needed. Drones (UAVs) would keep an eye on everything around us from the sky.

The vault access point was to the side of an existing structure, but the door was hidden under a layer of grass. A metal detector would be needed to locate it. Once we landed, we'd have twenty-four hours to determine if it was a viable find or not. I'd have to gain access to the vault and Lieutenant Hoffman would have to make an assessment. If everything looked good, he'd radio in a special code which would designate our area as a critical asset. A convoy of reinforcements would be immediately dispatched from Bangor while we figured out how to disperse the contents of the vault. The real Major Paladin had a general knowledge of the vault contents, but no specifics regarding the inventory.

My instructions were quite specific. I was to stay in my helicopter with my handler until Lieutenant Hoffman came to get me. I had one purpose: to access the vault. I would not be issued a weapon nor would I participate in any other aspect of the operation unless otherwise instructed. My notebook, the key, and the USB flash drive would be kept in the possession of Lieutenant Hoffman until he decided I would need them. I got the clear impression that they were carrying out this mission under the assumption that nothing about it was genuine until proved otherwise. Even though I was supposed to be a major in the U.S. Army, I was not a trusted asset.

* * *

A little over three hours later, we were on approach to the old Loring field. It was my first time in a helicopter of any type and I desperately hoped it would be my last. I disliked the hard banks and the aggressive maneuvers the pilot took to the landing site. It was a cloudy day with some rain showers in the area, and we were occasionally buffeted by gusts of wind.

The first helicopter approached and touched down. Soldiers hopped out and scrambled off in all directions. Once emptied, it took off again to provide close support air cover until the area was secured. Lieutenant Hoffman was sitting next to me shouting commands into his headset. He soon waved to our pilot and we began our descent while the soldiers readied themselves. Our Blackhawk settled at the far end of a stretch of pavement and all but one soldier spilled out. The remaining soldier would be my handler, and there was no mistaking that he'd rather be out with his comrades instead of babysitting me.

Our helicopter eventually powered down as the second continued to slowly orbit the airfield. After about fifteen minutes, it landed on the other side of the lot. It soon shut down and everything was silent. We patiently waited for any word of progress.

"They found the door," my handler reported to me a little while later. "The Lieutenant will be back here soon."

I looked forward and saw the helicopter gunners scanning around. The pilot and copilot continued to sit while listening on their radios for updates. So far, the area seemed quiet, but a pair of Blackhawk helicopters were noisy. We could have easily drawn unwanted attention to us.

"Roger, *Oceans Eleven* up," my handler replied on his headset as Lieutenant Hoffman came into view and waved us out. We hopped out and jogged over to the area where they had dug out the secret doorway. It resembled a basement bulkhead door with a stairway leading down.

"Okay, Major, it's your gig now," Lieutenant Hoffman said as he gave me a flashlight and gestured to the stairway.

I counted twenty steps down before we encountered a steel door. Looking it over, I found the slot for the key.

"I need the key."

Lieutenant Hoffman reached into his bag and retrieved it. I inserted it and turned it clockwise once, and then counter clockwise twice. A clanking sound rang out and we all gave the door a push. A creak wailed and a single light on the ceiling turned on to reveal a room inside. It couldn't have been more than twenty feet by twenty, but it contained a heavy round door at the opposite end. It looked exactly like a bank vault door. I turned and shared a smile with Lieutenant Hoffman.

"Looking good," he said as we glanced around. The room was cold, smelled musty, and was dimly lit by an automatic light which likely ran on solar batteries. A small desk with a computer workstation was to the left side of the vault door.

"I hope this thing still works," I muttered as I looked it over.

"The clock is ticking, so you need to get this thing open." Lieutenant Hoffman then handed me my notebook, which drew a snicker from my handler.

"Not a fan?" I jokingly asked, which drew my first laugh from him. I still had no idea who the cartoon character on the cover was.

Major Paladin had dictated to me a detailed set of start-up instructions. I carefully followed them step by step, and the LED monitor came to life.

"I've got the computer going," I told Lieutenant Hoffman. "After I key in the start-up sequences, a large generator will turn itself on. You might want to alert your team in case they see or hear something. I'm not sure where this generator is, but I'm told it's pretty big and might make some noise."

"Is the fuel still going to be good?"

"It's supposed to be powered by a huge tank of propane."

"Our fucking tax dollars at work," Lieutenant Hoffman wisecracked before he called out a warning about the generator over his radio.

I sat, took in a deep breath, and turned to my handler in time to see him cross his fingers. I keyed in the start-up sequence, which triggered a series of numbers and screen changes. After the start-up sequence was complete, a single empty box was displayed on the screen. It was time to enter the combination sequences. There would be three in all, and I slowly entered the first two. I paused before entering the third. It was the longest of the three combinations.

"Can you read this out loud?" I asked Lieutenant Hoffman.

"Problem?"

"I need to get it right. If I botch it, there's no second chance. This thing will stay locked for good."

"That I can help you with," Lieutenant Hoffman agreeably replied as he picked up the notebook. "This line?"

"Yes," I replied as I turned to my handler. "Watch him to make sure he correctly recites them?"

"Gotcha. I'll echo each one."

Lieutenant Hoffman called out each number and letter in military phonetic code, while my handler repeated each one. I slowly keyed in the third password and we double checked it before I pressed the enter button.

When I did, a pair of warning strobes over the vault door lit up, accompanied by a buzzer. There was an area on the floor in front of the vault painted in bright yellow stripes. It became obvious that we needed to stay out of the striped area as the door slowly unlocked and swung open.

Lieutenant Hoffman's mood changed. He was quite pleased. "You fucking did it!"

Reports of faint smoke rising from a distant structure came in over his radio. The generator had started itself.

We passed through the vault door and walked down a hallway. It led us into a large control room, which was lined with dimly lit and idled workstations. I found the main workstation and sat.

"I'll need the USB flash drive."

Lieutenant Hoffman handed it to me with a pleasant smile. Suddenly, I was his best friend. After plugging it in, the main monitor started flashing a sequence of numbers and dialogue screens. All the workstations came to life.

"We have a heartbeat."

I consulted my notebook and was able to bring up a master inventory list on the large monitor. It was staggering. Even after spending a few minutes exploring all the sub-inventory lists, we could hardly believe what we read. I finally keyed up a map of the complex.

"Is this all real?" Lieutenant Hoffman asked.

"That's what it's telling us."

"Holy shit! This is all actually under us?"

"It used to be a vault for nuclear weapons, but they expanded it."

"Can we get our eyes on it?"

I pointed to a door at the side. "Through there, but you might want to wait until I find a map. Looks like we could easily get lost."

I found a PC tablet that contained schematics and took it with me. We spent the next couple of hours walking through the most overwhelming collection of inventory I could have ever imagined, and I had plenty of experience to imagine more than most. It made what we had in the Supermarket look like a broom closet. We walked through cavernous warehouses and saw things that made us wonder what wouldn't be found there. One section even contained several types of aircraft and helicopters.

"We hit the goddamn mother-load," Lieutenant Hoffman said with a beaming smile while he stared at a stack of F22 Raptor fighter-jets.

I quickly studied the operational aspects of the vault on the PC tablet as we took our tour. "According to this, everything is part of a fully-automated inventory management system."

"What does that mean?" the handler asked.

"It means we don't need to touch anything to get at it. We just key in what we want and the warehouse automatically retrieves it. There's a whole network of automatic forklifts and robotic cranes. It'll prep anything for shipment by rail at the main loading dock."

"Main loading dock? Where's that?"

"It's a little north of here and buried. There's a rail-line that runs right beside it."

"Why?"

"How do you think they got all this stuff up here? This system will even tell us how many and what type of rail-cars we need in order to ship whatever we select."

"Jesus, our government never did anything small."

I stopped walking as something new popped up on the tablet.

"What's the matter?" Lieutenant Hoffman asked.

"Unbelievable," I replied as I showed the tablet to him. "This place has massive storage tanks containing millions of gallons of crude oil. There's also a small built-in refinery. We can produce fresh fuels."

"Somebody pinch me."

* * *

Back on the surface, Lieutenant Hoffman called in the phrase: *Danny cracked the vault.* It was a simple code to indicate that the old

Loring airport was now the most valuable piece of real estate in the Maine Republic. Dozens of military vehicles transporting hundreds of soldiers streamed up the Maine Turnpike. More helicopters dropped off additional soldiers to protect the area until the Bangor reinforcements arrived. General Osgood came up with the second flight of helicopters and met up with me in the vault control room. I kept myself busy learning the systems and getting more detail on the inventory.

"Damn nice work, Major," General Osgood announced as he entered. "Lieutenant, I need the room alone with Major Paladin for a little while."

"Yes, sir."

"I was praying you were right about this," General Osgood said after everyone else left. "Now that I see it, I'm trying to wrap my mind around the extent of what this will do for us."

"Just do me a huge favor and use it wisely. I have a rather keen appreciation for this sort of thing. It's nothing like what we unearthed for the BSA Supermarket."

"The President is being briefed along with Senate committee leaders. It'll really be up to them. I only follow orders."

"Can you arrange for me to meet the President?"

"She's already requested a meeting with you as soon as you get back."

"Do you think I should tell her everything?"

"I already have. She's very impressed with you. I understand she's having Molly over for dinner this evening."

I chuckled. "Good for her. Now, what about getting all this inventory out of here?"

"We've put out the call for anyone with railroad experience. Inspection teams should start looking over the rails and bridges between Auburn and here very soon. There's plenty of mothballed rail equipment in the Auburn freight yard."

"Good. All we need to do is come up with a list of what you want shipped and the inventory system will determine which rail-cars and how many locomotives we'll need."

"We'll get it all here. We're burning up most of our fuel reserves to do it. Have you prepped the communication system?"

"Whenever you're ready," I said as I pointed over to a workstation at the back. "That's the comm station. I've already sent activation signals to the satellite network. Everything should be ready."

General Osgood smiled. "Let's see who's still out there."

I sat at the workstation and keyed up the communication protocols. "The first step is to broadcast a wake-up call. It'll hail any surviving U.S. military communication systems. Then we wait and see who answers. Ready?"

"Let it rip."

I keyed in the codes and triggered the signal.

"How long will it take?"

"Not sure. Paladin said to give it at least a couple of hours, maybe sooner. It basically sets off the alarm clock that should wake everyone up."

"And he was sure someone would be listening?"

"He told me that it was the only thing they'd be listening for, at least for five years. All foreign U.S. bases were to defend their facilities while waiting for orders on this communication network. Beyond that, I have no idea what might have survived out there."

We sat for a while and watched the monitor. Forty minutes went by before a return signal registered. General Osgood was on the other side of the control center working on a master list for the first shipment. I was fighting to stay awake at the comm workstation.

"Hey, we got a return!"

I immediately opened my notebook and General Osgood rushed over.

I grabbed the microphone. "This is Major Joseph Paladin, U.S. Army Phoenix Command. Authentication lima, bravo, niner, alpha, fife, niner, zulu. Please identify."

There was a pause before a reply came. "Phoenix Command, this is Colonel Howard, acting commander of Ramstein Air Base. Authentication alpha, one, niner, zulu. Please tell me I'm not dreaming."

The General and I shared big smiles. "Colonel Howard, I'm initiating a Phoenix initiative recall. Repeat, this is a recall. Your airbase destination is Bangor - Bravo, Golf, Romeo. Seabase destination is Portland, Maine. Please confirm."

There was another pause. It lasted longer than the first.

"Did we lose them?" General Osgood asked.

"I don't know—"

"Phoenix Command, this is Ramstein. Please confirm. Is this really happening?"

"This is Phoenix Command. The recall order is confirmed. It's time to come home."

"Sweet Jesus, thank you! We never thought we'd ever hear anything. What in the hell has been going on back there?"

"Colonel, it's not ideal, but we have a nice corner of the country left in Maine. What do you have left out there?"

"Ah, it's complicated. I have remnants from a couple dozen bases consolidated here. All branches are represented, along with some NATO units. The flu is history but law and order is breaking down around us. It's a complete mess over here in Europe and getting worse by the month. We hunkered down and held out. Not too much flying these days, but I can get a couple of Globemasters in the air."

"Any other assets?" I asked, after being prompted by General Osgood.

"Plenty, but we don't have the gas to put them in the air. The army has a lot of equipment here, too. I heard the Navy has some ships tied down in Gaeta, Italy. That's about all I can tell you."

"How many people do you have?"

"About six thousand, counting dependents."

CHAPTER 17

Over the next couple of days, more overseas military bases checked in and General Osgood took over coordinating the recall. A mass return was being organized. The use of aircraft would be minimal due to lack of fuel. All operating naval vessels were instructed to make room for as many people as they could fit. Many ships had to be left behind because they lacked the fuel to make the voyage home. The nuclear-powered aircraft carriers would become the new ocean-liners.

A week after I opened the vault, the first empty freight train made its way north. We restarted the rail loading system and programmed the first load to be assembled. It was comprised mostly of supplies and spare parts, we needed more time to deal with the heavier equipment. The rail-cars were automatically loaded and the train was configured. The trio of locomotives would haul a forty-car train back to Auburn. I requested to ride on the train back, mainly because I didn't want to take another helicopter trip. General Osgood happily granted my request and assigned Lieutenant Hoffman's insertion team to handle train security.

We set out late at night so that we'd make the trip in darkness. Several UAV's orbited above to keep a close eye on our route. Helicopters swept over high-risk areas to keep any trouble away. I rode in the lead locomotive with Lieutenant Hoffman. The rest of the team rode various freight cars to help guard our shipment. The trip was slow and uneventful, although we kept a vigilant watch for sabotage. A noisy, slow-moving freight train was a tempting target. There were plenty of fringe groups out there who might have gone out of their way to score such a prize.

Many of the regions we traveled through had been uninhabited even before the pandemic, but there was always the chance of encountering a stray group of paramilitary survivalists looking to score a huge windfall. There was one instance of suspicious activity while traveling through a remote area. An obstruction was discovered over the tracks in a place where it wasn't possible for a branch or tree to fall on them. The UAVs didn't pick anything up on their IR detectors, but an ambush was suspected. We slowed the train to a crawl while select team members hopped off to establish a perimeter around the area. Two soldiers soon removed a large branch and everyone got back on the train without incident. The train never came to a stop during the procedure.

It was early morning when we approached our destination at the Auburn freight yard. I decided to step outside and stand on the front railing as we slowly pulled in. A contingent of soldiers was there to greet us along with a few other government officials. I recognized one person in the small crowd right away: Kathryn.

"Well, look at you," Kathryn said as she greeted me with a long hug. "You look like you're in charge."

"I'm the ranking officer, technically."

"Technically? Technically you're not even an officer. You're not even in the same army."

"Ouch, thanks for the reminder."

"Someone has to keep you grounded."

"I heard you had dinner with the President. How did that go?"

Kathryn smiled. "It was very nice and so is she. I bragged a lot about you."

"Oh," I groaned. "More attention. Just what I need. I've been invited to see her, probably tomorrow."

"I think you'll like her."

"Did I ever tell you how much I hate politics?"

"Not really. Just relax and enjoy yourself. She's easy to talk to"

"Most politicians are."

"So did you really find a lot in the vault?"

"Remember the end of *Raiders of the Lost Ark*?"

"Never saw it."

"Well, I'll just say it made Tony's old vault look like a walk-in closet."

"Tony had a vault?"

"I keep forgetting how little we talked on our way up here."

* * *

The next morning I was picked up by a chauffeured car which took me to the capitol building in Augusta. I was summoned to meet with President Maureen Tillman and maybe stay for lunch if time allowed. I continued to play my identity as Major Paladin, which forced me to scramble in order to wash my uniform after the Loring trip. I hadn't anticipated having to assume Paladin's identity for as long as I did, so having only one uniform presented challenges.

The car dropped me off to a waiting aide who ushered me into a large office. At one time it had been elaborately decorated, but looters had stolen or trashed most of the expensive furniture and decor. It was now a collage of cheaper, generic furnishings. Despite its more modest appearance, the office still had an unmistakable bureaucratic feel to it. I had entered the realm of politics that I always tried to avoid. I attempted to relax myself by looking over several paintings, but they did little to calm me. A minute later, President Tillman entered, leaving a posse of aides at the door.

"Major, it's a real pleasure to finally meet you," President Tillman said as the door closed us in. She stepped closer and extended her hand for a handshake. She was in her late fifties, taller than I was, and had a surprisingly firm handshake. Her short silver hair highlighted her dark gray pantsuit. Her accent wasn't typical of Maine because she hadn't lived there long. She had relocated to Maine from Oklahoma a few years before the pandemic to work for a defense contractor. "Please sit. General Osgood filled me in, so you don't need to keep up appearances here."

"Yes, the General told me."

"And while we're on that subject, you'd better get used to being Joseph Paladin. It's going to be a long-term assignment."

"Why?" I grumbled, caught off-guard by the perception that Paladin's work was somehow unfinished.

"Well, for one, I don't think trying to revert to your true identity would go over very well. You know, that you're actually a defecting, high-ranking manager from a territory we all regard with a deep mistrust? But mostly, the Major's legacy is spreading faster than gossip at a potluck dinner. Currently, you're part Santa Claus and part Jesus Christ, which is giving our people a healthy dose of much-needed hope. That's something we haven't seen enough of lately."

"I'm not sure I'm comfortable with that."

President Tillman allowed a labored smile. "I understand your feelings. Politicians tend to regard truth as a tool instead of policy. I'm not a career politician myself, but I tend to be pragmatic. Do you know what I was in my PPL?"

"PPL?"

"That's our abbreviation for pre-pandemic life. I was one of those corporate lawyers who knew when to lie through my smile to protect something important. Trust me, Walt, this is one of those times when a well-placed lie will benefit everyone. We've been scraping by since the pandemic, and as much as that vault's a god-send to us, it still doesn't guarantee the improvements we all need. Progress requires management of perception, which can be far more important than what comes out of that vault. It's the perception that things will improve that will drive the actual improvements. So, like it or not, we all need to suck it up and keep Paladin's legacy going."

"But I expected it to be over. Now I have to continue this lie?"

"Most definitely. Besides, we wouldn't be spreading around any lies about what you really did. I might be asking you to maintain a false identity, but your accomplishments while playing the Major are quite real. We'd just be withholding all the other remarkable things you did as Walter Johnson."

"How did you--"

"Molly told me a lot about you, including when you first saved her from that close call in Waltham. Wow, too bad we can't share that one. It would've put a nice, big cherry on top of Paladin's image. But politics aside, I'm very impressed by the difficult decisions you've made and the sacrifices you endured before you became Major Paladin. It's hard to believe that someone like you came out of the BSA mafia."

"Thank you, but--"

"I know this isn't what you hoped for, but playing Paladin is the only condition I'm putting on you. Consider it an executive order, which also means you won't be handling it alone. We're all going to be equally invested in this charade. We'll help you to establish a plausible backstory and to navigate through any PR issues that might arise."

I recall shifting in my chair and thinking about how much I

desired to slip back into a quiet life. I suppose it was naive of me to think that I could just walk away after opening the vault.

"It's just that Paladin's mission was to try to pull the country back together. Honestly, I don't have any clue about how I'd even start to do that. He never got the chance to share that with me."

"I have absolutely no expectation that you'd take that on. Hell, I don't even know if that's possible. All I want to do is to begin here, in Maine. Let's cultivate something in our small corner of the world and see what happens."

I was bothered because the more I pondered her argument, the more reasonable it sounded. That's when I realized there was still too much of Walter Johnson with me. I was supposed to have left him behind at the border with Glenn.

"Okay, I'll play along."

A warm smile came to President Tillman's face. "Thank you. I know we don't have as much to offer as the BSA, but please let me know if there's anything we can do to show our appreciation."

"I just want to do something productive, in addition to being paraded around as some sort of hero."

"Well, that I can help you with. At the risk of upstaging General Osgood, I'd like to be the first to welcome you into the Maine Militia. Osgood will arrange a formal ceremony, but you'll be inducted at the rank of colonel and assigned to head up supply logistics. Your experience running a supply operation as big as the BSA needs to be put to work here, particularly after opening up that vault. I understand there are three more of these vaults around the country?"

"Yes, North Dakota is the closest."

"All out of reach. Well, we've got more than enough to keep us occupied. With the mass repatriation of former U.S. military personnel heading our way, we're going to be growing faster than anyone anticipated. There were many programs you ran in The Supermarket that we need to replicate. In particular, we need to grow more than just potatoes."

"You're aware of my old operation?"

"We kept tabs on the BSA, and yes, I was always jealous of your Supermarket. Forming something like that up here was impossible. It violated too many rights of prior property owners. We couldn't just march into places and grab anything we wanted. A legal process needed to be followed."

"That must have slowed things down."

"Yes, I'll be the first to admit that it dragged on us for a while, but I strongly believe we're a lot better off because of it. No matter how much of a pain in the ass it was, and at the risk of sounding like a wind-bag politician, it was important for us to respect the rights of individuals and reestablish a democratic form of government. We even wrote up a new constitution. I think it's a significant improvement over the old one, but you'd probably get an argument from a lot of our senators."

"I was always prodding Glenn to transition to an elected government. He always thought it was too soon."

"I had a long talk with Molly about what happened to Glenn. She feels awful about having to shoot him."

"She was put in a situation where she didn't have a choice."

"I agree. Awful. I can't imagine having to shoot someone dead."

"Both of us just want to move on from that part of our lives."

"Joe, you're among friends now. We want you to settle down, start over, and make a new home here. I'm also a bit old-fashioned, so please, marry that girl, will ya? She's a real gem."

"I know. Did she tell you who she really is?"

President Tillman laughed. "Oh, the secrets we're keeping. Our Senate ethics committee would have a conniption."

"Is all this putting you at too much risk?"

"Oh, please. It wouldn't be politics if we didn't have secrets."

"Can I ask one more favor?"

"Certainly."

"A close friend of mine escaped to Providence in order to help protect our secret. Is there any way to have him located and brought here? His name is Doctor Chung-Hee Kym, and he was Chief Surgeon at Boston General Hospital."

President Tillman leaned back in her seat. The expression on her face shifted to a look of concern. "Why didn't he come with you?"

"I wanted him to, but he insisted he would slow us down, particularly with his young daughter along. It was much easier to get them to Providence."

"I see. You're aware that Providence is a shit-hole that's hardly worth anything?"

"I know. The BSA always felt the same way. That's why it was easier to get them there."

"Well, I have to give you an answer you probably don't want to hear. I'll try to have them located, but honestly, that's about all we can do. Please don't get me wrong - I'd love to have someone like him up here, but we don't have the assets in place for a retrieval. It'll take a lot of effort just to find them. But in time, we'll see about getting them out."

"Wouldn't he represent a security threat if the BSA ever found him?"

President Tillman smiled. "He must be a very good friend. I admire your dedication to him, but in reality, any security threat he represented has lapsed. The BSA obviously doesn't know where he is, or Bradshaw would've had a little talk with you about the vault at the border, and you wouldn't be here with me now."

"I see."

"Joe, they should be safe if they stay put. They picked a place that nobody's really interested in. If we can find them, I'll see what can be done. I can't make any promises."

"I understand."

We talked more and had lunch together. Kathryn was right, I did like President Tillman. She was down to earth, tough, reasonable, and didn't apologize when she needed to throw a cold bucket of reality on you. Despite my turbulent experiences with Glenn, I quickly grew to respect her.

* * *

A week later, I put on my new uniform with the rank of colonel. General Osgood and I traveled up to Bangor International Airport to meet the first flight of returning military personnel from Ramstein Air Base, Germany. We stood out on the tarmac on a chilly day with a number of other officers and a band.

"A second supply train made it to Auburn," General Osgood said as we waited. "Our tech guys still haven't been able to find any trace of what we were looking for."

The General was referring to nuclear weapons. They didn't appear on any inventory list, nor on the master computer list from known facilities. He was alarmed that they weren't accounted for.

"I still think they intentionally separated and locked them away," I said with a nod.

"Oh, God, I hope so. If just one of those things got out we're all screwed."

"I'll keep looking."

General Osgood paused and looked around. "You know, Joe, I hope you realize that all this was your doing. Thousands are on their way home now because you took that first step back in Lunenberg to get here."

It was good timing that someone announced that the airplanes were on final approach, because I had no idea what to say to that. The avalanche I had started was picking up momentum and the true extent of it still hadn't sunk in.

The bright landing lights of the first transport plane came into view, followed by the hulking silhouette of a light gray-blue airplane. It touched down gently on the far end of the runway. Its engines surged to slow the plane as it passed by a long row of military vehicles filled with waving soldiers. A red pickup truck with a yellow strobe led the transport off the runway as the second aircraft came into view.

The fife and drum corps played an impressive rendition of something I didn't know the name of, which was soon drowned out by the loud whine of the engines as the plane rolled to a stop. The rear ramp opened and a group of people cautiously walked out. One soldier, holding his young daughter by her hand, dropped to his knees and kissed the pavement. Jubilant cheers erupted. Everyone broke rank and rushed to greet the returning soldiers. It was difficult not to get caught up in all the elation. Vigorous embraces, fist pumping, hooting, raised arms, and tears of joy followed. Most were total strangers to each other, but that day they acted like they were part of the same family. I stood beside General Osgood and watched the spontaneous reunion. The chain of events that had been planned became an impossibility. The General and I grinned and he shrugged his shoulders. He had no intention of stopping the joyous celebration to observe a more reserved ceremony.

A muscular black officer broke free of the throng around the airplane and approached General Osgood. He gave the General a bold salute.

"Sir, Colonel Howard reporting."

"Welcome home, Colonel," General Osgood replied with a return salute. "May I introduce you to our newly minted Colonel Joseph Paladin."

Colonel Howard stepped closer and started to salute, but instead he embraced me abruptly. It was the tightest squeeze I've ever experienced. Both of us had trouble holding our composure, but him especially. When he finally released his hold, tears were streaming down his cheeks.

"You're fucking Moses to us, you know," he managed to say in a raspy voice. "Thank you for leading us to the promised land."

The celebration was repeated for the second aircraft. Once Colonel Howard made it known to everyone who I was, a crowd surrounded me and clamored for a chance to express their gratitude. At one point I was almost lifted up on their shoulders. General Osgood stood and watched with a mischievous grin on his face. He enjoyed every second of me trying to endure my sudden fame.

I will never forget that day. It was one of the most joyous of my life.

* * *

There were parades and other celebrations as more airplanes arrived over the next couple of weeks. In early November, Kathryn and I traveled to Portland to help welcome the first ship to arrive. The massive aircraft carrier U.S.S. George H.W. Bush crept into the harbor, its flight deck covered with tents and shipping containers. Thousands of people came home that day, but no matter how hard I tried to stay inconspicuous, everyone seemed to know who I was.

Despite all the repatriation celebrations, I tried my best to settle into my new responsibilities. It took me a while to respond to my new name, Joe. Kathryn had a far easier time because she had been known as Molly for much longer. We found new homes around Auburn and got to spend more quality time together. Our relationship deepened and romance finally blossomed. We had occasional meals with President Tillman, who was delighted to see us as a couple. I also worked closely with General Osgood on a number of projects.

The inventory continued to stream out of the Loring vault. To this day I'm still blown away by how much had been packed in there and the massive effort it must have taken to stock it during the pandemic. I had a team of over two hundred managing the vault extraction and supply distribution around the Maine Republic. Besides the hundreds of vehicles, tanks, aircraft, ammunition, and support equipment, items came out of there that went well beyond military applications. The most important of these was the nano-tech manufacturing initiative. It would eventually completely change how things were made.

The winter was harsh, though, and even with the extra food and fuel from the vault, keeping everyone supplied was a challenge. Our population had swelled dramatically with the influx of returning military personnel and their surviving families. This included a number of foreign citizens seeking refuge alongside our returning soldiers. Still, for a vast majority of those who returned, our living standard was well above what they were accustomed to. I heard very few complaints.

* * *

By the end of May, my agricultural efforts were gaining traction. The militia's engineering corps was assisting and training a new generation of farmers. Fields were being cleared, prepared, and planted. Greenhouses were being set up everywhere.

General Osgood and the militia were busy pushing out into remote areas. At the same time, President Tillman expanded the police force to bring law back to places that had suffered under the harsh rule of paramilitary survivalists. There was no shortage of willing ex-military to become sheriff's deputies. All the notoriously violent gangs of survivalists that had plagued the remote areas were captured, killed, or driven away. Several tried to mount a guerrilla-style resistance. They were no match for our seasoned special forces teams who had once fought against insurgents in Afghanistan.

* * *

In early June, I was called into a special meeting with President Tillman and General Osgood. I had no idea what they wanted to talk about, and the fact that they didn't tell me ahead of time made me uneasy.

"Thanks for coming, Joe," President Tillman said as I entered her office. "Great to see you. How's Molly doing?"

"She's doing well, busy setting up a local greenhouse these days."

"Yeah, I hear you've been setting up farms everywhere."

"Just trying to grow more than potatoes."

President Tillman laughed. "Is the vault almost empty?"

"Pretty much so. We're mostly refining fuel there these days."

"You've been doing outstanding work, Joe," General Osgood said.

"I agree," President Tillman added. "Now we need your advice on something else. Please sit."

"Joe," General Osgood started as we sat, "We're planning to push out into New Hampshire and Vermont this summer."

"What do you mean?" I asked.

"We've decided to expand," President Tillman replied. "Very few people are left out there and there isn't any form of government to speak of."

"What happened to respecting the rights of property?"

"We're not going in to take things away from people but to assert control. We also have a lot of former New Hampshire and Vermont residents that would like to reclaim their properties. Above all, we want to claim the area before someone else does."

"Like the BSA?"

"Exactly."

"Are they getting ready to make a move?"

"No, not that we're aware of, but we wanted to get a reading from you on how you think they would react if we beat them there."

"I'm sure they won't like it, but I doubt they're in a position to do anything to stop us. They're not nearly as well equipped as we are."

"I know they're no match for our military these days," President Tillman explained. "But I'm trying to avoid hostilities. If we clash with them, it'll likely have a detrimental effect on future relations we want to establish in places like the Virginia Commonwealth. We don't want to be perceived as conquerors, but as a uniting presence. We want to start fulfilling what Major Paladin and the Phoenix Initiative set out to accomplish: pulling this country back together again."

"What can I do?" I asked. "I haven't really been keeping up with the BSA."

"Glenn Bradshaw's death set off a cascade of bloodletting," President Tillman explained. "It was only last month that we learned Richard Smithfield is now the leader."

"Smitty?" I said with a chuckle. "It figures."

"We know that you worked closely with him before," General Osgood said. "We were hoping that you could give us a read on him."

"Well, I think having Smitty in charge opens up a very big opportunity."

President Tillman smiled. "That's the type of thing I want to hear. How do you suggest we proceed?"

"I wouldn't go into New Hampshire or Vermont until you have a sit-down with Smitty. I think you should offer the BSA something radical. Give them the opportunity to become a part of the Maine Republic under our laws and protection."

"A merger?" President Tillman replied. "That's pretty bold. Do you think they'd even consider it?"

"Smitty's not stupid. He's going to understand that there's too much going against them if they don't. If he wavers, I'd be willing to talk with him and set him straight."

"I thought he warned you not to show your face down there," General Osgood cautioned.

"Yeah, don't you think that would be risky?" President Tillman added. "I'm not asking you to go down there."

"Yeah, but I know how to talk to him. He won't like it, but my being there will at least demonstrate how serious our deal is. I also have a couple of other ideas that should help."

President Tillman rose and paced in thought. "So you're thinking if we can get the BSA to join us, we can take New Hampshire and Vermont without objection?"

"I think the BSA is a key domino to push if you want to start reuniting this country. If they join us, we'll have Massachusetts, New Hampshire, Vermont, and probably a good part of Connecticut and upstate New York without anyone balking. Then you can start approaching the other regional governments with a more compelling case to join us."

President Tillman sat down with a wide smile. "If you help us pull this off, do you understand what this could lead to?"

"I think it's best we don't get ahead of ourselves," I cautioned. "Smitty may not be stupid, but he can be stubborn. It's not a sure deal."

* * *

It was July 5th when a special meeting was set up with the BSA, held at Hanscom airfield in Bedford, Massachusetts. It was bold to meet on their territory, but I thought it was ultimately beneficial to our strategy. They needed to feel secure and confident so that my special plan with General Osgood would have a more pronounced effect.

A flight of three Blackhawk helicopters brought in our negotiating and security teams. I was in one of the three helicopters as they set down in front of the old civilian air terminal. Thankfully, it was a shorter flight than my first trip up to the Loring vault, and we noticed a strong BSA military contingent waiting for us. That's when the first part of my plan with General Osgood was put into play.

As soon as our trio of helicopters landed, another pair swooped in from just over the treetops. They were heavily armed AH-64E Apache attack helicopters. They slowly circled the area so everyone could get a good look at them and the rockets slung under their pylons. They eventually settled to a landing further out on the tarmac. The message was sent. We might have been on their turf, but we brought big guns with us.

I stayed inside my helicopter while the negotiations took place. Newly-promoted Major Bill Hoffman sat with me and we made bets over how long it would take before I got called in. Two hours elapsed before someone came out to retrieve me. I won the wager.

"Are you really sure about this, sir?" Major Hoffman asked as he handed me a small radio.

"Don't worry," I reassured as I tucked it away in my pocket. "I've known this guy for a while."

"Okay, *SpongeBob*," Major Hoffman wisecracked, using a nickname he'd given me upon returning from Loring, "just don't make me come in there and rescue you. Molly will give me all kinds of shit if it ever comes to that."

I gave him a sly grin. "You're smart to be afraid of her."

I put on a cap to obscure my face and followed my BSA escort inside. I was checked for weapons and led into a bleak, empty room. Only one window let in narrow rays of sunlight to shine on its drab, gray walls. Smitty entered with his bodyguard a few minutes later.

"I was told you had something important for me."

I turned to him and took off my cap. "I most certainly do."

Smitty showed no reaction as he turned and nodded at his bodyguard. The dour bodyguard left us alone after giving me a quick look over.

"Holy shit, Walt?" Smitty fumed as soon as the door closed. "What the fuck is going on?"

"I guess your story about Glenn falling into a river was a pretty easy sell. Was General Anderson the first person you got rid of?"

Smitty laughed and shook his head. "Walt, I'd say it's been too long, but it really hasn't. Please tell me you're not going to make me regret letting you go."

"I'm actually here to do you a favor."

"Really? How's that?"

"Advice. Take the merger offer. It's the best you're going to get."

"Let's back the fuck up for a second. What the hell, Walt? Look at you. You're what, a colonel in the Maine Militia? Colonel Paladin? Is this you turning on me and the BSA?"

"It's not what you think."

"The hell it isn't!"

"Smitty, I know you think I'm a bit dim, but I'm trying to help you here. Maine is a lot stronger than you think."

"What, so you show up here with a few helicopters and think we're going to shit our pants?"

"You have no idea what you let walk away last summer. Want to see a little something of what you let slip through your fingers?"

Smitty rolled his eyes. "Do I have a choice?"

I smiled and got out my radio. "Commodore flight, this is Ambassador-Two. Are you in position?"

"Affirmative, Ambassador-Two. Commodore flight is on station."

"Commodore flight, gates out, now, now, now."

"Affirmative, Commodore flight is inbound. Hold on to your nuts."

"What the fuck was that all about?" Smitty asked as I pocketed my radio.

"Why don't you go out and get some air? Keep an eye to the north."

Smitty snickered at me as he left the room. I watched from the window as he exited the building and looked around the sky. Soon, three groups of fighter jets came streaking overhead at near tree-top level. Everyone standing with Smitty didn't see them until they were almost overhead. The thunderous roar of their engines in afterburner shook the building. Everyone instinctively ducked while covering their ears. The jets were gone as quickly as they arrived.

Smitty came back into the room with a sheepish look and a ciga-rette hanging from his lips. "Subtle."

"I thought that might bring some clarity to the situation."

"Where did all that shit come from?"

"Maine had more treasures hidden away than anyone ever thought, and I knew where to dig."

Smitty bit his lip and chuckled. "I always wondered if it was more than a nice piece of ass that led you up there."

"Yeah, but Kathryn alone would've been worth it."

Smitty took a long drag on his cigarette. "All right, you have my attention. So what do you want for all this generosity?"

"Just merge with the Maine Republic and step down. That's it."

"Step down?" Smitty echoed with a chuckle. "That's all?"

"No strings attached."

"And if I don't?"

"Come on, Smitty, think it through. Even I know what would happen. It'll get ugly in a hurry. We can have hundreds of Humvees, tanks, and APCs storming over the Tobin Bridge by the end of the day. But it'll start with a volley of cruise missiles launched by ships that no one will ever see. Then all the jets roaring overhead will start the real panic. You know how crazy things get when it looks like authority is breaking down. Your organization will evaporate within an hour as they run for Provi with half the BSA chucking stones at them. Then there's all the looting that will follow. We'd rather not start things off like that. I don't want to see good people hurt or killed."

Smitty sighed, looked out the window, and took another drag on his cigarette. I hadn't seen that look of concern on him since the time he sat in my office and pleaded with me to forget about the civilian slaughter in Westford. "Do you know how many people will line up to cap my ass the minute I step down?"

"You mean you left people alive that would?"

"Oh, you're fucking hilarious."

"I heard you cleaned house and made a new bridge over the Charles with all the bodies."

Smitty smirked. "You know how it is around here. Oh, wait, you don't. Glenn took care of that for you."

"Look, you'd have my word that we'd relocate you somewhere safe."

"Where? Cow Hampshire? No suh, I'm not going to get stuck out in the fucking woods. I'll make my own arrangements if I decide to step down."

"Your choice. I'm just trying to help."

"Jesus," Smitty lamented as he looked out the window. "I can't fucking believe this. I finally get somewhere after years of shoveling someone else's shit and this falls on me."

"Karma's a bitch, isn't it?"

Smitty blurted a laugh. "Look at you with a shiny new sense of humor to go with your new set of brass balls."

"Smitty," I pleaded in a somber tone, "Please don't let change run you over. You know I wouldn't do anything to tee you up for the vultures."

"I'll think about it," Smitty muttered, dropped his cigarette on the floor, and headed for the exit. Then he stopped and turned back to me. "Oh, there was something I meant to tell you last summer. I decided not to, considering what had happened to Glenn. Back when you first bolted and everyone started looking around, we found someone else trying to escape. Your friend, the doctor from Boston General, was caught just outside of Provi. The stupid sonofabitch tried to run but was shot dead. He wouldn't surrender. I'm sorry that happened. I liked him. He was a good shit."

It felt like I had just been kicked in the stomach. I turned to the window to collect myself.

"Actually," Smitty continued, "it turned out to work in your favor. All our search parties were pulled south thinking that you were with him. It probably gave you a couple more days to get further away. It also gave Glenn some time to cool off and calm General Anderson down. I don't think things would've turned out the same if we caught up with you earlier. Anderson was so pissed that he wanted you shot on sight."

"What about the doctor's daughter?"

"She wasn't with him."

I nodded while staring out the window. "Thanks for telling me."

Smitty exited. I remember standing there for a minute before I looked down and stepped on Smitty's cigarette to extinguish it. I walked out, returned to my helicopter, tried to step in, but I suddenly couldn't get my legs to work. Major Hoffman hopped out to see what was wrong.

"You okay, sir?"

"I don't know. I can't get in. Something's wrong with my legs."

He turned back to the helicopter cabin. "Can I get some help here?"

It was the last thing I remember hearing before I got dizzy and blacked out.

* * *

I woke up that evening in a hospital bed back in Maine. The first face I saw was Kathryn. Her smile beamed and she gently put her hand on my cheek.

"Hey, are you okay?" she asked.

It took a few seconds before my memory returned and a terrible melancholy came crashing down on me.

"He's gone."

"Who?"

"They shot Chung-Hee."

Her face crinkled and she pulled me into her arms. We held each other over the next hour. I was still in such a state of shock that I couldn't even shed a tear. General Osgood was waiting outside, took one look into the room, and knew something terrible had happened. He left us alone to console each other.

The doctors found nothing physically wrong with me. I was referred to a psychiatrist who had a long visit with me and was ultimately concerned about PTSD. I was embarrassed that I had to talk to a shrink and found the whole experience uncomfortable. It was something I didn't take very seriously at the time. I just wanted to get back to work.

The loss of Chung-Hee was devastating. It took me weeks to get over the initial shock, and I grieved for a long time after that. I had always expected that we'd meet up again once he was located and the situation improved. I thought of him every time I helped allocate medical supplies to our hospitals. I had been looking forward to helping find him a new practice and had even talked with some of the hospital administrators. They were all eager to meet him.

I eventually learned that his daughter, Soon-Yi, was alive and safe. She had been separated from Chung-Hee as he tried to lead the BSA search team away from her. Their underground contact found her and took her to the church that was supposed to help them get settled. The reverend took her in and raised her as part of his own family. I didn't get a chance to see Soon-Yi for a while, and she was a young woman by the time I met up with her. It was an emotional reunion for both of us. She became a doctor a couple of years later and took up a residency at the New Providence General Hospital. I know Chung-Hee would have been proud of her. I certainly am.

* * *

Soon after our meeting, Smitty agreed to step down and merge the BSA with the Maine Republic. It took several weeks to stabilize the area and start organizing a new government. Meanwhile, General Osgood ordered the militia to charge into New Hampshire and Vermont. They met with practically no resistance and easily took control. Our forces soon took most of upstate New York and western Massachusetts. The only governing entity in the area, the Buffalo Consortium, freely joined us.

By the end of the summer, the Maine Republic stretched as far south as Hartford, Connecticut, and north into New Brunswick. The Montreal and Quebec territories were also eager to join. We were growing at a frightening pace. Word was out that we were the biggest kid on the block, which tended to blunt notions from any other territories about giving challenge.

* * *

On a warm, beautiful September day, I proposed to Kathryn. President Tillman had been putting a great deal of pressure on me to propose and even jokingly declared that she would compel me under executive order if I waited any longer. I took Kathryn to Ogunquit and proposed to her on the beach. She accepted before I even had a chance to finish proposing, quipping that playing Paladin came with long-winded speeches. We planned to have a wedding sometime in the following summer.

In the fall, our crops yielded more than anticipated. The influx of returning overseas personnel had dwindled to a trickle, but the population surge was still taxing our food supplies. The greenhouses were still developing and needed a bit more time to produce significant quantities of food. The BSA food surplus was able to fill the shortfall. It also helped that I knew their system. The final acting Supermarket manager was perplexed by how well our liaisons understood how things worked. There was nothing they could hide from us. By the following summer, the Supermarket was disbanded.

By the end of the year, we were in merger negotiations with the Virginia Commonwealth, the Great Lakes Alliance, and Chicagoland. There was an exodus of refugees out of Providence because most were convinced that our tanks were going to roll in there at any minute. We didn't bother with them until the following year when they threw a parade to welcome us. So far, military conflict had been avoided. President Tillman was working a miracle.

There was also no sign of any surviving United States leadership. Visits to the Virginia Commonwealth were held in Richmond because Washington, D.C. was in ruins. Gangs had run amok and destroyed just about everything in sight. The cultural losses were devastating, as the city museums and monuments were looted and burned. Very little survived in our lawless former capital before the Commonwealth finally asserted control. It would never regain its former glory. The new country would be run from Maine.

Almost lost in all the activity was a small piece of news that Smitty had disappeared. It wasn't a surprise to most, but I found it sad. The circumstances behind his disappearance were murky, but it was well known that he had many people seeking revenge on him. Some thought that he was somewhere at the bottom of Boston Harbor, but most couldn't have cared less about what happened to him. I have no idea what fate he met. I never saw or heard from him again.

I had always liked Smitty more than most people did and probably more than many think he deserved. He was smarter than many gave him credit for, but he was ultimately brutal in his short stint as leader of the BSA. In the end, Smitty had obtained the position that he was always angling for but quickly lost it in the bigger picture. Progress pushed him aside. All published accounts of his brief but bloody purge cast a decidedly negative light on his legacy, but there was always a troubling truth about it which many historians are reluctant to admit. Smitty's violent clean-out inadvertently paved a smooth road for the Maine Republic by eliminating several troublesome characters who would've given us a difficult time during the merger.

The lone area of instability was New York City. Millions there had already died, victims of the pandemic and the horrible aftermath. Nobody could be sure of how many died of what cause, because the city was engulfed in a nightmarish mishmash of gangs who fought endlessly with each other. For years they were ensnared in wave after wave of oppressive violence, and very few escaped the carnage.

Finally, a single gang emerged to control everything east of the Hudson River. They would proudly call themselves the Long Island Kingdom. Stories of their atrocities were appalling. The few refugees who escaped during their reign told us frightening and gut-wrenching stories that hardly seemed imaginable. If we were to believe the reports, something horribly depraved dwelt in the pock-marked landscape of the Big Apple.

CHAPTER 18

The following spring our military units formed a blockade around the newly minted Long Island Kingdom, or The Kingdom, as we came to call it. We established a forward base in White Plains, New York to help keep everything bottled up down in Manhattan, as well as several other outposts to keep everything on The Kingdom side of the Hudson River. I was called in to help with an anticipated round of negotiations. I'm not sure why, but I suspect it was to demonstrate our seriousness by bringing in a name they seemed to know. My reputation over helping merge the BSA into the Maine Republic was known even to them.

Tensions were high because The Kingdom proved to be aggressive and unpredictable. Most of the scouts we sent in never made it back, and the couple that survived urged us to nuke the place and move on. I was convinced that most of the stories they told were exaggerations. Despite all the horror I had seen up to that point, the reports seemed too outlandish and grotesque to believe. They were later proven to be accurate.

Maureen Tillman was in her final year as President. She had decided not to seek reelection because of exhaustion and shifts in the political landscape, mainly due to the addition of new territories. The Kingdom was a thorn in her side. Peaceful solutions to that issue constantly eluded her. She was running out of ideas on how to handle them without resorting to violence. Her patience was wearing thin, and with the threat The Kingdom represented to future territory mergers, she was politically forced to take a tougher position with them.

We had successfully negotiated several trade agreements with southern territories that produced and refined oil. It allowed us to fuel many idled naval vessels, several of which continued to make trips to our old foreign military bases. They retrieved any remaining personnel, but they also brought back equipment that base commanders couldn't bear to leave behind. We recovered so much military hardware and ordnance that we ran out of storage facilities. It augmented our already strong military, which at the time was arguably the most potent in the world.

A fight was brewing with The Kingdom and our willingness to employ a military solution was at an all-time high. By the time I reached White Plains, I sensed something terrible on the horizon.

I met up with General Osgood and we prepared to travel to a designated no-fire zone located at the edge of the Woodlawn Cemetery, a few miles south of our base. We were supposed to meet with a negotiating team from The Kingdom to discuss a treaty. No one really knew what to expect. Several of these meetings had been set up before, but the representatives from the other side always failed to show up. In one case, our negotiation team had been ambushed.

Our convoy of armored personnel carriers rolled down Route 87 to the East 233 street exit. That's when a frantic call came in from our forward patrol that they were taking fire. A UAV soon detected a large force of Kingdom raiders swarming into the cemetery. That's when I saw General Osgood reach for his radio with the angriest look I've ever seen from him. He was always a highly disciplined officer who kept his temper in check.

"This is White Plains Actual, execute *Dark Thunder*! Repeat, execute *Dark Thunder*!"

Our convoy stopped and waited. Ten miles away, nearly fifty pieces of artillery and missile launchers fired off their salvos. Over the years, I've been asked numerous times if this was the point when I took over one of the fifty-caliber machine-guns and started gunning down Kingdom raiders. I'm not sure how that exaggeration got started, but the only shots our convoy fired came from the lead Stryker APC. It provided short bursts of cover fire as our forward patrol sped out of the cemetery. I never touched a weapon. In fact, I never even saw a Kingdom raider that day. We never got that close to them.

(In order to settle a number of exaggerations on that subject, I will here and now state that I have never once fired a weapon in combat. In fact, this was the one and only time I was ever close to a combat zone.)

Once our forward patrol sped past us, I looked up, hearing a chorus of shrieking and roaring noises. Hundreds of projectiles rained down on the cemetery. Some exploded on contact while others detonated above the ground and sent hundreds of smaller explosive projectiles shooting down. I felt countless percussion thuds rock our APC and reverberate in my chest. I've never seen or felt such an awesome display of firepower in my life. I fought dizziness and nausea as I held my hands over my ears. Within a minute, dozens of acres were consumed in exploding ordnance. Hundreds of attacking Kingdom raiders were instantly blown to shreds or vaporized. Our convoy backtracked to the highway and left a massive wall of billowing smoke behind us.

The Dark Thunder order set off a larger chain of events. By the time we returned to the White Plains base, large formations of aircraft were converging on Manhattan Island. This included dozens of bombers along with smaller combat aircraft. They blanketed the remnants of New York City with thousands of bombs. We could hear what sounded like a constant rumble of thunder in the distance. I had never heard so many aircraft fly overhead, even before the pandemic. The bombardment would last for the rest of the day at a near constant pace.

At night, the horizon was lit up by several firestorms ignited by the bombings. Flashlights weren't needed on that windy night as we watched Manhattan burn to the ground. I was later told that the firestorms caused the wind as they drew in fresh air to feed their intense appetites. The blistering infernos raged for several days, and it took a couple of months for them to completely burn out. Nothing survived. Even those who had sought shelter deep underground were found dead. The fires had sucked all their oxygen away.

History has marked this event as the most controversial action of the young American Confederation. General Osgood and President Tillman were eventually scrutinized by several Senate committees. They were not found negligent, but lingering doubts always dogged their contentious decision. General Osgood never talked to me about it, but I know it deeply affected him. It had not been an order he was ever proud of giving.

Many historians and pundits have interpreted General Osgood's

so-called initial flash of anger to be motivated by revenge, outraged
over once again being duped by The Kingdom. I strongly disagree
with this assessment, because I know he wasn't the type of person
who let his anger control the larger decisions. He expected this
behavior from The Kingdom, and it was his frustration that boiled
over because of it. Despite giving The Kingdom one last chance to
make a peaceful settlement, one last chance to prove they could
change direction, they instead followed a predictable pattern of
treacherous behavior. Their actions forced General Osgood to give an
order that he didn't want to, but had to.

President Tillman was a bit more forthcoming with me in the following years. After stepping out of politics, Kathryn and I got to
know Maureen much better. She would occasionally talk about that
terrible decision, but even she had her limit. Her reluctance to fully
discuss it wasn't due to confidentiality issues - she trusted me with
many other sensitive issues which probably shouldn't have been
shared. It was because she was privy to such disturbing information
about The Kingdom, she felt it was best never to repeat it. One of the
few unreleased facts she did share with me was how our captured
spies were treated. I won't get into the gruesome details of the
grotesque tortures inflicted on them, but after their eventual executions, they were consumed. It was part of a bizarre cannibalistic ritual
to make their warriors stronger by absorbing the essence of their
enemy.

From my vantage point, the Dark Thunder operation was deeply
unsettling. Untold thousands died in the bombing and New York
City vanished from the face of the earth. The lingering question
through the years has always been was it really necessary? The Big
Apple had been deeply scarred by several years of conflict, and many
thought we mercifully put it out of its misery. To be perfectly honest,
as appalling as it was to watch, I have to reluctantly agree that the
destruction was an unfortunate necessity. The unspeakable atrocities
committed by The Kingdom are well corroborated. Their nean-
derthal-like raiders and Machiavellian politics were about to be
turned loose on a young and fragile Confederation. If we had allowed
them to continue unchecked, it would've undermined our recent
mergers and probably sparked a civil war. I don't think our new Confederation would've endured under those circumstances.

Dark Thunder became a watershed event, as it drove many other territories to pursue peaceful merger negotiations. Doubts about our military strength were extinguished. It became clear that we possessed enormous firepower, and we had, when threatened, demonstrated the will to use it. I'm thankful that we've never had to unleash our military might like that again.

* * *

I went back home a couple of days later and took some time off to process everything I'd experienced. Kathryn watched me wander around my apartment in a state of near shock. I had just been moving past the death of Chung-Hee when this dreadful event had dropped into my lap. Kathryn thought I should seek counseling, but I was resistant to that idea. After a week, I went back to work but was quickly reaching a breaking point.

Kathryn was deeply concerned and contacted General Osgood, who sat me down in his office that same day. He ordered me to seek out psychiatric help and arranged an appointment with a trusted military doctor. I was a bit upset with Kathryn for going behind my back but soon saw that she was looking out for me in ways that I truly needed. The appointments helped and I was able to confront issues I never knew I struggled with. This also led to some needed changes.

Kathryn and I talked about everything that I was dealing with. We came to an inescapable conclusion that I had reached my limit. I felt that I didn't have anything more to contribute to the rebuilding efforts and she didn't feel compelled to tell me otherwise. Our nation was moving forward and entering a new phase of growth. The scale of this growth, and the new challenges that came with it, called for a far more refined set of skills than I possessed. I was fatigued from what I had already contributed. The usefulness behind the symbol of Joseph Paladin had peaked. It was time for me to step off the stage and slow down our lives.

I told General Osgood what Kathryn and I had discussed and decided.

When I was done, he smiled, rose, and shook my hand. "Joe, you've done more for us than anyone could have ever imagined. I can't argue with your decision because it makes too much sense. I've been thinking the same thoughts myself."

"You'd retire too? I couldn't imagine things working around here without you."

"Well, maybe not retire right away. There's still a little more work ahead of me." General Osgood paused and stepped over to a minibar in the corner of his office. He took out a couple of glasses and poured a small serving of brandy in both. He handed me one glass while he raised the other. "To Major Paladin."

"To the Major," I echoed as we drank a toast.

"Now I'm going to get terribly sentimental on you. Paladin's mission was to rebuild this country and it's remarkable what you've helped to start. I have no doubt he'd be overjoyed at what you've accomplished. Hell, I'm very proud of what you've pulled off. You more than deserve a rest. Go get married and raise a family. That's what this world needs right now."

* * *

President Tillman reluctantly agreed to my plan. She was sad to see me step down, but she was heading in the same direction and understood. It was time for a new generation of leaders to take up the reunification effort.

"I've already told this to General Osgood," President Tillman said to me in her office, "but my last order to you as President is to remain Joseph Paladin. The true story behind your odyssey must be kept secret."

"Are you serious? I can't be Walter Johnson ever again?"

"Joe, let's be realistic. Ongoing reunification efforts are extremely fragile. If the truth about Paladin came out now, it could easily blow-up into a devastating political scandal. It would undermine the trust that we've worked so hard to build in our government."

"Politics again," I grumbled.

"Consider it the price of being a hero."

"For how long?"

"At least twenty-five years."

"Twenty-five years?!"

"People should be a bit more understanding at that point, but I'm going to leave that to you."

"Leave what to me?"

President Tillman sighed and leaned back in her chair. "Brendan and I will probably be dead by then, or too senile to care, so it'll be up to you to determine if the country is ready to hear the truth. If you think the time is right, you can write a book and make a fortune. If not, stay silent and the secret will die with you."

I sighed and looked around her office which had been redecorated the month before. "I don't think I'm comfortable making that call."

"Well," President Tillman said with a wide smile, "the good news is you've got twenty-five years to get comfortable with it."

"What about your legacy?"

President Tillman laughed. "Oh, I won't be caring about it at that point, and I'm sure Brendan won't either. Being dead tends to change your priorities."

I paused, gazed into her eyes, and saw a familiar determined look. "I don't have a choice in this, do I?"

"I'm issuing a sealed executive order."

"What? You don't trust me?"

"You misunderstand. It's for your protection. It'll shield you from prosecution, if you decide to say anything after twenty-five years."

"Okay, you win," I reluctantly conceded.

"Good, then our bodyguard of lies will remain in place."

* * *

My retirement date was set for mid-August. That allowed me plenty of time to transition my responsibilities to other officers. I also designated several alternates who could open the remaining three vaults when they became accessible.

The only major item of unfinished business was our search for the disposition of nuclear weapons. It was clear that another directive had been put into motion at the same time Phoenix was initiated. While untold tons of equipment and supplies were being routed to the vaults, the entire nuclear arsenal of the United States had been moved somewhere else. This included nuclear material from all idled nuclear power generators and nuclear submarines. Only a few surviving military personnel could confirm the movement of nuclear material during the final days, but no one knew where it all went. One of my last tasks was to come up with a list of possible sites to investigate.

Kathryn and I also had a wedding to plan and the end of August was a perfect time to schedule it. I would be retired and have plenty of time to start a new life with her. Our plan was radical. After the wedding, we would relocate far from our old lives. I had grown up outside of Chicago, and since that region was now part of the Republic, I sought out places to live in that area. Kathryn was equally as eager to start fresh somewhere new.

I wanted to first settle a couple of details. The biggest was the restoration of the Lexington Battle Green. It was easy to obtain a presidential order and get the work started. It took a couple of years to restore the area and I saw pictures of the progress. However, I never saw the finished project in person. In fact, neither Kathryn or I ever went back to Massachusetts. It was not out of fear that anyone would've recognized me. Most who dealt with me as the boss of the old Supermarket were dead, victims of Smitty's intensely violent clean-out of the Bradshaw regime. Anyone else who knew the name Walter Johnson wouldn't remember a face to go with it. Regardless of how safe it would've been to go back, neither of us felt any urge to make a visit. There was nothing there for us to go back to. It belonged to a past that we didn't want to dredge up.

* * *

August came and I gladly retired. General Osgood threw me a retirement party at the Capitol. It was a formal affair involving many familiar faces and countless others I maybe met once or twice. During the ceremony, I was awarded the Republic's Medal of Honor. It was the highest honor that could be bestowed on a military officer and I was the first to ever receive it. The special forces team that accompanied me to the Loring vault stood beside me while I was awarded the medal. Major Hoffman and the team later presented their own medal to me: *the SpongeBob Legion of Merit*. I'd never laughed so hard in my life.

I have to admit that, although I dislike the attention my past exploits typically draw, I really enjoyed receiving that Medal of Honor. It was a symbol of what I, Kathryn, Chung-Hee, and others had really accomplished. My medal is still in a small frame sitting in the middle of my desk. I see it every morning and think of all the people who paid the ultimate price to help bring back civilization.

I said my farewells and breathed a sigh of relief that I no longer had to act the part of a military officer. Although I had become proficient at keeping in character, I was most satisfied that I had completed Major Joseph Paladin's mission. It probably wasn't with the same bravery, skill, and finesse the real Major would've employed, but I helped get the job done.

Our wedding came next, which was the crescendo to our year. It too was held at the Capitol at the insistence of President Tillman. Kathryn looked stunningly beautiful in her gown. Up to that point, I'd never seen her dress up so nicely, and she took my breath away. Countless pictures were taken and she was later offered a modeling job. We had a good laugh over that because we both knew the primary motivation was to exploit our name. However, Kathryn really enjoyed being glamorized for that occasion, and reading the numerous press accounts comparing her to past royalty brought a special smile to her face.

Our good friend President Maureen Tillman presided over the ceremony and married us on that hot afternoon. She later confessed to us that it was the most meaningful thing she had done in a long time. We were the first and only couple she ever married.

A presidential limousine took us to the airport in Bangor so we could board a private jet to Chicago. We enjoyed every minute of luxury on that Gulfstream jet. It was the only honeymoon we would have, or really wanted. There really wasn't much to do for a vacation in those days. Neither of us was particularly fond of the beach because the water was always so cold. The only other option was camping in the mountains, which did not appeal to us at all.

CHAPTER 19

Kathryn and I entered a new phase of our lives which would last for decades. The majority of it was spent out of the public eye, and without further dramatic exploits, it was the time we cherished the most. Our new frontier was something that wouldn't garner any headlines, nor make for a thrilling read.

We settled in a suburb of Chicago called Glen Ellyn. Like countless towns, it was in the midst of rebuilding when we moved into a sizable, reclaimed home. I suppose it was unrealistic to think we could escape our notoriety, as everyone around us knew who we were. Our neighbors were nice about it, and Kathryn was always far more gracious about handling the extra attention than I was. The people there were different, more open and friendly than we were used to.

Life finally slowed down for us. We took the first few months to settle in and got to know everyone in town. I enjoyed learning to play golf, to fish at a small local pond, and simply to relax. Our new friends, who loved to go camping in the woods of Wisconsin, were always puzzled by our lack of interest. I'm sure Wisconsin is nice, but sleeping in a tent was something Kathryn and I never wanted to experience again.

General Osgood kept me in the loop about any developments in his hunt for nuclear weapons. It was an unresolved mystery and he continued to seek out my advice. I didn't mind helping him at all, and we'd spend hours in video conference reviewing the latest intelligence reports. General Osgood had no surviving family and was totally dedicated to this one remaining assignment. Also, I think he simply enjoyed talking to me. Kathryn and I were among the few who he held in high regard, and he missed having us around. I also enjoyed a good mystery, and there was no one better than Brendan

Osgood to partner with for the investigation. He had a very keen mind.

Former President Tillman dropped in for visits. It was nice to be able to sit and have an extended conversation without interruption. She looked far more relaxed in those days. Retirement did her good.

As we settled into a quiet life, I had time to reflect back on everything I had been through. The more I pondered over my exploits, the more questions arose. How had I managed to get through it? Could anyone really be that lucky? What did it all mean?

At that point, I'd always come back to something Chung-Hee had told me on the evening after I shared my encounter with Major Paladin with him. He insisted that I was clearly chosen to carry on that task. I knew he was talking about God, but I just didn't believe that I could have anything to do with something like that. I wasn't religious, so why would God have any interest in placing such a huge responsibility in my hands? Why not just continue it in the far more capable hands of Major Paladin? It just didn't make any sense to me. At the same time, I couldn't reconcile how the numerous fortuitous coincidences in my life could be simply attributed to blind luck.

I came to an acceptance that Chung-Hee and Major Paladin shared a faith I couldn't comprehend; yet I couldn't escape how profoundly it had affected my life. So I decided to seek out what drove their incomprehensible attitudes and conduct. I wanted to find out what had caused a highly trained and seasoned officer, on the verge of death to place so much trust in a complete stranger. I wanted to understand why a skilled neurosurgeon saw so much worth in someone who was involved in some highly questionable acts.

Maybe it was out of a sense that I owed them something, but one day I told Kathryn that I wanted to start attending a local church. She was totally surprised but delighted. She had grown up in a traditional Catholic family that faithfully attended church at least once a week. While she rebelled against it in her teenage years, she yearned to get back on track. However, she was less than thrilled over my choice of churches. I had settled on a modest Protestant Church in the next town. After a brief protest, and with some prodding, she attended weekly church services with me. It didn't take long for it to grow on her, despite lacking the traditional sacraments of Catholicism.

My search for answers began.

Life also went on. Kathryn found work doing what she loved at a local greenhouse. She had always enjoyed cultivating, studying, and developing advanced greenhouse techniques. We also got a pleasant surprise the following spring. Kathryn was pregnant.

* * *

Our young nation progressed and grew. Several new territories joined what had been recently renamed *The New American Confederation*, soon commonly called the NAC. Waves of reunification and rebuilding swept across the old country, which kept everyone busy trying to shape something new and better than before. The nano-tech manufacturing processes we had brought out of the Loring vault dramatically changed our industrial output. They provided an important foundation to hasten the rebuilding process. Nanorobotics was capable of fashioning almost anything out of the abundance of rubble and junk.

General Osgood eventually gained access to the remaining three vaults. What he reported astonished me. None of the newly opened vaults had nearly as much stored in them as the Loring vault. Apparently, Loring was the first vault to be prioritized. By the time the pandemic had crippled the infrastructure, the Phoenix supply initiative had shut down before completely filling the other three vaults. It was yet another fortuitous coincidence to put on my list to ponder over.

The flu strain that had triggered the pandemic had completely disappeared, much like it had back in 1918. There are no shortage of theories, but most scientists agree that it simply mutated into a less harmful variant. It's currently estimated that the flu was directly responsible for the death of five-hundred million worldwide. More tragically, nearly three billion more died in the aftermath due to other diseases, violence, hunger, exposure, and suicide. Industrialized nations seemed to take the brunt of these losses, because once modern conveniences broke down, people lacked the skills, strength, and social willingness to quickly adapt in order to produce basic life-sustaining staples.

Globally, all nations suffered during the pandemic. For a long while it was difficult to assess what had transpired in other countries.

At first we had a good handle on most of Europe and the United Kingdom, but it took longer to establish communication with regions like the Russian Federation, the Middle East, and China. China was particularly hard hit and had fragmented into numerous provinces. They took nearly as long as we had to reunite. Once they did, they eventually became an adversarial superpower, much like Russia had been during the Cold War.

Trade was slowly reestablished and we were no longer a country that relied on imports. Our new manufacturing processes allowed us to recycle most materials. The ruins of our past supplied the materials to rebuild our nation and to fuel a thriving export market. We were the first nation to start producing complex products and technologies, which helped other nations to get back on their feet. Our best friend in the world, the United Kingdom, was our first priority. They weathered the pandemic storm with remarkable poise.

* * *

Justice also progressed. Prisons were filled with those who were charged with what the justice system called P.P.A. (Post-Pandemic Atrocities). The day of reckoning was at hand for those surviving criminals who had taken advantage of the helpless. Special tribunals were formed to handle the overload of cases. Many books and case studies were written over the years about the worst offenders. I've read a few, they were truly sad and disappointing accounts of just how far the depravity of the human race had progressed during that time. One thing I can conclude for those of us who lived during that period is that it either brought out the best or the worst in us all. There was little middle ground, and it seemed for a time that the worst outnumbered the best. While things looked grim, I'm thankful that eventually more of us became better in order to overcome the many who had descended deep into degeneracy.

I'm particularly amused at those books about Smitty. I hope my first-hand account will clear up the many misconceptions that have been spread around about him. It's too bad, however, that Glenn Bradshaw has so far escaped the interest of authors.

* * *

Glen Ellyn was growing and I was spending my spare time

helping people to restore their homes. We formed a group who helped finish projects around houses of those who lived by modest means. I never tired of doing that sort of work. It reminded me of the secret supply drops I had arranged for The Pit. In fact, one of my fondest memories was seeing the expression on Chung-Hee's face when I took him the antibiotics for Soon-Yi. I've seen that same expression often here and I always look forward to it.

Our first son was born and we named him Brendan Walter Paladin. Both mother and son were healthy. Our lives were about to change again. We were now a family and raising kids was one of our new priorities. Little Brendan would eventually be joined by a brother, Raymond, and a sister, Sarah Kathryn.

* * *

Just after Brendan's birth, my search for answers came to a key juncture. Our time spent at church finally helped me to unlock a better understanding of the past events of my life. I finally found God, or as my pastor put it: I might have just found God, but He always knew exactly where I was.

From that point on, I dedicated my life to God's service. I quietly enrolled in classes at a local seminary. After years of study, I received my Masters of Divinity. I was ordained as a minister and accepted a senior pastor position at the First Bible Church of Lombard. It took me a while to settle in and get comfortable with that role. I was absolutely horrible as a speaker and still apologize to many in my congregation for putting people to sleep. It took me a few years to get better at delivering a decent sermon, but my heart was always with community service. I also had the privilege of offering guidance to every President since being ordained. Maureen had a hand in getting me started in that role, but I quickly became the first to be called to the Capitol when moral dilemmas weighed on our country's leadership. I can't be sure how many times my advice was followed, but I was honored just to be consulted.

I don't intend to use this memoir to proselytize. I'll save that for my sermons and let people decide for themselves what they want to believe. However, each day I continue to gain a better appreciation for those turbulent years in the wake of that great flu pandemic. I have no doubt that God was with me through every step and at every crossroad. Each time I ponder the details of my strange odyssey, the more I'm in awe of how all the strange, fortuitous twists worked to help so many – despite my shortcomings. I once complained to Chung-Hee that I didn't believe I was qualified to carry out my tasks, but it didn't matter. I'm certain that God filled in all the gaps, as He does to this day.

* * *

General Osgood finally discovered what had happened to the nuclear arsenal of the United States. We were correct to assume a special directive had been issued which consolidated all nuclear materials. The key break in the case came from a former United States Air Force junior NCO (Non-Commissioned Officer) living in Arizona. As the pandemic broke, he had been assigned to a special underground facility in Utah where all nuclear materials were sent. Most of his duties didn't put him in contact with the true purpose of this facility, until enough officers succumbed to the flu that his responsibilities were upgraded. His assignment ended after almost half of the warheads had been dismantled. The facility had been idled and sealed when it became impossible to continue. He swore an oath to keep it all a secret until it was obvious that it was best to come forward. Once the facility was located, it took almost a year to safely access some of the deeper vaults. The old Air Force did a superb job securing these dangerous weapons. I applaud their efforts, which is in sharp contrast to how some other nations had handled their nuclear weapons.

Tragically, as we've all seen, nuclear weapons from other nations have turned up from time to time. Despite the efforts of the United Nations Nuclear Task Force, atomic attacks have occurred. I pray that we've seen the last of these senseless and horrific bombings.

A year after settling the nuclear mystery, General Osgood retired. His final task was finished. I had the privilege to attend his retirement ceremony and deliver the prayer.

A few months later, the general died of heart failure. What had driven him was gone and he was weary. He had given everything of himself to the military forces of our country. I consider him one of the greatest men I've ever known. I'll never forget the chance he took on such a wild tale of buried treasure.

A few days after returning from the funeral, I spent a free afternoon sitting in our backyard under a maple tree. It was a beautiful,
sunny day in early June. As I reclined and relaxed myself, a memory
resurfaced. For a moment I was in my old backyard on the day after I
graduated high school, enjoying that moment of perfect contentment.
I heard some footsteps and felt a hand tap my shoulder. Little Sarah
smiled at me and I pulled her into my arms. She lay with me and
soon wondered why I was quietly weeping. I told her it was because I
had just been given a repeat of a wonderful gift that I'd been convinced would be just once in a lifetime.

* * *

In April of 2045, we received the sad news that Maureen Tillman
passed away. We traveled back to Maine for her memorial and
funeral. Now a reverend, I had no excuse not to participate and was
honored to perform the eulogy at her memorial service. Many probably remember my speech or can easily look it up, so I won't get into
it. I will say on a more personal level that my family and I very much
miss Maureen. She was the grandmother our children never had, and
she enjoyed every second of that distinction. We were a surrogate
family to her because she lost her entire family in the pandemic.
Kathryn and I also considered her our surrogate mother. She was
truly a remarkable woman.

I was never able to find out what happened to my parents in
Florida. There is no doubt that they perished sometime during the
pandemic's aftermath. Most of us who lived through that period have
similar stories. Maureen took it on herself to investigate their fates.
She worked diligently but wasn't able to uncover any information. Of
all the things she ever did for me, and despite her feelings of failure
in that regard, I always deeply appreciated her intention and deter-
mination.

While investigating the fate of my parents, Maureen scored an
unexpected success. She found my little sister alive and well in the
Texas Territory. I was reunited with Mary and introduced her to
Kathryn (Molly) and her nephews and niece. She moved nearby and
became a part of our everyday lives. It's taken years for her to tell me
everything that happened in her life after the pandemic. Her story is
tragic and full of heartache. She's found much needed peace and

healing around her surviving family, and eventually started one of her own.

* * *

As I finish this memoir, it's clear that our new nation has come a long way. Most of us couldn't have imagined something like this emerging from the cesspool of the post-pandemic era. My time of contribution is long past, but we are fortunate that so many more have stepped up to help advance our country to what it is today. There has never been a more powerful civilization on the face of the Earth. The NAC currently encompasses all of what used to be the United States of America, most of Canada, Cuba, Puerto Rico, and about half of old Mexico. Those born after the pandemic simply won't be able to comprehend how impossible a union of these territories would have been in the old culture.

I hope and pray that future generations will never forget what it was like to live in anarchy, and how our old narcissistic culture categorically failed to cope with a global disaster. I'm convinced that while we possessed the knowledge and technology to stop the flu virus, we lacked the capacity to control a far more difficult element within the situation: ourselves. I strongly believe that the flu started the decline of our old culture, but it was our rampant selfishness that nearly sealed our fate.

I think back to how most of us lived our lives after the pandemic raged and wonder how different it would've been if just a few more of us had developed the moral courage to confront the nefarious kingpins that sprouted up like weeds. I wonder how it would've played out if people like Glenn Bradshaw had had better friends to help guide his leadership, just as Chung-Hee Kym helped to mold my future. The lessons of how we behaved in the post-pandemic aftermath should always remind us of the depths of depravity that the human race can sink into. I personally look forward to an eternity where such behavior is unfathomable.

As for keeping the falsehood of Major Paladin going for longer than ordered, I have no legitimate excuse. At the time President Tillman set the twenty-five year limit, I was concerned for what people would think of her. When the time expired, my outward excuse was the same. However, I must confess that it actually became more about my pride.

Despite what some well-meaning pundits have tried to project about me, I'm not quite the courageous hero who selflessly served his country. It's hard to listen to people sing your praises for years and not wonder what they'd think if they knew the whole truth. I was also afraid of other repercussions, as if someone would come and take away that medal which prominently sits on my desk. I feared that the memories of Major Joseph Paladin, Doctor Chung-Hee Kym, President Maureen Tillman, General Brendan Osgood, Glenn Bradshaw, and even Smitty would fade away if that medal ever left my possession.

While I had the authority to decide if and when to let the truth out, it took too long for me to make up my mind. However, I finally came to a realization that what people might think is up to them. There is only One in my life whose opinion counts the most, and shockingly, it's not Kathryn. She has no problem with the fact that I care about what God thinks above all. She shares the same priority.

For many years, the truth has been protected by a bodyguard of lies. I hereby retire them.

THE END

EPILOGUE

A note from Julian Ferrin, Literary Agent
July, 2061

As this memoir went to press, I was profoundly saddened that Reverend Joseph Paladin died on June 10, 2061. He passed away while doing what he enjoyed best, simply helping someone out. He was working at the renovation site of a church outreach project with his wife, Molly, and oldest son, Brendan, when he collapsed of a heart attack. He peacefully passed in Molly's arms with Brendan beside him.

Dignitaries from around the world attended his grand state funeral a week later in Bangor, Maine. His beautiful oak casket was wheeled past countless thousands of mourners and rows upon rows of soldiers and officers in dress uniform. He was given full military honors and I think our entire air force flew over the ceremony on that beautiful, sunny afternoon.

I'll never forget assisting an elderly man in a wheelchair to get a better look at the procession. Once my sons helped him and his caretaker find a good vantage point, he turned to me and struggled to say something. I leaned in closer and asked him to repeat himself. He whispered to me in a raspy voice: "Walt was always a good shit."

I had the distinct pleasure of knowing Joe Paladin for the past few years. Despite the notoriety he couldn't seem to escape, he was an ordinary man who enjoyed all the small things. He shunned the spotlight and lived a quiet life dedicated to God and his family. He rode the train to his church in Lombard every morning and always made time to talk to well-wishers. He never once referred to his past exploits in a Sunday sermon. No matter how many times we talked about his past, he steadfastly refused to take credit for much of anything. He attributed all the credit to God. He often scoffed at being called one of the founding members of the New American Confederation (I added this to the memoir), when in reality he was *the* founding member. I'm convinced that nothing would have come to pass if it weren't for what he risked.

Many would argue that Joe's greatest contribution was seeing the Phoenix initiative through. I would disagree. As I got to know him better, the one thing that quickly became apparent was how many lives he's touched since he stepped away from public service. From presidents to ordinary people, many have stories about how Joe helped them out. Whether he was painting a house, visiting the sick, or giving advice to national leaders, he approached each task with equal importance. What brought him the greatest joy, however, was inspiring many to seek out a greater power in their lives. Even a hardened cynic such as myself was moved to reconsider personal priorities and worldviews.

On the day his statue was dedicated in the new capitol building, he found it hard to believe that someone had shown the artistic vision to recreate that picture of him at the front of the locomotive. He was thrilled to have retired General William Hoffman, the team leader who rode with him in the locomotive at his side for the unveiling. They were both overcome with emotion as an overflow crowd cheered while the NAC Fife and Drum Corps played our national anthem.

The casket that millions saw on the day of the funeral was only a temporary container for Walter Johnson's body. At his insistence, the official grave of Joseph Paladin at the national cemetery contains the actual recovered remains of Major Joseph Paladin. Walt's body was cremated and a few days later Molly took his ashes to Brownfield Road outside of Eaton, New Hampshire, where he last confronted Glenn Bradshaw. I was with Molly as she lovingly spread his ashes around the area where Glenn was buried. She told me that Walt wanted it that way, because he always felt that it was the place where the old Walter Johnson perished. The crude wooden cross that once marked Glenn's grave was long gone, but a couple of the rocks which Molly placed there decades ago still peeked out from beneath the weeds.

After Walt's ashes were spread, we stood for a while and listened to the calm of the warm afternoon along that secluded stretch of road. Molly soon let out a chuckle, and I asked her what she was thinking about. She told me she had just pictured the reunion Walt must be having with Joe Paladin. Walt had recently told her it was something he was looking forward to after his life here ended. She turned to me, smiled, and said with certainty that she'd have to wait a while longer to see how it all went.

Other novels by Bruce Fottler:

Chasing Redemption
Dover Park
The Juncture

24470313R00144

Made in the USA
Middletown, DE
26 September 2015